A MATCH MADE
IN TEXAS

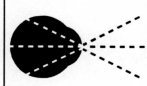 This Large Print Book carries the
Seal of Approval of N.A.V.H.

A MATCH MADE IN TEXAS

MARGARET BROWNLEY

THORNDIKE PRESS
A part of Gale, a Cengage Company

Farmington Hills, Mich • San Francisco • New York • Waterville, Maine
Meriden, Conn • Mason, Ohio • Chicago

GALE
A Cengage Company

LIBRARY OF CONGRESS CIP DATA ON FILE.
CATALOGUING IN PUBLICATION FOR THIS BOOK
IS AVAILABLE FROM THE LIBRARY OF CONGRESS

ISBN-13: 978-1-4328-4593-3 (hardcover)
ISBN-10: 1-4328-4593-4 (hardcover)

Published in 2018 by arrangement with Sourcebooks, Inc.

Printed in the United States of America
1 2 3 4 5 6 7 22 21 20 19 18

I dedicate this book to my three grand-daughters, Summer, Courtney, and Bry-anna, the inspiration behind the three Lockwood sisters. In the interest of family peace, I'll let each girl decide for herself which sister she most resembles.

ONE

Could she trust him? *Dare* she trust him?

The man — a stranger — looked like one tough hombre. Perched upon the seat of a weather-beaten wagon, he sat tall, lean, and decisively strong, his sunbaked hands the color of tanned leather. The only feature visible beneath his wide-brimmed hat and shaggy beard was a well-defined nose. The beard, along with his shoulder-length hair, suggested he had no regard for barbers. From the looks of him, he wasn't all that fond of bathhouses either.

"Need a ride?" the stranger asked, looking down at her with open curiosity.

She hesitated. It wasn't as if she had a lot of choices. If she didn't accept his offer, she might have to spend the rest of the day, maybe even the night, alone in the Texas wilderness with the rattlers, cactus, and God knows what else.

"Where you headin'?" he asked.

This time she answered. "Two-Time."

"Same here," he said with a gruff nod, as if that alone was reason to trust him.

His destination should have offered no surprise. Two-Time was the only town within twenty miles. "Why there?" she asked.

Her hometown had grown by leaps and bounds since the arrival of the train but still lagged behind San Antonio and Austin in commerce and population. Most people, if they ended up in Two-Time at all, did so by mistake.

He shrugged his wide shoulders. "Good a place as any."

Moistening her parched lips, she shaded her eyes from the blazing sun as she gazed up at him. No sense beating around the bush. "You don't have a nefarious intent, do you? To do me harm, I mean?" A woman alone couldn't be too careful.

The question seemed to surprise him. At least it made him push back his hat, revealing steel-blue eyes that seemed to pierce right through her. What a strange sight she must look. Stuck in the middle of nowhere dressed to the nines in a stylish blue walking suit.

"Are you askin' if your virtue is safe with me?"

She blushed but refused to back down. The man didn't mince words, and neither would she. "Well, is it?"

"Safe as you want it to be," he said finally. His lazy drawl didn't seem to go with the sharp-eyed regard, which returned again and again to her peacock feathered hat, rising three stories and a basement high above her brow.

It wasn't exactly the answer she'd hoped for, but he sounded sincere, and that gave her a small measure of comfort. Still, she cast a wary eye on his holstered weapon. The Indian Wars had ended, but the possibility of renegades was real. The area also teemed with outlaws. In that sense, it wouldn't hurt to have an armed man by her side. Even one as surly as this one.

"If you would be so kind as to help me with my . . . um . . . trunk. I'd be most grateful."

He sprang from the wagon, surprising her with his sudden speed. For such a large man, he was surprisingly light on his feet. He was also younger than he first appeared, probably in his early thirties. He would have towered over her by a good eight inches had she not been wearing a hat gamely designed to give her height and presence.

Gaze dropping the length of her, he visually lingered on her small waist and well-defined hips a tad too long for her peace of mind.

"Name's Rennick," he said, meeting her eyes. "R. B. Rennick."

A false name if she ever heard one, but for once, she decided to hold her tongue. He was her best shot for getting back to town. He might be her only shot.

"I'm Miss Amanda Lockwood." She offered her gloved hand, which he blithely ignored. Feeling rebuffed, she withdrew it.

The man was clearly lacking in manners, but he had offered to help her, and for that she was grateful.

Thumbs hanging from his belt, he gazed across the desolate Texas landscape. "How'd you land out here, anyway? Nothing for miles 'round."

"I was on my way home from Austin when I . . . had a little run-in with the stage driver."

He raised an eyebrow. "What kind of run-in?"

"He was driving like a maniac," she said with an indignant toss of the head. "And I told him so." Not once but several times, in fact.

Hanging out the stage window, she'd insisted he slow down in no uncertain terms. When that didn't work, she resorted to banging on the coach's ceiling with her parasol and calling him every unflattering name she could think of. Perhaps a more tactful way of voicing her complaints would have worked more in her favor, but how was she supposed to know the man had such a low threshold for criticism?

She gritted her teeth just thinking about it. "Thought he would kill us all." He pretty near did. The nerve of him, tossing her bag and baggage out of the stage and leaving her stranded.

Mr. Rennick scratched his temple. "Hope you learned your lesson, ma'am. Men don't like being told what to do. 'Specially when holding the reins." It sounded like a warning.

Turning abruptly, he picked up the wooden chest and heaved it over the side of the wagon like it weighed no more than a loaf of bread. It hit the bottom of the wagon with a sickening thud.

She gasped. "Be careful." Belatedly, she remembered his warning and tempered his order with, "It's very old."

The hope chest was a family heirloom. If anything happened to it, her family would never forgive her. The chest had been handed down from mother to daughter for decades. She inherited the chest after the last of her two sisters wed. Since she had no interest in marriage, she used it mostly to store books. Today, it contained the clothes needed for her nearly weeklong stay in Austin.

He brushed his hands together. "Sure is heavy. You'd have an easier time haulin' a steer."

"Yes, well, it's actually a hope chest." While packing for her trip, she discovered the latch on her steamer trunk broken. The hope chest was a convenient though not altogether satisfactory substitute. For one, it was almost too heavy for her to handle alone — the most she could do was drag it.

"Don't know what you're hoping for, ma'am, but you're not likely to find it out here."

He gazed into the distance for a moment, then suddenly spun around and climbed into the driver's seat without offering to help her. "Well, what are you waitin' for?" he yelled. "Get in!"

Startled by his sharp command, she reached for the grab handle and heaved herself up to the passenger side.

No sooner had she seated herself upon

the wooden bench than Mr. Rennick took off hell-bent for leather.

Glued to the back of the seat, she cried out. "Oh dear. Oh my. *Ohhh!*"

What had looked like a perfectly calm and passive black horse had suddenly turned into a demon. With pounding hooves and flowing mane, the steed flew over potholes and dirt mounds, giving no heed to the cargo behind. The wagon rolled and pitched like a ship in stormy seas. Dust whirled in the air, and rocks hit the bottom and sides.

Holding on to her hat with one hand and the seat with the other, Amanda watched in wide-eyed horror as the scenery flew by in a blur.

The wagon sailed over a hill as if it was airborne, and she held on for dear life. The wheels hit the ground, jolting her hard and rattling her teeth. The hope chest bounced up and down like dice in a gambler's hand. Her breath whooshed out, and it was all she could do to find her voice.

"Mr. R-Rennick!" she stammered, grabbing hold of his arm. She had to shout to be heard.

"What?" he yelled back.

She stared straight ahead, her horrified eyes searching for a soft place to land should the need arise. "Y-you sh-should s-slow down and enjoy the s-scenery."

Her hat had tilted sideways, and he swiped the peacock feather away from his face. "Been my experience that sand and sagebrush look a whole lot better when travelin' fast," he shouted in his strong baritone voice.

He made a good point, but at the moment, she was more concerned with life and limb.

He urged his horse to go faster before adding, "It's also been my experience that travelin' fast is the best way to outrun bandits."

"W-what do you mean? B-bandits?" It was then that she heard gunfire.

She swung around in her seat, and her jaw dropped. Three masked horsemen were giving chase — and closing in fast.

Two

"Oh no!" she cried.

"You better get down, ma'am," Mr. Rennick shouted. "They look like they mean bus'ness."

Dropping off her seat, Amanda scrunched against the floorboards. Her body shook so hard, her teeth chattered. "G-give me your g-gun," she cried.

"Know how to use it?" he yelled back.

"N-no, but I'm a f-fast learner!" She pulled off her gloves, which flew out of the wagon like frantic white doves.

Holding the reins with one hand, he grabbed his gun with the other. After cocking the hammer with his thumb, he handed it to her. The gun was heavier than she expected, requiring both hands to grasp. Keeping her head low, she balanced herself on wobbly knees and rested the barrel on the back of the seat. She held onto the grip with all her might. Still, the muzzle bobbed up and down like corn popping on a hot skillet.

Aiming at a specific target was out of the question. The jostling wagon made control impossible. The best she could do was to keep from shooting the driver. She wasn't all that anxious to shoot the bandits either. She just wanted to scare them away.

Eyes squeezed shut, barrel pointed in the bandits' general direction, she pulled the trigger. The blast shook her to the core, and her arm flung up with the recoil. She fell back against the footrest and fought to regain her balance.

"Good shot!" he yelled, looking over his shoulder. "You stopped your hope-a-thingie from attackin'. Now see if you can do the same with the bandits."

Her heart sank. Oh no. Not the hope chest. Her family would kill her. That is, if the bandits didn't kill her first. Forcing air into her lungs, she fought to reposition herself. The horsemen kept coming. They were so close now, she could see the sun glinting off their weapons.

Bracing herself against the recoil, she fired again, this time aiming higher. The wagon veered to the right, and she fell against the side, hitting her shoulder hard. Her feathered hat ripped from its pins and flew from the wagon in a way that no peacock ever had.

"Oh no!" That was her very best hat, and the fact that it landed on the nearest high-wayman gave her small comfort. His horse stopped, but the bandit kept going.

"Stay down!" Rennick yelled.

"But my hat . . ." It was one of the most elaborate hats she'd ever created. The peacock feathers matched the color of her eyes. "I loved that hat!"

"Yeah, well, too bad it didn't return your affection."

Of all the rude things to say. Blinking away the dust in her eyes, she hunkered close to the floorboards and struggled to catch her breath.

The wagon continued to race over uneven ground, jolting her until she was ready to scream. Just when she thought her battered body could take no more, the wheels merci-fully rolled to a stop.

She shot Rennick a questioning look. "W-what are you doing?"

"Seems like our friends deserted us."

She raised her limp body off the floor-boards on shaky limbs and flung herself onto the seat, breathing hard. All that was visible in the far distance was a cloud of dust that seemed to be moving in the opposite direction.

Relief rushed through her. "W-why do you suppose they gave up the chase?"

He lifted the gun from her hand and holstered it. "Guess the hat was enough to convince them that whatever chunk change we might have wasn't worth the trouble."

She glared at him. He didn't seem to notice.

Her hair had fallen from its bun, and she did her best to pin back the loose chestnut strands. She brushed the dust off her skirt and rubbed her shoulder.

"You okay?" he asked.

She nodded, though without her hat and gloves, she felt naked.

He drank from a metal flask and wiped his mouth with the back of his hand. "Here." He handed her the canteen.

She hesitated before bringing the spout to her mouth. The water was warm and tasted metallic; still, it helped quench her thirst. Pulling a lace handkerchief from her sleeve, she poured a few drops on it before handing the canteen back.

She dabbed her face with the moist handkerchief, but it offered little relief from the heat. The sun was almost directly overhead, and though still early spring, the temperature hovered in the high eighties.

"Do you mind if I retrieve my parasol from my hope . . . trunk?"

"I'll get it." Before she could object, he jumped to the ground and walked to the back of the wagon.

She tossed him an anxious glance and tried to remember how she'd packed. Were her intimate garments on the top or bottom of the chest? She'd packed in a hurry and couldn't remember. Shaking her head in annoyance, she blew out her breath. They had almost been robbed, maybe even killed, and here she worried about — of all things — a few pairs of red satin drawers and corset covers.

He returned to his seat with her parasol, his expressionless face giving no clue as to what unmentionables he had been privy to.

"Much obliged," she said, taking it from him.

He regarded her with curiosity. "What were you doin' in Austin?"

She opened the sun umbrella, casting a welcome shadow over her heated face. "I was at a Rights for Women meeting."

He made a face. "I should've known." He picked up the reins. "You're one of those suffering ladies."

She leveled a sideways glance his way. "They're called suffragists," she said. "I take it you don't much approve of women having the right to vote, Mr. Rennick."

"I have no objection to women votin'. But it's been my experience that you give women an inch, before you know it, they'll want the whole kit and caboodle."

"Right now all we want is the right to the ballot." She pursed her lips. "Are you married, Mr. Rennick?"

"Nope."

She narrowed her eyes. Had she only imagined his hesitation?

He met her gaze. "What about you? Got any marriage prospects?"

"None," she said, looking away. "And I plan on keeping it that way."

His passenger fell silent as they drove the rest of the way to town, and that was fine with R. B. Rennick. A loner by circumstance, he wasn't even sure how to act in front of a woman anymore. Especially one as independent as Miss Lockwood.

She was something, all right, sitting there all prim and proper in her conservative suit like a trussed up turkey. No one would guess from looking at her that she favored red satin petticoats and matching under trousers. Recalling the intriguing contents of her hope chest, his gaze traveled down the length of her. For a woman who had no interest in marriage, she sure did arm herself with enough trappings to catch an army of men if she so chose.

Clearly, she was a woman who could cause a man all sorts of trouble if he didn't watch out. Even so, the way she'd handled herself in the face of danger had earned his begrudging respect.

He also felt sorry for her. It was hot and humid and dusty, the air thick as a wet blanket. She had to be downright miserable but was either too polite or too stubborn to admit it. If he was a betting man, he'd put his money on the latter. He urged his horse to go faster. The lady looked like she could use some shade and a cold drink. The last thing he needed was her passing out on him.

The sun hung low, and shadows ran long by the time they reached Two-Time. The town was larger than he expected. A railroad stretched the length of the town, along with a string of saloons. A street two wagons wide separated rows of adobe and brick buildings, each with false wooden fronts. They passed a general store, bakery, gun shop, post office, and barber along with other businesses.

"What kind of name is that, anyway? Two-Time?" he asked. "Doesn't sound like a very trustworthy name for a town."

"It's not what you think," she said. "Until last year, the town had two time zones." She gave him a short history of the two feuding jewelers, including her father, who kept the town divided for years by refusing to agree to standard time.

Rick had little interest in town history. He was more concerned about the lay of the land. "Where shall I drop you off?" he asked abruptly.

She hesitated. "At my father's place. It's two blocks up yonder. At the Lockwood Watch and Clockworks shop."

He tossed a nod toward a knot of people blocking the street. "Looks like trouble."

She craned her neck. "No more than usual."

He raised an eyebrow. Where he came from, trouble didn't usually start till the sun went down. Something about the night made prisoners restless.

But here in broad daylight, the mass of people spilled off the boardwalk and into the street. Traffic had come to a complete standstill, preventing him from driving any farther. Tugging on the reins, he guided his horse to the side of the road and parked behind a dogcatcher's wagon.

"You can let me off here," she said.

"Sure?" He slanted his head to the back. "Your hope-a-thingie weighs a ton."

"I can manage," she said.

Setting the brake, he leaped to the ground and hauled her chest out of the wagon and onto the wooden sidewalk. This time, he showed more care in setting it down. A chip in the wood the size of a quarter drew his attention, and he rubbed his finger over it.

He heard her gasp and looked up. For an independent woman, she sure did put a lot of stock in that old chest. Or maybe it was the finery inside . . .

"It's just a bullet hole," he assured her. "Probably passed right through all that satin and lace."

Her slender frame stiffened, and her cheeks turned a most beguiling red. She really was a looker. Especially now that she'd lost that ridiculous hat.

At first glance, her turquoise eyes had seemed too large for her delicate features and her body too slight to support such an independent spirit. Now that she was in familiar surroundings, she'd dropped her guard, and all the mismatched parts worked together to create a very pleasant whole.

He touched the brim of his hat with the tip of his finger. "Sure you don't need help with your —"

"No, that's fine," she said quickly, avoiding his eyes. "I can manage from here. Much obliged."

He watched the late afternoon sun play with the golden highlights of her brown hair. Why a woman would want to hide such a fine mane beneath a ridiculous bunch of bird feathers was one of the mysteries of life.

She gazed up at him through a fringe of lush lashes. "If you need a place to stay, we passed the hotel back a ways. There're also a couple of boardinghouses in town. Some of them are even respectable."

"In that case, I'll stay at the hotel." With a tip of his hat, he forced himself to turn away, starting off on foot. Since the street was still blocked, there was no sense trying to drive his wagon. He'd come back later to stable his horse. Without the distraction of Miss Lockwood, he could concentrate more fully on the town. This time, he paid particular attention to the location of the bank, the sheriff's office, and the hotel.

This town was everything he hoped for and more. It was large enough for a man to remain relatively unnoticed, yet small enough to escape quickly should a need arise.

All in all, it was a perfect hideout for a cold-blooded killer.

THREE

Surprised to find herself staring at Mr. Rennick's retreating back, Amanda grasped the handle of her hope chest and dragged it along the boardwalk toward her father's clock shop. The cedar-lined chest bounced up and down over the rough-hewn wooden sidewalk.

The bullet hole worried her. Maybe the carpenter, Mr. Woodman, would take a look at it. If anyone could make the hope chest look like new again, he was the man.

Right now, her main concern was reaching her father's shop before closing time so as to hitch a ride home with him.

The weeklong suffragist meeting had been exhausting but also exhilarating. She'd learned much from the other attendees and was in awe at the many things that had been accomplished since the last quarterly meeting. Her own efforts for the cause seemed woefully lacking in comparison.

One member got her hometown to change the law forbidding women to own businesses. Another was elected to a school board, the first woman in Missouri to do so. Even that annoying Marilyn Hock had something impressive to brag about. She had single-handedly persuaded a New Orleans cotton mill to cut women's work hours from fourteen to twelve hours a day.

When it came her turn, Amanda was one of only two women with no meaningful news to report. All the marches and rallies she'd spearheaded had failed to produce a single positive outcome for women's rights. All she got for her efforts was a ruined reputation and more jail time than she cared to admit.

The next suffragist meeting was scheduled for June. That was only three months away, and she had no time to lose. Next time, she would have something positive to report if it killed her. But what?

Her thoughts scattered as she neared the knot of people blocking both the street and boardwalk. Angry voices escalated, and fists punched the air. Curious, she moved closer, dragging her hope chest behind her. What had the town up in arms this time? It didn't take much to get folks riled, but this dispute sounded more serious than most.

The blacksmith's strident voice rose above the rest. "I'm tellin' you, this town is goin' to the dogs." Mr. Steele paused to make sure he had everyone's attention, his powerful arms hanging past his knees like an ape's. "We ain't got nottin' but crime and disorder, and it's smudgin' our town's reputation. It's time to put a stop to it!"

"You tell 'em!" someone shouted.

Furrowing her brow, Amanda moved closer. Something must have happened in her absence. Not too surprising. Crime had increased at an alarming rate in recent months and was now the main topic of discussion at every gathering. Horse theft and cattle rustling were the least of it. There had been two bank robberies in the last couple of months alone.

Some blamed the railroad. Others held the slowing cattle trade responsible, as many cowpunchers were now out of work. A few suggested it was a sign of the times.

Anxious to find out what happened to cause such an uproar, Amanda rose on tiptoes and craned her neck. Still, the high-crowned hats blocked her vision.

Hiking her skirt above her ankles, she stepped atop her hope chest. This gave her the height needed for a clear view.

Mayor Troutman faced the crowd, thumbs

hooked from the pockets of his waistcoat. A round-bellied man with heavy jowls and bushy sideburns, his girth was impressive even if his leadership was not. A year in office and already his campaign promises had turned into excuses.

"The stage robbery is the last straw," he said in a deep-chested voice.

Amanda's jaw dropped. The stage was held up? The one she had been kicked off of?

Unbelievable!

The mayor's voice grew more insistent. "What we need is a sheriff who will clean up this town once and for all. I have asked for Sheriff Appleby's resignation effective immediately. That means we have no time to waste in selecting someone to take his place."

Amanda groaned. Not again. The town changed sheriffs more often than fashion changed styles. The Texas constitution specified a two-year term for sheriffs, but things like that never bothered the residents of Two-Time.

If citizens saw no results in a few months — and, in some cases, weeks — the sheriff was booted out and another one installed, usually less capable than the one they'd replaced.

"So who's it gonna be this time?" called the postmaster.

"That's what we're here to find out," Mayor Troutman said. "We're gonna do this in the usual dem'cratic way. Everyone interested in the job will get their name added to this here board. Then Friday, we'll have a fair and proper vote." He pulled out a square of paper from his vest pocket and unfolded it.

"Just so there's no question, here's what the job entails." He then began reading aloud. "The sheriff's duty is to quiet and suppress all riots." He glanced pointedly at Amanda, no doubt recalling the riot she caused after trying to close the saloons on Sundays.

He continued reading. "The sheriff will furthermore appr'hend and secure any person guilty of committin' a felony or" — his gaze lit on Amanda — "disturbin' the peace."

Amanda glared back. She was still riled about the night spent in jail for carrying a picket sign during the mayor's speech. Disturbing the peace indeed!

Since Two-Time was a relatively small town and the only one of any consequence in the county, the sheriff's duties also included the unpleasant task of collecting taxes.

"Any questions?" Troutman asked, folding the paper and stuffing it back in his pocket.

When no questions were forthcoming, the mayor continued. "All right, men." He peered at the crowd from beneath bushy eyebrows. "Who's gonna be the first to step up and do his civic duty?"

The pox-scarred butcher everyone called T-Bone raised his hand. His stained white apron reached his ankles but barely stretched around his equator. "I am."

"Whatcha want to be sheriff for?" the mayor asked.

"Give me a chance to catch the culprit who stole me side of beef."

"What's your qualifications?" someone yelled.

The butcher looked insulted, and his horseshoe mustache quivered. "Grinding meat," he said to appreciative laughter.

Amanda gritted her teeth. The man thought nothing of shortchanging his customers. The idea of him in charge of law and order horrified her.

The mayor wrote his name on the board. "Anyone else?"

Mr. Mutton, the dogcatcher, raised his hand. A thin man with a flat face and reced-

31

ing jaw, he bore a striking resemblance to a bulldog. "Trackin' down outlaws can't be any harder than trackin' down stray dogs."

Amanda clenched her hands by her side. The man was as unscrupulous as they came, and no dog, licensed or otherwise, was safe from his greedy paws.

The mayor wrote the dogcatcher's name on the board. "So far we have two candidates. Anyone else brave enough to put their name where their mouth is?" Hands went up all around, and soon, a dozen or so candidates had tossed their hats in the ring.

Amanda was just about to step down from her hope chest when something occurred to her. Running for sheriff would surely score points at the next women's suffrage meeting. No other member had run for sheriff. She would be the first. Now wouldn't *that* be something to crow about? Even that annoying Marilyn Hock would have to be impressed.

She raised her hand. "Add my name."

Never in a million years did she expect to be elected to such a post, but neither did she want to pass up the opportunity to promote her cause. Adding her name to the growing list of candidates would send a message that women were just as qualified to serve as men. Certainly, she couldn't do any worse than the men already listed.

Silence brittle as glass followed her declaration, and all eyes turned to her.

The mayor dismissed her with a shake of his head. "You can't run. You're not qualified."

"Why aren't I qualified?" she demanded.

"You're a woman, that's why!" he bellowed back. "And it's against the law for women to vote."

"I'm not asking to vote," she argued. "I'm voicing my intention to run. Far as I know, that's not against the law."

What she was doing wasn't all that groundbreaking. That honor went to Victoria Woodhull, who ran for president of the United States against incumbent Ulysses S. Grant. The fact that Miss Woodhull couldn't vote for herself didn't stop her, and neither would it stop Amanda.

Banker Mr. Mooney spoke up. "She's got a point there." His curling gray mustache twitched as he fiddled with his watch fob. "Nothing in the law says she can't run."

"*I* say she can't run," T-Bone said. "Not only is she not a man, she ain't got no qual'fications."

"He's right," the owner of the Lazy B Ranch yelled. "What makes ya think ya got what it takes to be sheriff? What do ya know about law and order? What experience ya got?"

Amanda folded her arms across her chest and glared down at him. Thanks to the hope chest, she stood several inches taller than any of the men, and that gave her a definite advantage. "I'll have you know I have lots of experience. I've been arrested a time or two." Or three. Once for voting in the mayor's election, a second time for trying to close a saloon on the Sabbath. A third time, she and a dozen other suffragists were arrested for blocking traffic and frightening the mayor's horse as they marched down the middle of Main Street. "How many times have *you* been arrested?"

"I . . . I . . ."

"Just as I thought," she said. "If you've never been arrested, how can you possibly know how the system works?"

"She has a point," Mr. Mooney said and scratched his head. A pompous man with a muttonchop beard, his body bore a striking resemblance to an overstuffed money bag. "Least I think she does."

"Have you ever fired a weapon?" Mayor Troutman asked.

"Yes," she said, nodding. Now they were getting somewhere. "I have fired a weapon." Less than four hours ago, as it turned out.

The mayor's lip curled. "Has anyone ever *seen* you fire a weapon?"

"I have."

Recognizing the gruff voice, Amanda nearly fell off the hope chest.

All eyes turned to the newly arrived stranger.

"And who might you be?" the mayor asked.

"R. B. Rennick's the name."

Troutman frowned. "Under what circumstances did you see Miss Lockwood fire a weapon?"

"She fired at three outlaws who were out to do us both" — he locked gazes with her — "*nefarious* harm. Once she got to firin', they took off like a bunch of skinned mules. Lest I'm mistaken, those were the same thieves who robbed the stage."

Everyone started talking at once. Grimacing with impatience, the mayor waved his arms. "Quiet!" He waited until he had everyone's attention. "It seems that despite having the misfortune of bein' of the female persuasion, Miss Lockwood is indeed qualified to run for sheriff."

He turned toward the board and scribbled her name beneath the names of the other candidates . . . albeit in a much smaller print. "Anyone else?"

No one else spoke up, and Troutman continued. "All right, men. Voting will commence on Friday at noon sharp."

The crowd quickly dispersed. Leaving her hope chest behind, Amanda rushed to catch up to Mr. Rennick. "Why'd you do that?" she asked, falling in step by his side.

He swung around to face her, reminding her once again of his height. "Why not?"

"You said you were against women's rights."

He grimaced. "I have no problem with female rights. I just don't like sufferin' women."

"If you're so against suffragists, why the endorsement?"

"That was no endorsement. Just telling it how it was. You and your crazy hat sent those hombres fleein' like a bunch of yellow hounds. Can't deny that." He narrowed his eyes. "You aren't serious about runnin', are you? It's a joke, right?"

"I don't joke, Mr. Rennick. And, I suspect, neither do you."

He regarded her with a look of surprise. "Now what do you know? Seems like you and me have a lot in common. We have the same taste in women's under-riggin's, and we're both serious-minded." Without another word, he walked around his horse

36

and, with one easy move, swung onto his wagon's driver seat.

Refusing to be intimidated, she glared up at him, hands at her waist. "A gentleman wouldn't mention a woman's personal . . . garments," she called.

"Probably not," he said, and this time, she detected a touch of humor in the blue depths of his eyes. "Fortunately, no one's ever accused me of bein' a gentleman. I suspect no one's ever accused you of bein' a lady, either. Somethin' else we have in common." With that, he clicked his tongue and drove away.

FOUR

Amanda answered the door early the very next morning to find her two sisters standing on the porch, staring at her over the morning paper. The headlines screamed out the news in big, bold headlines. WOMAN RUNNING FOR SHERIFF. Below in smaller but equally bold type, she read: POLITICS HAVE BEEN RAISED TO A NEW LOW.

"Have you seen this?" Josie demanded. She followed Amanda into the parlor and shoved the newspaper into her hands. It was unusual for her calm and mild-mannered sister to look so upset. The oldest and tallest of the three, Josie had Mama's turquoise eyes, but her dark-brown hair was from Papa's side of the family.

Amanda quickly scanned the front page with growing dismay. The article couldn't have been more inflammatory. Words like *lunatic, fool,* and *hysteria* made her sound more fit for an insane asylum than public office. Worse, the article made no mention of the other candidates. An outsider might think she was the one and *only* candidate and that Two-Time was going to the dogs.

If that wasn't bad enough, every offense Amanda had committed through the years was cited. Papa jokingly claimed she emerged from the womb demanding equal rights for female infants, which was only a slight exaggeration.

The article went all the way back to when she was in second grade. That was the year she picketed the schoolhouse for showing favoritism toward male pupils by placing the boys' outhouse in a more convenient location than the girls'.

She thrust the paper back at Josie. Had she not returned from Austin with a new sense of purpose, running for sheriff would never have crossed her mind. It looked like her plan to make the town more favorable to women had failed miserably.

"You must be out of your cotton-picking mind!" her sister Meg said with a shake of her blond head. At age twenty-three, Meg was older than Amanda by two years and had recently married. "A sheriff is a danger-ous job even for a man. But a woman . . ."

"Poor, poor Mama," Josie said, tossing the newspaper on an upholstered armchair.

"She won't be able to show her face in public."

Just thinking of the shame she brought to her family made Amanda groan. Why, oh why, couldn't she be more like her sisters? Josie hid her writing talents behind a nom de plume. Mama and Papa only recently found out that their oldest daughter wrote the *Two-Time Gazette*'s Miss Lonely Hearts column and had done so for more than two years. Somehow, Josie managed to maintain a certain independence without calling undue attention to herself.

"You must withdraw your name at once," Meg insisted. "It's the only way."

Amanda glared at her. "I'll do no such thing." When did Meg become such a wishy-wash? If that's what marriage did to a woman, thank goodness Amanda wanted no part of it.

"But you must," Josie said. "No good can come of this. You know you haven't got a chance of winning the election. So why put yourself through all this ridicule?"

"It's for a good cause," Amanda said stubbornly.

Since her trip to Austin, she felt even more restless than before. Just hearing what the other suffragists had accomplished had filled her with a burning desire to do something more to change the town and lay the tracks for future generations of women.

Meg gave her a sympathetic look. "Oh, Mandy, I know you mean well, but there are other good causes. What about your work with orphans and war veterans? The way you're going now will get you nowhere."

"That's where you're wrong," Amanda argued. "Times have changed. Women can now vote in Wyoming. And in Austin, I met a woman from California studying to become a lawyer." Two-Time had grown in many ways during the last few years. The train and telegraph had changed the way people traveled and communicated. Once the Texas railroads were completed, even stagecoaches would be a thing of the past, but the same old biases existed.

"A woman's place is not just in the home. It's wherever she wants it to be. She no longer has to marry, have children, obey her husband, and meet society's expectations."

Josie threw up her hands. "There you go again, disparaging marriage and family."

"I'm not disparaging anything. I'm just saying that women today have other options. My running for sheriff proves it."

A shout came from the top of the stairs. *"What?"* Papa demanded. "What did you say?"

41

Josie and Meg exchanged worried glances. Papa had a heart scare a while back, and the doctor warned him to stay calm. That was like trying to contain a newborn pup.

Amanda balled her hands at her sides. It was much too early for this. She hadn't even had her morning coffee. Besides, it wasn't as if she was running for a *national* office.

Bracing herself with a deep breath, she turned toward the staircase. "They said I can't be serious about running for sheriff."

"Running for —" Papa thundered down the stairs with his suspenders flapping at his side. A tall, barrel-chested man with liberally salted dark hair, he still maintained the energy of youth despite his bulk. He snatched the newspaper from the chair and glanced at the headline. As his gaze traveled down the page, his wide girth shook like a trembling leaf.

"What is the world coming to indeed!" he bellowed, waving the paper in Amanda's face.

"Now, Papa," Josie cajoled. Married to her husband, Ralph, for more than five years, she had nursed him through some serious bouts of pneumonia due to his poor lungs. If anyone could calm Papa, it was Josie. "Remember your heart . . ."

"Remember your heart!" her fathered par-

roted. *"Remember your heart!* That's all I ever hear. You sound like that Houston fella. Save your battle cries. I don't want to hear them!"

Ignoring her father's protests, Josie slipped her hand around his arm, her voice gentle enough to soothe a child but firm enough to overcome Papa's objections. "Let's all sit down and discuss this calmly."

The veins in Papa's neck stuck out like thick cords. "I don't want to be calm. I want to know why my youngest daughter is making a fool of herself yet again!"

Quick footsteps announced Mama's arrival. "Henry! Why are you shouting?" She looked from one to the other.

As always, Mama's fair hair was perfectly coiffed despite the early morning hour, her voice properly modulated and slender frame composed. Whereas Papa was always hanging from a high wire, Mama was solid as a rock, providing the calming influence the family so often needed.

"What are you all doing here so early?" A shadow of alarm touched her face. "Is Ralph . . . ?" Josie's husband's lung condition had grown progressively worse through the years.

"No, it's not Ralph, Mama," Josie assured her.

Papa turned to Mama with a scowl. "Do you have any idea what our daughter has done this time?"

Mama shot Amanda a worried frown. There didn't seemed to be any question in Mama's mind which daughter had Papa so upset. "No —"

"She's gone too far, that's what!" he bellowed. "Thanks to her, we are now the laughingstocks of the town. Who ever heard of a woman running for sheriff?"

Mama's mouth dropped open. Hands on her chest, she stared at Amanda. "You're running for sheriff?"

"I can explain —"

"Explain?" Her father's eyebrows bounced up and down. "You think an explanation will make this right? Do you know what a dangerous job that is? You were too hard to raise to take chances with your life, and I won't have it!"

"You needn't worry," Amanda said. "There's no way I can become sheriff. I mean, who's going to vote for me?"

"Who indeed?" Papa threw up his hands as he glanced at the ceiling. "Where did I go wrong? Hmm? Would you tell me that?" Papa wasn't especially a religious man, but his habit of directing his frustrations to the Man in the sky had increased along with his daughters' ages.

He sounded so distressed, Amanda felt sorry for him. It couldn't be easy to remain stuck in the past. Not with the speed at which society was changing.

"You should be happy, Papa, for raising us with minds of our own."

"Minds of your own? Is that what you call it? I call it plain stupidity. Do you have any idea what a sheriff does?"

"You mean besides sit with his feet on the desk and take bribes?" She'd spent enough time in jail to know that the last sheriff was more of a crook than anyone he managed to put behind bars.

"A sheriff carries a gun and puts himself in danger, that's what!" he thundered.

"If that's what you're worried about, you can relax. I've got as much chance of winning the election as a mule."

"Then why run?" Papa frowned. "Hmm? Do you think this a game?"

"No, Papa. But you must admit I'm just as qualified as the other candidates and am entitled to equal rights."

"Equal rights, equal rights!" he thundered. "Now you sound like that rock woman."

"Stone."

"What?"

"Her name is Lucy *Stone.*"

If Papa knew she'd just spent a week with the activist, he would have a conniption. She told him she had gone to visit her cousin, which was only part of the truth. She hated lying to him, but in this case, it was for the greater good.

Papa tossed the paper to the floor. "Equal rights doesn't mean you can run for office."

"And why not?" she demanded.

His nose was practically in her face. "Because it's a man's job to run for office, that's why! You don't see us bellyaching to give birth or clean house. So why should women insist upon taking on a man's responsibility?"

Amanda gritted her teeth. Josie signaled her with a mute shake of her head to back down, but Amanda was too incensed to heed the warning.

"That's the most ridiculous, outrageous, and —"

Fortunately for Mama's delicate ears, the dozens of clocks that graced the parlor and dining room walls sounded the hour of eight a.m., effectively drowning out Amanda's voice with a chorus of bongs, bells, and cuckoos. A horologist by trade, Papa collected clocks like a squirrel collected acorns.

Muttering something known only to himself, Papa spun around and stomped from the room.

FIVE

Amanda rode out of town early that Wednesday morning on her brown-and-white pony, Molly. Though it was still early, the sun already felt warm on her back.

White puffy clouds dotted the sky like tossed hats. Texas was in the throes of a drought. It was yet another blow to farmers affected by the railroad and availability of produce grown in other parts of the country. Mesquite trees were usually the last afflicted by lack of rain, after livestock deaths and failed crops, but already the spiny and normally hardy trees were starting to wilt. Not a good sign.

Even the bluebonnets that normally covered the rolling hills like a colorful counterpane this time of year had yet to bloom, and the air lacked the usual perfume fragrance.

She followed the dirt road to the Wendell farm. It was actually a home for indigents, but Mr. and Mrs. Wendell refused to call it a poor farm, much to the irritation of county supervisors.

Amanda rode the well-trodden road toward the two-story adobe farmhouse. She waved at residents working in the cotton field. Old Mr. Jacobs waved back, his dark face split by a wide grin. A former slave, he supervised the other workers. Now he and his men were preparing the soil for planting — an act of faith in a time of drought.

She rode her horse to the fence, where he met her.

"How are you, Miz Lockwood?"

"I'm fine, Mr. Jacobs. How's your wife?" Mrs. Jacobs had some stomach problems a while back.

"Sukey's fit as a fiddle. One good thing about being poor . . . the doctor cures you faster," he said and laughed.

Amanda laughed too. "Give her my best." After a few more pleasantries, she broached the subject very much on her mind. "I'm forming a new group, and I wonder if you would care to join."

"What kind of group?"

"A women's rights group."

The national women's movement had seen a few bright spots in recent months. The women's suffrage amendment proposal sent to Congress three years prior had still not been voted on, but former California-senator-turned-lawyer Aaron Sargent was still pushing it. Inspired by his efforts, some women had convinced other men to join the fight — a brilliant plan. Men had the power, so why not recruit them to the cause?

Mr. Jacobs's white teeth flashed against his dark skin. "You want me to join a women's rights bunch?"

"Why not? You have the vote. That gives you a voice."

He shook his head. "The Fifteenth Amendment might give us the right to vote, but that doesn't mean beans. The polls are generally blocked to the likes of me. Even an act of Congress can't change the way people think."

She sighed. Suffragists believed their troubles would be over once they gained the right to vote, but that might only be wishful thinking. "There's strength in numbers," she said. "And that's what's going to change people's minds, not some silly law."

"What you say is true, but I'd probably do you more harm than good."

"I wouldn't have asked you if I thought that was true," she said.

"Oh, it's true all right." He reached

beneath the brim of his straw hat and rubbed his glistening forehead with the back of his hand. "A black man living in a poorhouse ain't likely to win you any favors."

"Are you sure I can't change your mind?"

He shook his head. "I wish you luck. But don't go expecting any miracles."

A miracle was exactly what she hoped for. "I'll let you know when the first meeting is. In case you change your mind."

She rode off with a wave and moments later reined her horse in front of the two-story farmhouse.

Mrs. Wendell walked out to the porch to greet her. She wiped her hands on the spotless white pinafore worn over a blue gingham dress.

"What brings you here today?" she called, patting the figure-eight braid pinned to the back of her head.

Amanda slipped from her mount and wrapped the reins around the fence post. "Brought you some tin goods."

"Mercy me. What would we do without your generosity?"

"Miss Lockwood, Miss Lockwood!"

At the sound of children's voices, Amanda turned. The brother and sister ran up to her, and she greeted them with hugs and smiles.

"Did you bring somethin' for us?" eight-year-old Libby asked. She was a pretty child with big blue eyes that looked too serious for such a young age. Today, two yellow plaits tied with pink ribbons fell down the length of her back to her waist.

"I most certainly did." Amanda reached into her saddlebags and pulled out two peacock feathers. "One for you and one for your brother."

Six-year-old Charley gazed down at the eye-spotted tail feather, a look of awe on his freckled face. Small for his age, the little shaver didn't talk much, but now as always, he greeted her with a big smile.

Libby held the feather in her hands like it was cast from delicate glass. "This is so pretty."

"It is pretty," Amanda agreed. "The eyes on the feathers protect the peacock from harm. For that reason, some people think they're good luck."

"I'm going to keep this forever and ever," Libby exclaimed.

"You can wear it in your hair," Amanda said. "Nature always saves its most colorful creations for the top. That's why flowers bloom on the tip of stems where we can most enjoy them."

"Is that why you always wear those funny hats on your head?" Charley asked.

"Charley!" Mrs. Wendell exclaimed. "Mind your p's and q's!"

"That's all right," Amanda said and laughed. "He's not the only one who thinks my hats are funny."

Mr. R. B. Rennick didn't think much of her fancy peacock hat either and had stated his opinion in no uncertain terms. Whenever he came to mind, her cheeks flared, and today was no different. It was the strangest thing. Hoping Mrs. Wendell didn't notice her red face, she turned to her horse and dug into the saddlebags.

"I brought you some penny candy and a book." She handed Charley the bag of candy and Libby a copy of *Mr. Fox.* "I thought you might like to read it to Charley."

Libby nodded. "Charley can now write his name."

Amanda looked down at the beaming boy. Charley had definitely put on some much-needed weight while under Mrs. Wendell's care, and his little legs no longer looked like they belonged on a chicken.

"Sign your own name? Why, that's wonderful, Charley. You'll have to show me."

The two youngsters held a special place in her heart. Being poor and receiving help from the county was considered shameful, but in this case, their mother didn't have much choice. Her husband deserted the family, leaving them destitute. Mrs. Wendell found them living down by the river in an old army tent.

"Thank you, Miss Lockwood," Libby said.

"You're very welcome. Say hello to your mama for me."

"I will."

Amanda smiled as she watched the two children race off. She untied the package of tin goods from her saddle and joined Mrs. Wendell on the porch.

"You're very good with them," Mrs. Wendell said, smoothing her apron. "One day, you'll make a fine mother."

"That will be difficult, as I don't intend to marry."

Mrs. Wendell's eyes crinkled at the corners. "Ah, I forgot. You're one of those, what do you call them? *Modern women.*" She laughed. "One day, you'll change your mind. You'll see. When the right man comes along." She took the package from Amanda and backed toward the door. "You look hot. Do you have time for some lemonade?"

"Always have time for that."

Fanning her heated face with her hand, Amanda followed Mrs. Wendell into the house. Three older women — all widows down on their luck — sat in the parlor mending trousers and darning socks.

An older man with a Welsh name that no one could pronounce sat in a corner whittling. Since he spelled his name with a lot of Ls, everyone called him Mr. El for short. Long white hair fell to rounded shoulders, and one front tooth was gold. He blamed his dry, hacking cough on gold mining.

She guessed he was in his late forties, maybe early fifties, but he acted much older. Miners aged early, that's for sure. Still, there was something odd about the man. Like he'd been hobbled together with spare body parts, none of which seemed to fit.

"Hello, Mr. El," she called, but her greeting got no reaction. He just kept whittling away as if in another world.

The house was simply furnished with sagging sofas and Shaker-type tables and chairs. The upstairs rooms were arranged barrack-style to fit as many bodies as possible. Women and children shared one dormitory, men another. Because his cough kept others awake, Mr. El was the only resident with his own room.

Mrs. Wendell led the way to the large but

cozy kitchen. A brick fireplace and oven took up one wall. An icebox and large free-standing cabinet with built-in bins for flour and rice occupied another.

Mrs. Wendell arranged the tin cans on a pantry shelf, careful to turn the labels outward. "Why are you so against men?" she asked when they were alone again. "You have a fine father and two very nice brothers-in-law."

"I like men fine. It's just . . ." Amanda searched for words. Some women took offense at any perceived criticism, and she didn't want to hurt Mrs. Wendell's feelings. For that reason, she chose her words carefully.

"Women have more opportunities today than ever before."

Mrs. Wendell wrinkled her nose. "Trust me, the right man will support you in whatever you want to do."

"Like your husband," Amanda said, knowing it would do no good to argue. Billy-Bob Wendell and his wife had created a fine home for the county's poor and had gotten many down-and-outs back on their feet. Still, like most men, he was a traditionalist and frowned on Amanda's advocacy work. "Speaking of which, where *is* Mr. Wendell?"

"He rode into town to report a theft, for

all the good it will do us."

"Oh no! Not another."

Mrs. Wendell sighed. "They stole a couple of our good horses this time." Last time, it was their small herd of cattle.

"I'm sorry. Is there anything I can do to help?"

"Don't know that there's anything anyone can do." She reached into a cupboard for two drinking glasses and set them on the table.

Amanda pulled out a chair and sat. "Something's got to be done about the crime in Two-Time." It wasn't that long ago that people felt safe in their own homes. Now, people had resorted to installing locks on their doors. "Even the stage was robbed." She then described her own close call with outlaws.

"Mercy! You're lucky to have escaped alive." Mrs. Wendell threw up her hands. "The thing that worries me is that the candidates running for sheriff aren't worth a plugged nickel."

Amanda bit her lower lip. "Did you know that I'm running too?"

Mrs. Wendell laughed. "So I heard. Billy-Bob and I had a good laugh over that one." She grew serious. "You're the best of the lot, and I'm not just saying that to be nice.

It's true. Too bad you're a woman." She lifted a pitcher of lemonade out of the ice-box.

"Actually, I think it's an exciting time to be a woman," Amanda said and then described her trip to Austin. "Women are capable of doing all sorts of things, but unless we gain the right to vote, we'll always be second-class citizens. That's why I'm starting a women's rights group; I'd like you to join."

Mrs. Wendell tittered. "Oh, mercy, not me. I've got about all the rights I can handle right here. Don't know why you young folks want to take on more responsibilities. If you ask me, it's unwomanly, not to mention exhausting."

Mrs. Wendell's opinion wasn't all that surprising. Many women had expressed similar views, even Amanda's own mother.

"But don't you want a say in how the country is run? Wouldn't you like to vote for our next president?"

Mrs. Wendell leaned forward and lowered her voice. "We women might not have the vote, but that doesn't mean we don't have influence. I told my husband bad things would happen if Mr. Garfield became president, and I was right. That's why he voted for that Hancock fellow. Most men wouldn't admit it for the world, but they do listen to their wives, even in political matters. So why bother to vote?"

"What about the women who are orphans or widows and have no men in their lives? What influence do they have?"

Mrs. Wendell scoffed. "I doubt that such women have a notion to vote. They're too busy trying to survive to care about politics."

Amanda sighed. Gaining the vote was only the first step. She hoped to see the day when women could own property under their own names and take out bank loans to start businesses. But it seemed as if women of a certain age had little or no interest in such things, so arguing was a waste of time. "If you change your mind —"

"The only mind that needs changing is yours, and I'm a-hoping and a-praying that a man comes along and does just that."

Amanda smiled. Mrs. Wendell meant well but was clearly a product of her generation. "That would be some man," she said and laughed. Some man indeed.

Six

R. B. Rennick bellied up to the long, polished bar of the Golden Spur Saloon and rested a well-worn boot on the shiny brass foot rail. The bar and walls of the saloon were buried beneath an onslaught of campaign handbills promising everything short of the moon in exchange for votes.

But none belonged to the lady candidate. Far as he could tell, Miss Lockwood was the only one running for sheriff not actively campaigning. Not that she had a snowball's chance in hell of winning. Still, he didn't expect her to give up without a fight. Maybe he read her all wrong. Maybe she wasn't as determined and independent as she wanted everyone to believe.

Not that it mattered to him one way or another. He had no time for women, even a looker like her. Didn't even know why she was on his mind. Especially now that he was close, so very close, to the man he had traveled all this way to find.

All that mattered was regaining some of what had been taken from him. Was that even possible? Hard to remember the time he'd lived a normal life.

Pushing his thoughts aside, he focused on his current surroundings. A haze of blue cigar smoke stung his eyes. The smell of whiskey permeated the air, along with the potent body odor of a group of cattlemen fresh off the trail. Every so often, he caught a whiff of sickly sweet perfume from one of the good-time gals. Except for a passing glance, the women left him alone. Either they sensed he was trouble or too lacking in funds to make it worth their while. They were right on both accounts.

Five long years spent in prison had sharpened his senses and taught him to keep up his guard. Now, he could usually smell trouble a mile away. Mostly, he could tell if someone recognized him or had seen through his disguise. The wrong person knowing he was out of prison could ruin his plans.

At the moment, he was safe from detection. The beard and long hair helped, as did the buckskin pants and fringed shirt, a stark change from his usual dungaree trousers, collarless shirt, and vest. The hand-tooled boots and bead-banded hat, however, were the same. A mistake, perhaps, but a necessary one. Anyone who knew him and took the time to look would instantly recognize the boots if not the hat, but the risk was worth it. Sometimes, a man needed a reminder of who he was and from whence he came, but never more than now.

Except for a few curious stares when he first walked in, everyone ignored him, even the bartender, who had yet to take his order.

Hat pulled low, Rick riveted his gaze to the large mirror on the wall behind the bar. His spine stiffened, and the hackles rose at the back of his neck. He could view practically everything behind him, including the man he hated more than anyone in the world. The man who'd brought him to town in the first place.

Rick clenched his fists and fought to suppress his anger. One wrong move on his part could spoil everything. Spoil months of planning, years of waiting.

Rick had searched high and low for this man. Had practically turned the state upside down. He'd followed every trail, no matter how faint or remote. At long last, he'd found him.

The man's name was Michael Cooper. And unless Rick's eyes were deceiving him, the man he'd come all this way to find was standing but fifteen feet away . . .

Amanda rode her pony the length of Main Street and couldn't believe her eyes. The town looked like it had been hit by a blizzard. Every window, door, wall, and post was plastered with campaign handbills, all of them handwritten.

Some candidates were more creative than others. Calling himself a human hound, the dogcatcher Mutton's campaign motto was *Sniffing Out Outlaws with Dogged Determination.*

Vote for me, proclaimed the butcher's handbills. *No bones about it; I'll make mincemeat out of crime.*

Vote for Baker

Vote for Miller.

Your troubles will be over
if you vote for Simpson.

If the handbills weren't nuisance enough, candidates stood on soapboxes at practically every corner yelling insults about their opponents. They were like a bunch of angry birds fighting over a single morsel of food.

"Unprincipled usurper," snarled Mr. Mutton, the dogcatcher, calling attention to the butcher's money-grabbing ways. With his bulldog jowls and disagreeable expression, he looked more dangerous than even the most rabid canine in town.

T-Bone yelled back from his soapbox across the street. "And you, my friend, have all the chara'teristics of a dog 'cept loyalty."

"Place your bets here, place your bets here," called a faro dealer who'd apparently decided the real action was not in the saloons but on the street. No one bothered placing bets on the possibility of Amanda winning.

"Hey, Amanda!"

Amanda reined in her horse when she spotted the baker's boy. "Hi, Scooter."

He rested his broom against the building and moved to the edge of the boardwalk. The sparse mustache he'd managed to grow did nothing to make him appear older. He stood six foot two, but his face forgot to keep up with his body, and he still looked half his age.

"I don't see any of your handbills around town," he said. "I'll make you some, if you like."

"That's okay, Scooter. Voters have already decided they don't want a woman sheriff.

Handbills won't change anyone's mind."

He pushed his lips outward. "That's a pity. I was kind of hopin' I could talk you into lettin' me be your deputy sheriff."

Amanda leaned over her saddle horn. "I didn't know you were interested in law and order."

He grinned, and his face got beet red. "Been inter'sted in law and order ever since I was knee high to a milk stool."

His enthusiasm made her smile. "Why didn't *you* run for sheriff?" Despite his youth, he had a better shot of getting elected than she did. For crying out loud, even a gnat would have a better chance.

"By the time I heard about the election, it was too late to throw in my hat." He grinned. "Maybe next month," he said, alluding to a sheriff's short shelf life.

Some people considered Scooter lazy, but she always thought there was more to him than met the eye. Turns out she might be right.

"I'd vote for you if I could," she said.

He gave her a lopsided grin. "Maybe you can be *my* deputy."

The thought made her laugh. "That's all you need."

He laughed too. "So is it a deal? If you become sheriff, can I be your deputy?"

"It's a deal," Amanda said. "Meanwhile, I have another idea. I'm organizing a women's rights group. Any chance you might like to join?" She told him a little about what she hoped to accomplish.

He shook his head, and his hair flopped from side to side like a dog's tail. "Any man joinin' your group better know how to die standin' up. That's fer sure."

"Other men who joined the women's movement have lived to tell about it. A lawyer in California is helping us."

"Yeah, well, Texas ain't California."

She sighed. "I'll let you get back to work," she said. She pressed her heels against her horse's flanks and continued on the way to her father's shop.

Papa stood outside his shop, mumbling to himself and angrily ripping campaign posters off his windows. Soap and water would be needed to remove the paste left behind.

She dismounted and tethered her horse to the hitching rail in front.

Papa greeted her with a nod. "There ought to be a law," he complained and tore Mutton's promises off the glass.

"The election will soon be over," she said.

"Humph! You know full well that no matter who's elected, he won't last past the next full moon."

"Unless they vote for me," she said in an effort to tease him out of his bad mood.

Her father yanked a handbill off the nearby lamppost. "That's all we need. A woman sheriff. Heaven help us." He spun around and tramped into his shop.

Spirits sinking, she followed him inside. All her life, she'd had to choose between pleasing Papa and following her heart. Only one person had accepted her for who she was — her now deceased grandmother. Would she ever find anyone like Grandmama again? She doubted it. Certainly no man wanted a woman with a mind of her own.

The walls of the shop were alive with ticking clocks and swinging pendulums, bringing her out of her reverie. The familiar smell of sperm oil and old wood tickled her nose.

Her sister Meg looked up from behind the counter where she stood marking the prices on a new batch of men's pocket watches, a bright smile on her face as Papa walked to the back of the shop, leaving the two of them alone.

Amanda studied her sister. Something was different about her face — a new maturity, perhaps. Marriage certainly seemed to agree with her, and today, her eyes sparkled like two turquoise gems.

Meg insisted upon keeping her job at the shop even though married. Papa couldn't understand how his new son-in-law could let his wife work. Papa held the old-fashioned belief that no respectable man would allow such a thing. In his mind, a man's job was to support his family, and shame on him who couldn't or wouldn't.

She watched Meg write a number on a small tag, preceded by a dollar sign. "I came to ask if you want to join the new group I'm starting."

Meg arranged the watch in a square cardboard box. "New group?"

Keeping her voice low, Amanda told her about the trip to Austin and what she hoped to accomplish. "So what do you say?"

Meg looked over her shoulder to where Papa sat at his workbench oiling a regulator clock. Pushing a stray strand of blond hair behind her ear, she walked around the counter and motioned Amanda to the front of the store.

"It sounds exciting, but . . . Belonging to your group wouldn't be a good idea right now. I'm afraid I couldn't be any help to you."

Amanda frowned. It never occurred to her that either of her sisters would turn her down. "Oh? Why not?"

Meg glanced at Papa and lowered her voice to a whisper. "I'm expecting."

Amanda grabbed her sister's hands in hers. "Oh, Meg!"

"Shh!" With a nod of her head, Meg mutely indicated she didn't want Papa to hear. "We haven't told anyone yet. You're the first to know."

"That's the best news ever," Amanda whispered. "I can't believe it. I'm going to be an aunt. Mama will be thrilled!" All Mama ever wanted was for her daughters to marry and fill her lap with grandbabies. Meg was about to fulfill her mother's wishes, and that was bound to take the pressure off the rest of them.

"But why aren't you jumping up and down with joy?" Amanda released Meg's hands. "It's what you want, right? To be a mother?"

Meg relieved Amanda's mind with a smile as wide as all of Texas. "Of course I do. Grant and I can hardly wait to welcome our first child."

"So why all the secrecy?"

Her sister's smile faded, and the corners of her mouth turned down. "Josie . . ."

Amanda groaned. Of course. She should have known. So far, their oldest sister's marriage had produced no children. It was a sore subject with Josie, though she tried not to show it.

"She'll be happy for you," Amanda said. Josie was always happy to hear other people's good news. Even news about a blessed event.

"I know but . . . it's got to hurt. I've only been married for a short time, while she and Ralph have been married for ages."

"I know, Meg, but you can't let Josie's problems spoil your happiness. She would be the first to tell you that."

"I'm sure you're right." Meg bit her lower lip. "Promise you won't say a word until I figure out how to break the news to her myself."

"I promise."

"As for your new group . . ."

"It's okay. I understand. You'll have your hands full with a new baby."

She was thrilled for her sister, of course, but oddly enough, it felt as if the chasm between them just got a whole lot wider.

SEVEN

On Friday, a line of male citizens waiting to vote snaked from the mayor's office halfway down Main.

The voices of candidates rent the air, turning Two-Time into the land of promise. Despite the inherent dangers the job entailed, many were drawn to the benefits of a regular salary and free living quarters. Some even saw the job as a stepping stone to a political future. It was well-known that state Senator Ross once served as county sheriff, and there was talk of him running for governor.

"Vote for me," blacksmith Steele shouted, "and I'll give each of you a 'get out of jail' pass free."

Not to be outdone, T-Bone railed, "Vote for me, and I'll put a steak on every table."

"A wooden stake!" Amanda shouted from her saddle as she rode by, and this brought a roar of laughter from the crowd.

T-Bone yelled something back to her, but by then, she was out of earshot.

I suspect no one's ever accused you of being a lady.

The voice in her head was so clear and distinct that at first, she thought its owner was in the vicinity, but a quick glance around relieved her of that notion.

Now why in heaven's name did Mr. Rennick pop into her head? And it wasn't as if it was the first time. The way he kept intruding on her thoughts, one might think she was interested in him — which she definitely was not.

Even if she wanted a beau, which, of course, she didn't, she would never set her cap for the likes of him. He was too . . . arrogant and far too surly. Furthermore, he was totally without manners. Wild and woolly didn't even begin to describe the man.

Reaching her destination, she dismounted. So far, only three people had joined her women's rights group. One man had signed up — her brother-in-law Ralph — but even he had shown reluctance and joined only as a favor to his wife. Nevertheless, she wasn't giving up.

Bells tinkled as she walked into the general store. The welcome smell of freshly ground coffee, spices, and candle wax greeted her like an old friend.

She'd barely made it inside when she was accosted by a store customer, Mrs. Aldridge.

"Oh, I'm so glad I bumped into you," Mrs. Aldridge said, walking toward her as if a steel rod ran up her spine. An older woman with a figure round as a pot-bellied stove, she had recently purchased one of the fancy headgears Amanda created. She pointed to the top of her head. "I'm afraid my hat will fall off."

Women, especially the older ones, were leery of giving up bonnet strings and didn't trust pins to keep hats secure.

"Let me see," Amanda said. She stood on tiptoes and tried to move the hat, but it held fast. It was a black lace toque with hand-made silk flowers, designed to pull the eye away from the woman's ungainly figure. The hat was a work of art, if Amanda did say so herself, and suited the woman to a T.

She pulled a hatpin from her own hat, more for Mrs. Aldridge's peace of mind than necessity, and fastened it onto the woman's hat.

"There," Amanda said, stepping back to better observe her handiwork. "That should withstand even a tornado."

"Does it look all right?" Mrs. Aldridge

asked, turning her head ever so carefully.

"It looks wonderful, and you can wear it different ways." Amanda demonstrated with her own hat, a confection trimmed with blue silk rosettes. "Pushed back like this gives the wearer a friendly, open look. A perfect way to wear it to church, don't you think?" She continued, "Tilted over one eye will make you look mysterious." She posed to show what she meant. "But if applying for a loan at a bank, you really must wear your hat straight to show you mean business."

Mrs. Aldridge laughed. "No hat will convince a banker to make a loan to a woman, no matter how she wears it."

"That's why you need to join the new group I'm forming." Amanda quickly explained what she hoped to accomplish.

"Sorry, but personally, I think women have enough to do as it is. Though I do thank you for inviting me." With a wave of her hand, she tottered toward the door, balancing the hat on her head like a waiter one-handing a tray. "Good day."

After she left, Mr. Spencer called from behind the counter. "Those peacock feathers you ordered haven't arrived yet."

"That's all right. I'll check back tomorrow." She hesitated. "Actually, I'm here for another reason. Would you consider renting out space? Perhaps over there by the window." Real estate in the town was at a premium. What little money she earned designing hats wasn't enough to pay for rent on a shop of her own, no matter how much she wanted it.

Spencer blinked. "Rent out space?" He made it sound like she had asked him to turn over his profits.

"Just a shelf or two," she assured him. A proper place to display her hats was bound to help her sell more. If things went according to plan, she would be able to afford rent on a shop of her own, maybe sometime next year. Eventually, she hoped to earn enough money to pay for her trips out of town to fight for women's rights.

Her trip to Austin revealed a gift for public speaking, but she was still unknown and would have to pay her own way until she had made a name for herself.

"I hardly have space enough to display my own goods," Spencer said.

She sighed. So far, every shopkeeper she'd queried had turned her down. The only two places she hadn't tried were the gun shop and casket company, neither of which suited her purpose.

Refusing to be discouraged, she asked him

if he would join her new group.

"Women's rights?" He looked like he'd bitten into a lemon. "Any man joining a group like that ain't working with a full deck."

"I'll join."

At the sound of the familiar male baritone, she spun around. This time, she hadn't imagined his voice, for there stood Mr. Rennick in the flesh, looking tall and very much in charge. How could she have missed knowing that such a commanding presence was in the shop?

Today, he wore a buckskin shirt with fringed cape, his hair pulled back and tied with a piece of rawhide. He was the most masculine man she'd ever met, and her pulse quickened.

"I thought you didn't approve of suffragists, Mr. Rennick."

"Nothing's changed in that regard," he said, tilting his wide-brimmed hat rakishly over one eye.

His derisive grin irritated her. Gaining the right to vote was serious business, and she didn't appreciate him making fun of it. "Then why would you want to join my group?"

"Sounds like it might be good for a few laughs." This time, he adjusted his hat to show he meant business. So he'd been eavesdropping.

She lifted her chin. "If it's laughs you want, Mr. Rennick, I suggest you join the circus." With that, she whirled around, petticoats flapping against her ankles, and left the shop amid a frantic jingle of bells.

EIGHT

It was nearly ten o'clock that night before Michael Cooper left the saloon and walked the short distance to the hotel, seemingly unaware that he was being followed.

For three days, Rick had shadowed the man. Cooper was up to something, but what? Every night, he dropped a bundle on faro, women, and whiskey. He seemed to be rolling in dough but had no visible means of employment.

Money like that almost always came from illegal activities. Murder might be his worst crime, but it sure in blazes wasn't his only.

Tonight as usual, Cooper walked through the lobby and up the stairs. Looking neither left nor right, he talked to no one. The years hadn't been kind to Cooper. In his younger days, he'd stood straight and tall, as quick in mind as he was on his feet. Though he was barely out of his thirties, his skin was sallow, eyes puffed, and he walked like a man with gout.

Following behind at a discreet distance, Rick debated whether to confront him now or wait till the new sheriff was installed to place Cooper under arrest.

The fact that Cooper was staying at the hotel, rather than one of the boarding-houses, suggested he didn't plan on making Two-Time his permanent home. So what was he doing here?

Rick paused a moment before climbing the stairs. He arrived at the second-floor landing just as Cooper entered his room midway down the hall. Room 108 — three rooms away from Rick's own.

Watching him, Rick knew he could no longer wait. Tonight was the night he would confront his wife's killer, even it meant having to lock Cooper behind bars himself.

Rick curled his hands into fists by his side. He'd waited so long for this moment, he'd almost forgotten that his real name was Rick Barrett. Rennick had been his wife's maiden name. Using it was his way of keeping her memory alive and the promise made to find her killer the day he buried her. That was more than five years ago. Five long, hellish years.

For the last six months, he'd been on the road — ever since being released from prison. The vagaries of law made no sense to him. Steal a horse, you hang; kill your wife, it's prison. Not that he was complaining. The devaluation of human life by the justice system in some counties was what kept him alive.

He served five grueling years for a crime he didn't commit before he finally got lucky. A witness on his deathbed cleared his conscience by naming his friend as the real killer.

Rick swore up and down he was innocent, but no one believed him. Instead, it took the word of a dying man to free him.

He'd walked out of prison to a world he hardly recognized. A world that now included extended train lines. There was even talk about running trains to the border.

He walked out of prison a man without a home, a man without a future. A man without a country, or at least one that he recognized. But none of that mattered. The only thing on his mind was tracking down his wife's killer. He'd lived for the day he avenged her murder, and that day was finally here.

Instead of making a dash for the door, Rick stood rooted in place. He wanted to absorb the moment. It had been a long time coming. Five years, eight months, and two weeks to be exact.

But now at long last, it was payback time. The man had stolen everything from him, maybe even a little bit of his soul.

The prosecutor had painted Rick as a jealous husband who couldn't bear to think of his wife with another man. That was absolutely true, but not in the way the prosecutor suggested.

Christy had been forced against her will. Anger didn't begin to explain the rage that shot through him the day he found his wife huddled in their bedroom, sobbing.

Cooper had threatened her with harm if she told anyone what he'd done, but she told Rick. That's because she trusted her husband enough to know he would not blame her. He'd held her close that day, murmuring soothing words, while all the while, hate unlike any he'd ever known simmered beneath the surface like a volcano about to erupt.

Cooper had worked for Rick and was one of many wranglers who helped him with his horse ranch. Rick had trusted him, like he trusted all his men. That had been his first mistake.

His second mistake was leaving Christy alone that night while he went looking for Cooper. He never found the man, but

Christy did. Fearing what Rick might do, she'd gone looking for her husband. Instead, she'd found *Cooper . . .* and was shot through the heart. Rick still blamed himself for her death.

Rick was arrested, tried, and found guilty of her murder. No one believed him innocent, not even his in-laws. So for five long years, he sat in prison and would still be rotting behind bars had it not been for a previously unknown witness — Cooper's friend.

Never for a moment did he give up hope that this time would come. Never had the thought of revenge tasted so sweet.

A young couple stepped out of a nearby room. The man and woman looked like newlyweds. The woman had on a pretty floral gown fit for a dance. Such a handsome couple, so young. So vibrant. So full of hope and promise. *Hold on to that,* he wanted to tell them. *Don't let anyone take it away.*

They were so wrapped up in each other, they didn't seem to notice him as they passed by and headed down the stairs.

Two people having a good time. Living a normal life. Doing the same things that he and his wife Christy once did. He squeezed his eyes shut for a moment to block out the memories assailing him.

Can't think of that. Not now when he needed a clear head. He opened his eyes and was surprised to see a stranger hurry out of Cooper's room. The corridor was dimly lit, leaving the man's face in shadow, except for the tiny orange glow of his cigarette. Hat pulled low, the man glanced at Rick before turning in the opposite direction. He had a funny walk, like one leg was shorter than the other.

Rick waited until the man had vanished somewhere at the far end of the hall before making his move. It was payback time. His breath whooshed out of him as he walked to the room marked 108.

NINE

That night, Amanda woke from a deep sleep to the sound of something . . . hammering.

Willing the disturbance to go away, she buried her nose deeper in her pillow, but the banging persisted. Groggily, she lifted her head and struggled to make sense of the battering sound that shook the very foundation of the house. At first, she thought she was dreaming, but a man's gruff voice below her open window told her otherwise.

"Open up!" More pounding followed.

Wide awake now, she slipped out of bed. Grabbing her dressing gown, she ran to the window and moved the chintz curtains aside. The covered porch was hidden from view, but two horses were tethered by the gate, their dark, shiny hides glowing in the moonlight. She rubbed her eyes with her knuckles. Was that more horses in the street?

Alarmed, she spun around. Such a late-night visit could only mean an emergency.

Ripping open the bedroom door, she ran barefoot into the hall.

Mama stood on the top of the stairs, holding a lantern. "What do you suppose is wrong?" she whispered, her face pale as a winter moon.

Amanda shook her head. Shoving her arms into the sleeves of her dressing gown, she hurried past her mother and down the stairs. She reached the first floor just as Papa finished lighting the gas lamp in the entryway.

Papa's white nightshirt fell to his ankles in ghostly folds.

"Is it a fire?" Amanda asked anxiously, lifting her voice to be heard over the incessant banging. That was always the main concern.

"Guess we'll soon find out." Face stoic, Papa practically yanked the door off its hinges. "What's the matter? What's wrong?" he demanded.

Peering over her father's shoulder, Amanda was surprised to see Judge Lynch and Mayor Troutman on the porch. She glanced back at the tall clock in the corner. It was a little after eleven p.m.

"Sorry to wake you, Lockwood." Mayor Troutman pulled off his hat. "Trouble's brewing. Just outside of town. Some of the boys are getting ready for a lynching."

"So why the deuce are you telling me?" Papa's voice was prickly as the hair standing up on his head.

"Thought Miss Lockwood should know," Troutman said.

"What in blazes for? She can't do anything about it!"

"We were hoping she could. As the new sheriff, it's her respons—"

"What?" Amanda crowded into the doorway next to her father. "What did you say?"

The mayor shifted his gaze to her. "I said since you're now the new sheriff . . ."

Amanda's jaw dropped. She glanced at the judge for confirmation, but he remained silent. This couldn't be happening. She was dreaming. "There . . . there must be some mistake."

Papa blew out his breath. "If this is your idea of a joke —"

"It's no joke," Troutman said. "We counted the ballots a dozen times, and they always came out the same. We planned to make the announcement tomorrow, but this can't wait."

Amanda's mind whirled. "I couldn't have won." She hadn't even campaigned. "I mean . . . this is crazy. Who would vote for me?"

"Don't know," the mayor growled. "But if

I ever find out, I'll —" He stopped and cleared his throat.

Amanda pressed her hand to her forehead. She was the new sheriff? That didn't seem possible. This had to be a dream. Since the two visitors were staring at her, she willed herself not to panic or faint, despite the temptation to do one or both.

Papa's jaw hardened. "Go back to bed, Amanda. I'll handle this!"

"Papa, please . . ."

He shook his head. "I won't have my daughter putting herself in harm's way. Now go!"

She backed away — the good little daughter.

From the deepest reaches of her heart came a familiar echo: *You can do it, Mandy. You can do it.* The voice was so clear, so distinct, that for a moment, she imagined her grandmother standing at the top of the stairs instead of Mama. Her beloved grandmother believed Amanda could do anything she set her heart on and once dressed her in trousers, shirt, and male cap so she could enter a boys' sporting event. For a girl to participate in such an activity would have been impossible without help.

The memory made Amanda square her shoulders. Something that felt like a steel rod rose up her spine. Filled with a new sense of purpose, she lifted her chin as she had seen Miss Lucy Stone do when attacked by the opposition. *This is for you, Grandmama.* She took a deep breath. *This is for you . . .*

Braced with new determination, she rejoined her father at the door where he stood arguing with the mayor.

She tugged on his arm. "If I won the election fair and square, I'll do what's required of me." Lucy Stone and the other suffragists would do no less.

Papa shuffled back a step, his jaw dropping. It wasn't the first time Amanda had fought him, but never had she so openly opposed him in front of others. "You'll go against my wishes?" he asked, his voice hollow with disbelief.

"It's my duty, Papa," she said, beseeching him to understand before turning to the mayor. "Where's this lynching taking place?"

If the mayor was surprised at the sudden turn of events, he didn't show it. "Near the old Barstow place. There's a posse out front waiting for you."

Amanda sucked in her breath. A posse? Waiting for her? Sweat broke out on her forehead. "I'll . . . I'll get dressed," she said, her voice thin as air.

The mayor slanted his head toward the judge at his side. "You must take the oath of office before you can act in a professional capacity. That's the law."

"Very well. Let's get on with it," she said.

"Amanda." Papa's eyes flashed a warning. "I forbid it . . ."

Mama joined them and laid her hand on his arm. "Henry, the vote —"

"I don't care beans about the vote." Her father's voice rose. "I don't want my daughter hobnobbing with criminals!"

Hobnobbing? Amanda raised her eyebrows but said nothing. Papa made it sound like she planned on inviting outlaws to tea or something. If she took on this job, she would do it right or not at all.

The mayor stepped into the house. "Sorry, Lockwood," he said grimly. "It's outta your hands. Outta my hands too. Least," he added with a pointed look at Amanda, "for now."

Moments later, Mama and Papa stood on either side of Amanda like two bookends. Papa didn't move a muscle, and Mama wept softly. They couldn't have looked more miserable had this been her funeral.

Judge Lynch stood directly in front of her, holding a hearing trumpet shaped like a ram's horn to his ear. The man was deaf as a doorknob but refused to retire. Practically every lawyer in town was hoarse from shouting to be heard in court.

"Raise your right hand and repeat after me." The judge spoke in a loud voice as if the rest of them were deaf instead of him.

Amanda did as she was told but had to be reminded to speak up. "I, Amanda Lockwood, do solemnly affirm . . ." Even though she shouted, it was still necessary to repeat herself several times for the judge's benefit.

Lynch shouted back. ". . . that I will faithfully execute the duties of the office of sheriff of Two-Time, Texas . . ."

Her mother's sobs grew louder. Papa's shoulders slumped, and his face twisted in anguish. The wall of ticking clocks sounded like a death knell.

Amanda hesitated. Suddenly, her earlier bravado deserted her. "M-maybe we should go over my duties again."

The judge thrust his hearing horn practically in her face. "Aye? What did you say?"

"I said —"

Mayor Troutman interrupted with a wave of his hand. "Don't worry about it. You won't be sheriff long enough to execute duties, let alone criminals." His heavy jowls quivered. "So take the blasted oath."

After she had been sworn in, the mayor thrust a tin badge into her hand. The silver star seemed to wink in the dim light as if enjoying a joke on her.

"Here's your weapon." The mayor handed her a gun belt. The Colt pistol was similar to Mr. Rennick's. "You have the right to appoint a deputy," he added. "I suggest you do so immediately. You'll need all the help you can get. Any questions?"

She blinked. Questions? She was pretty sure she had plenty, but right now, her mind was blank as an unpapered wall. She shook her head.

"You better get to work then. A vigilante hanging's not gonna look good on your record." He started for the door. "Hurry. You don't want to keep the posse waitin' any longer." With that, the mayor stormed out of the house, followed by Judge Lynch.

Mama dabbed her eyes with a handkerchief. "Oh, mercy."

"Forgive me, Mama . . ." Amanda glanced at Papa. His face was dark, remote, grim as a wintry storm.

Knowing it would do no good to argue with him, she turned. Taking the stairs two at a time, she then fled down the hall to her room. She lowered her shaking hands into the porcelain basin on the dry sink and splashed cold water on her face. Reaching for a towel, she dried herself and tried to breathe.

She was all thumbs as she pulled on a dark skirt and shirtwaist. "Sheriff Amanda Lockwood," she murmured. Gasping in disbelief, she covered her mouth with her hand. It didn't seem possible. She glanced at the rumpled bed and willed herself to wake from what surely must be a dream.

Her only hope was that the posse waiting for her outside knew what they were doing, because she sure didn't.

Not bothering to pin up the single night braid that fell down her back, she buckled on the gun belt. It was too large for her small waist, and the Colt fell to her knee. She unbuckled the belt and slid the gun in her waistband. The badge, she pinned to her shirtwaist.

Out of habit, she reached for one of her feathered hats but caught herself. None of her carefully designed headgear was up to the task of sheriff. In one of the many hat boxes stacked on top of her wardrobe was a Stetson, but she didn't have time to look for it. Tonight, she would go hatless.

Just before leaving the room, she glanced at the framed daguerreotype of her grandmother. Right now, she could use some cheering on. "If only you were here . . ."

The mayor greeted her outside with a solemn nod. She was surprised to find her pony already saddled and ready to go.

"Thank you." She took the reins from him and mounted. At least a dozen or more horsemen were gathered on the street in front of her house. Even in the dim light, she recognized the men. They were mostly business owners, but a few were farmers and one a railroad worker.

Most were built solid and strong, and that gave her a small measure of comfort. She felt no qualms about letting men handle the hard physical stuff.

"This isn't right, Amanda," her papa shouted from the porch. All that was visible was his dark bulk outlined in the doorway, but his harsh voice cut through the silence of the night like a hard-edged knife. "It's a job for a man. No woman should be sheriff."

"Whatcha talkin' about, *Sheriff*?" yelled a voice she recognized as belonging to farmer Kellerman. "I thought we were here to gather more posse members."

"Miss Lockwood is our new sheriff," the mayor said, sounding like he was announcing the end of the world.

The news was met with an outcry of protests.

"You didn't tell us that a dang female won the vote," shouted another.

"There's no time to deal with that right now," Mayor Troutman said, bellowing to be heard. "A man's life is on the line."

His shouts brought a loud objection from the neighbor across the street, whose head popped out of an upstairs window. "For the love of Henry, can't a man get any sleep around here?"

Lowering his voice, the mayor continued, "She's the sheriff, and I'm counting on you all to see that she does no harm. We'll figure out the rest tomorrow."

The men didn't take kindly to this news, and much dissent followed. Amanda expected opposition, but these men were downright hostile. One man even accused her of stuffing the ballot box.

Amanda tried to get a word in edgewise. "I wouldn't do such a —"

The heated argument grew in volume, bringing more complaints from farther down the road. For once, Mr. Crawford, who lived three houses away, wasn't hollering at his bagpipe-playing neighbor. Instead, he stood in the middle of the street yelling curses at the loudmouthed mayor.

The Double Bar Ranch owner's voice rose above the rest. "I ain't takin' orders from no woman sheriff, and that's final!"

"I didn't tell you to take orders from her," the mayor's voice boomed. "I just want you to make sure she comes back alive. Right now, we're wasting time. A man's about to be hung . . ."

"I'm not wasting time," shouted one of the men. "I'm going home to bed."

"You're part of the posse," the mayor snapped. "You can't go home."

"Wanna bet?" With that, the man whirled his steed toward town and took off helter-skelter, his horse's hooves pounding the road like a hammer on a blacksmith's anvil. His departure spurred others to do likewise. Soon, only the mayor and judge were left behind, plus a bunch of disgruntled neighbors hanging out of second-story windows.

Papa had moved to the edge of the porch. "Do you see how foolish this is? Now will you listen to reason?"

"Papa, please . . ."

Their gazes locked, hers pleading for understanding, his begging her to put a stop to this madness. Neither gave an inch. Out of his three daughters, she was most like him in temperament and stubbornness. The two of them had been at loggerheads nearly all her life . . . but never more so than tonight.

Papa stepped off the porch. "I'm going with you!"

"No, Papa. Your heart . . ." He hated being reminded of the restrictions the doctor placed on him following his health scare, but it couldn't be helped. Even riding a horse could put his life at risk.

Mama grabbed his arm, her face pale in the moonlight. "She's right."

A tortured look crossed Papa's face as he directed his next comments to the mayor with a pointed finger. "If anything happens to her, I'll hold you personally responsible."

With his threat still hanging in the air, he swung around and stomped up the porch steps and into the house, Mama by his side. The slamming of the door echoed in Amanda's head as she snapped the reins of her horse and raced out of town — alone.

Ten

"Sheriff! Sheriff!"

Amanda circled her horse around to face the direction of the horsemen galloping toward her. In the light of a full moon, the landscape with its gentle rolling hills looked like an unmade bed — one she wished she could slip into.

"Scooter, is that you? What are you doing out at this time of night? And how did you know I was the sheriff?"

He reined in his horse next to hers, and his white teeth flashed. "My pa helped count the ballots." His grin practically reached his ears. "I made my brothers all vote for you. Cousins too."

She blinked. That was no small number. "You . . . you did that? But . . . but why?"

He grinned. "Cost me a whole month's salary, but you said if you became sheriff, I could be your deputy."

"You *paid* them to vote for me?" she

gasped. Was that even legal?

"I can still be your deputy, right?"

She sighed. If only he were ten years older and a hundred pounds heavier. "Can you fire a gun?"

"Yes, ma'am." He pulled out a Colt and brandished it. "Sometimes, I even hit something."

It was no more than she expected from a baker's son. Great thunder. Could things get any worse? "Okay, follow me." Two was better than one, right? Had to be. "We're looking for a lynch mob." She had no idea how to stop a hanging. All she knew was that she had to try.

"Aren't you supposed to deputize me or something?"

She pressed her legs against her mount's side. "You're deputized!" she shouted.

Fifteen minutes down the road, they spotted pinpoints of light ahead. She reined in her horse and rose from her saddle for a better look.

"That must be them," her deputy called by her side.

Suddenly, the reality of what she was doing, or was about to do, hit her full force, and panic threatened to cut off her breathing. She had to be out of her mind to accept such a job. A man's life was at stake, and saving him had now fallen onto her shoulders. One impetuous moment, and look what happened! The tin badge on her chest suddenly felt heavy as a brick.

What if she was too late, and he'd already been hung? Worse yet, what if she reached him in time and still couldn't stop the lynching? A shudder of horror ran through her.

"You okay, Sheriff?" Scooter asked.

No, she wasn't okay. She was scared to the gills. Her hands were shaking so hard, she could hardly hold on to the reins. " 'Course I am," she managed. "I'm just planning my attack."

"I say we surprise them." He tilted his head. "Worked for Sam."

"Sam?"

"Yeah, you know, that Houston fellow. His surprise attack led to the state's ind'pendence."

She stared at him. He had to be kidding. "You do know that he had an entire army, and there's but two of us."

He grinned. "Guess we just have to plan a bigger surprise."

She heaved a sigh. Though they were close in age, his youthful exuberance suddenly made her feel very old. "I don't reckon there's a surprise big enough to get the jump on that mob." If the torch lights were any indication, there had to be at least a dozen men. Not good odds.

He shrugged. "Grandpappy always said that the longer you stare at trouble, the bigger it grows. I say what are we waitin' fer?" He took off at a fast gallop, waving his hat and shouting "Remember the Alamo!"

Chasing after him, Amanda muttered beneath her breath. As if she didn't have enough troubles, she now had to worry about Scooter's safety. Either he was a brave soul or had no clear understanding of the dangers. Whichever, she felt responsible for him. She would never forgive herself if something happened to him . . .

She rode her pony fast, shouting, "Wait!"

She caught up to Scooter just before they reached the group of vigilantes, but there was no stopping her enthusiastic sidekick.

Riding side by side — a terrified woman and a kid still caught between hay and grass — they galloped into the center of the circle. Men scrambled out of their way, cursing a blue streak.

Someone held up a lantern. Blinking against the sudden brightness, she brought her horse to a halt.

A gruff male voice shouted, "What's the

matter with you? You came chargin' in here like the brigade. Have you gone crazy or somethin'?"

"No," she cried. "I'm the sheriff!"

Her exclamation was met with brittle silence.

Next to her, Scooter pulled out his gun. "Shall I shoot, shall I shoot?" he asked, keeping his voice low.

"Certainly not!" she whispered back.

"Sheriff?" She recognized the speaker as farmer Tom Steckle. "Ya jokin', right?"

"Do I look like I'm joking?" She gazed straight at Ken Kerrigan, who appeared to be the ringleader. His hot temper had earned him the name of Pepper for short. He wore what he called "store boughten" clothes that were too small, his trousers stopping above his ankles. In contrast, his wide-brimmed hat extended way beyond his shoulders.

Amanda and Pepper had a history together and none of it good. After trying to get him to close his saloon on the Sabbath, she was ordered to stay away from him and his ilk.

"What's the meaning of this?" she demanded, suddenly aware of the troublemaker Buck Coldwell, a rail-thin man who resembled a telegraph pole. Everyone called him Gopher because of his nervous habit of digging holes in the ground with the toe of his boot.

Their animosity toward each other dated all the way back to third grade, when he purposely tripped her during a foot race and she retaliated by feeding him the wrong answers during a test.

Pulling her gaze away from Gopher, she focused on Pepper. "What gives you the right to take the law into your own hands?"

Fingers resting on the grip of his gun, Pepper glared at her from above a broken nose. "This man here's a bloody murderer."

She stirred uneasily in her saddle. Why couldn't her first duty as sheriff be something simple like rescuing a treed cat? It was just her luck that it involved a killer.

With a nudge of his head, Pepper drew her attention to the large cottonwood tree. Beneath it in the shadows sat a man astride a horse, hands tied behind his back. The rope around his neck hung from a branch above his head. The light from the burning torches failed to reach his face, but it was enough to know he was still alive. The rest was up to her.

"Found him at the scene of the crime goin' through the dead man's pockets," Pepper added.

She placed her hand on the firearm at her waist. It wasn't the first time Pepper tried taking the law into his own hands. "Who'd he kill?"

"A man named Cooper. Mike Cooper."

She didn't recognize the name. "If what you say is true, the suspect's entitled to a fair trial."

"We already had a trial. Fair and otherwise. Ya just missed it." Pepper spit out a stream of tobacco juice, which hit the ground with a plop. "The man has five minutes left to make peace with his Maker, and then we're gonna string him up good and high so they can meet face-to-face."

"Your kangaroo court has no jurisdiction here," she said.

"Oh yeah? Well, I've got news for you. Neither do you. Now git outta the way!"

One man made a move, and Scooter did some fancy maneuverings with his gun. He'd been reading too many dime novels.

"Shall I shoot now?" he whispered.

"No!" she said beneath her breath. Louder, she addressed the others. "I suggest you all leave or . . . or I'm running you in."

Pepper laughed as did his men. "You and what army?"

He had her there, but if she backed down

now, her stint as sheriff would end in disaster before she even got started. She nudged her horse to the prisoner's side.

"I'm taking him in and plan on doing it peacefully." Oh, how brave she sounded. How absolutely official. Little did anyone know her knees were knocking to beat the band and her mouth felt dry as the desert sands. "So if you would kindly let me do my job, it would save us all a peck of trouble."

Next to her, the prisoner spoke, his whispered voice directed to her ears only. "Been my experience that politeness is more effective when backed by a gun."

His voice resonated in some way. Did she know him?

Pepper looked about to call her bluff but stopped midstep when she pulled the Colt from her waist and pointed it at him.

His eyes rounded in surprise. "You don't mean that."

"Oh, I mean it all right," she said. "I'll shoot anyone who tries to stop me." Great thunder, did she actually say that?

"Better listen to her," called the prisoner. "The last time the lady fired a gun, she hit her target straight on the chest."

The deep baritone voice almost made her drop her weapon. Mr. Rennick? *He* was the murderer? She forced herself to breathe and gripped her gun tighter. Could this night get any wilder?

ELEVEN

Rennick's threat did the trick: Pepper's men were no longer laughing. They weren't moving either. Even Gopher had stopped digging with the toe of his boot. Instead, they gaped at her as if she had fangs and was ready to bite. Good thing they didn't know that the only chest she'd shot was a hope chest, and she wasn't about to enlighten them.

She drew her pony as close to the prisoner as possible, careful to keep her gun aimed at his would-be lynch mob.

"I didn't expect to find you here," she whispered.

"Didn't expect to find you here either," he whispered back. "You sure have a habit of showin' up in the most unexpected places."

Pepper raised a fist to her, his face tomato red. "If you know what's good for you, Lockwood, you'll take your baby-faced

106

deputy and go home where you belong. Me and my men are gonna clean up this town once and for all, and we don't need help from no petticoat sheriff." With a nod of his head, he motioned for his men to advance toward the prisoner.

Rennick leaned toward her, his voice hushed. "Now might be a good time to show them you mean business. The hammer . . ."

"What? Oh!" She thumbed back the gun's hammer, and the *click* stopped Pepper in his tracks. The sound didn't do much for her either; bile rose to her throat.

She swallowed and willed her voice to stay strong. "Stay right there." Gripping the Colt hard, she moved a finger onto the trigger. It took both hands and sheer determination to keep the gun from shaking.

One of the vigilantes made a sudden move, startling her. Her finger twitched, and her gun went off with a deafening blast, practically pulling her arm from its socket. Holding her gun in one hand, she pulled back on a rein to keep her frightened horse from bolting.

The gunshot had made the men jump back. Their horses whinnied and tugged at their picket ropes, but no one fell down dead . . . though Scooter looked like he was about to.

The bullet had hit the ground less than an inch away from Pepper's foot. Jumping back, he frantically patted himself up and down as if expecting to find his body riddled with bullet holes.

"Not bad," Rennick said next to her. "Next time, aim higher."

"You crazy dame," Pepper bellowed when he finally recovered. "You coulda killed me!"

Her ears still ringing, she tossed her head. "And it would have served you right for taking the law into your own hands." Something about the gun or badge — she didn't want to think it was Rennick — gave her more confidence than anyone in her position had the right to feel.

Since everyone was staring at her, she felt compelled to say more. "So whose chest am I going to shoot this time?" As if such a thing was possible.

No one uttered a word. Instead, the vigilantes stood frozen in place like a bunch of bronzed statues.

After a moment of silence, Rennick spoke up. "It wouldn't look good to be shot by a petticoat sheriff." For someone with his head in a noose, he sure did sound like a man in control. "I mean, that could permanently damage a man's reputation."

"It sure in blazes could," Scooter added, brandishing his gun.

At this, even Pepper backed away.

"I think they're waitin' for you to make the next move," Rennick whispered, egging her on.

She inhaled. "Scoot . . . eh . . . Deputy Hobson, would you be so kind as to remove the rope from the prisoner's neck?"

"Yes, sir, ma'am . . . I mean, Sheriff." With a click of his tongue, he galloped to the other side of the prisoner and slid out of the saddle. After untying the prisoner's horse, he handed her the reins.

Gripping the prisoner's reins with her free hand, she kept her gun pointed straight at Pepper while her deputy attended to the prisoner.

Scooter holstered his pistol and pulled a knife out of his boot. Mounted again, he cut the rope from the tree with one easy swipe and pulled the loop over the prisoner's head.

Rennick's hands were still tied behind him, and she meant to see that they stayed that way.

"Escort the prisoner back to town," she said, surprised at how calm and in control she sounded. If only they knew . . .

Scooter's eyes gleamed. "Will do!" He

sounded like he could barely contain his excitement. Pulling a rope from his saddle, he looped it around the prisoner's horse. She dropped the reins, and he rode away, towing Rennick behind him.

She held the lynch mob at bay with her gun. "Don't anyone move." It was as much of a command as a prayer. *Please, don't anyone make me fire my weapon again.*

Her order went unheeded, for as soon as Rennick's back was turned, Pepper raised his firearm and pointed it at the two departing men.

Her heart practically leaped to her throat, and her body tensed. "You sh-shoot, and I'll run you in for murder," she said, hoping no one noticed the tremor in her voice.

For a full minute, Pepper held his gun aimed at Rennick's back.

Gopher threw up his hands. "Dadgummit, Pepper. The lady has you over a barrel, and you know it. You shoot him, and I'll take you to jail myself. So take your loss like a man, and let's call it a night."

Pepper lowered his arm, and Amanda dared to breathe. Oddly enough, even a rabble-rouser like Pepper adhered to a code of ethics, which is probably why he surrendered. Lynching a man was one thing, but only a coward would shoot a man in the back.

Feeling a sense of victory, even though it wasn't entirely hers to claim, she motioned with her gun.

"Now git. All of you." She brandished her gun again, and the men scattered like buckshot.

They ran for their horses and raced off like their tails were on fire. Watching them bolt like a bunch of scared jackrabbits, she slumped with relief and slipped her gun into her waistband. Grandmama should see her now.

After waiting to make certain no lingerers remained, she turned her horse and galloped after her deputy. With luck, maybe she'd make it back to town with Rennick before anyone figured out that neither she nor Scooter could shoot their way out of a chicken coop. Least not on purpose.

TWELVE

Astride her horse, Amanda followed close behind the prisoner, ready to act at the first sign of trouble. Scooter kept a firm grip on the rope as he led the way back to town.

"I guess we showed them, Sheriff," he said. "Whoo-eee!"

As much as she wanted to share in Scooter's boyish delight, her earlier confidence, weak as it was, had now deserted her. Heart pounding, she held onto the reins with shaking hands and struggled to keep her emotions in check. Looking weak in Rennick's eyes could prove fatal. He already knew her skills with a gun were nonexistent.

Even so, she doubted he would try to escape. His hands were still tied behind his back, and Scooter had taken the added precaution of tying Rennick's boot laces to the stirrups — a trick he claimed to have read in a dime novel.

She was more concerned about someone

from the lynching mob ambushing them and wanting to make a name for himself.

The way back to town was lit by the silvery light of the full moon, but a slight breeze surrounded them with moving shadows — all of which suggested danger. From the distance came the howl of baying wolves. Her pony, Molly, nickered, and her already taut nerves grew as tight as the corset cutting into her ribs.

Sheriff Amanda Lockwood. Great snakes and thunder! She still couldn't believe it. The reality made her blood run cold, and gooseflesh crawled up her arms. She had to be out of her cotton-picking mind. She could no sooner track down outlaws than a three-legged goat. By some strange fluke, she'd saved Rennick's neck — at least temporarily — but that didn't mean she could do the job.

The lynch mob had been made up of misguided but well-meaning citizens. Crime had run rampant in recent months, with no end in sight. Who could blame them for taking the law into their own hands? Some of the vigilantes had known her almost all her life. She doubted any would have done her serious harm. But what if she met up with real outlaws? What then?

"When are you gonna let me go?" Rennick asked, his voice cutting through her worrisome thoughts.

She met his gaze. Big mistake, for now her worries doubled. He sat tall in the saddle, even with his hands and feet tied. What if he somehow worked himself free? Or had a partner somewhere waiting to ambush them? It wouldn't be the first time someone had escaped while in protective custody.

"Let you go, Mr. Rennick? Now why would I go and do a fool thing like that?"

He gave her a knowing look, as if reading her thoughts. "You don't have a nefarious plan for *me,* do you?" he asked, a blatant reference to their first meeting.

She glared at him. If his plan was to intimidate her, he was doing a good job. "Are you asking if your virtue is safe?"

"A man can't be too careful."

"Guess not," she said. "But if it will make you feel better, I'm taking you to jail."

"I thought you and me were friends."

Eyes narrowed, she studied a large granite boulder ahead. More than one outlaw had used it to prey on unwary travelers. "I don't make friends with murderers."

"Whatever happened to innocent till proven guilty?"

"Not my problem," she said.

"Case you're interested, I didn't kill nobody. He was dead when I found him."

Something moved, and she gasped, but it was only a coyote. She swallowed a mouthful of air to calm her nerves. "Tell it to the judge."

They rode in silence for several minutes before he asked, "Aren't you at least interested in who the real killer is?"

"Right now, I'm hoping it's you. It would save me a lot of trouble."

Rennick surprised her by laughing. Scooter turned his head to look at him but said nothing.

Gripping the reins tight, she lifted her chin. "What's so funny?"

He was laughing so hard, he could hardly get the words out. "Just thinkin' about the looks on their faces when you announced you were the new sheriff." His hoots rolled across the landscape like thunder.

Glancing nervously over her shoulder to make sure they weren't being followed, she then focused her gaze on the road ahead. Her only hope was that they reached town before anything sinister happened.

"Laugh if you must, Mr. Rennick. But if you recall, I've saved your neck twice." Who knows what those highwaymen would have done had it not been for her peacock-feathered hat?

"That you did, Miss Sheriff. That you did." He paused for a moment before adding, "Still, I can't help but wonder what those hombres would say if they knew you couldn't shoot straight if your life depended on it."

Scooter looked back at her before addressing the prisoner. "I thought you said the sheriff shot her target square on the chest."

"That she did," Rennick said and laughed again. The light of the moon made his eyes sparkle and his teeth glisten. For someone on the way to jail, he sure did look unconcerned. Looked mighty handsome too, even with his beard.

"Don't worry, Miss Lockwood . . . I mean Miss Sheriff. *All* your secrets are safe with me." His warm, smooth voice and knowing gaze left no doubt as to his meaning.

Cheeks blazing, she silently cursed him. If he hinted at the contents of her hope chest one more time, she might just use him for target practice.

Main Street was deserted when they reached town, but Amanda didn't dare let down her guard.

They rode single-file down the middle of Main to the sheriff's office. Scooter dismounted first and tied his horse to the hitching rail.

Amanda slipped out of the saddle and wrapped Molly's reins around a post. "Help him down," she said, resting her hand on the grip of her gun.

"Will do, Sheriff." Scooter untied Rennick's shoelaces and then helped him off his horse.

Amanda took up the rear as Scooter led Rennick up the boardwalk steps and through the office door. She took a quick glance around before following them inside. Everything went smooth as clockwork.

Until it didn't.

Just as they reached the door leading to the cellblock, Rennick kicked the gun out of Scooter's hand. Amanda cried out in alarm. Before the deputy could react, Rennick head-butted him with such force, Scooter went flying backward. He hit the door with a thud before slithering to the floor.

Somehow, Amanda had the presence of mind to pull out her Colt. "Stop or I'll shoot!"

"Like heck you will," Rennick growled.

He started past her, but Scooter reached up and grabbed him by the leg before he made his escape.

Rennick fell to the floor, and the two men scuffled. Just when it looked like Scooter had the advantage, one well-placed foot sent him sailing across the room.

Holding the barrel of her gun with both hands, Amanda hit the back of Rennick's head as hard as she could with the grip.

Body rigid, he turned, his face lit with surprise. He opened his mouth as if to speak . . . but instead crumpled to the floor.

Scooter scrambled to his feet and picked up his pistol. He and Amanda stared down at the prone body lying at their feet.

"Gee willikers," Scooter said, rubbing his shoulder. "He almost got away."

"Are you all r-right?" she stammered.

"Better than he is." Holstering his own weapon, Scooter grabbed Rennick under the arms and grinned up at her. "Like Grandpappy always said, a spur in the head is worth two in the heel."

Amanda drew in her breath. She was shaking so hard, she could hardly think. "I-I didn't mean to hurt him." The thought of seriously harming someone filled her with horror. "Is he . . ."

Scooter leaned over and poked Rennick with his gun. "He's still breathing."

"Thank God." She slumped against the desk. "We better get him into the cell before he comes to." And while she still had her wits about her.

THIRTEEN

What to wear, what to wear . . .

Amanda pulled the clothes out of her wardrobe one by one. She examined each skirt, shirtwaist, and dress with a critical eye before tossing it aside. One discarded skirt struck the wall, knocking a "Votes for Women" handbill to the floor.

Her bedroom looked nothing like her sisters' rooms had looked when they lived at home. They favored floral wallpaper, ruffled curtains, and dressing tables encircled with Swiss-dotted skirts.

In contrast, Amanda's stark white walls were plastered with handbills supporting all the causes she'd favored through the years. Books were crammed into every nook and cranny. Hat forms molded with felt in various sizes, shapes, and colors stood drying on windowsills and floor. Handmade silk flowers and colorful ribbons spilled out of drawers and haphazardly stacked boxes.

She yanked another skirt off a wooden peg. Nothing so far had suited her needs. What does a woman sheriff wear anyway?

"Watch it," her sister Meg cried, ducking to keep from being assaulted by an airborne frock.

Meg and Josie had rushed to the house the moment they read the election news in the extra edition of the paper. Both had expressed horror in no uncertain terms.

Meg looked especially upset. Today, blond wisps escaped an untidy bun as if she had pinned her hair up in a hurry. "I still can't believe people actually voted for you. Of all the crazy things you've done through the years, this has got to be the craziest."

Josie made a face. "And that's saying something." She stabbed her index finger at the Two-Time book of town ordinances that lay open on her lap. Amanda had brought it home from the sheriff's office to study.

"Listen to this," Josie continued. " 'It's against the law for a lady to lift her skirt more than six inches while walking through a mud puddle.' What do they expect you to do? Walk around with a tape measure?"

Amanda sighed. Two-Time had more laws than a dog had fleas. Unfortunately, most were aimed at regulating the behavior of women. Few laws actually dealt with the illegal activities of criminals.

Josie continued. " 'And women of uncertain chastity are not allowed on the streets after dark.' " She shrugged. "That takes care of half the women in town."

"And look at that one," Meg said, reading over Josie's shoulder. " 'It's against the law for women to raise their voices in public, curse, or wear fake mustaches.' "

Amanda rolled her eyes and placed the index finger from both hands beneath her nose to imitate a mustache. "Oh yeah, that's what I want. A hairy lip." Maybe then she'd look more official.

Josie laughed. "Just be sure not to raise your parasol on Main, or you might spook the horses and land in jail." She kept reading, each law progressively more ridiculous or impossible to enforce than the last. "Oh, here's one you should be familiar with. 'Women are not allowed in saloons, barbershops, or other domains sacred to men.' "

"Sacred my foot." Amanda made a face. Waltzing into the Golden Spur Saloon to demand it close on Sundays had earned her a stint behind bars. Nothing sacred about it.

"I especially like that one," Meg said, pointing over Josie's shoulder. " 'It's illegal for a volunteer fireman to rescue a woman wearing a nightgown. If she wants to be rescued, she must be fully clothed.' "

Josie burst out laughing. "Look at this one . . ."

Amanda scowled. "You two are supposed to be helping me pick out an outfit." She had to *look* like a sheriff, even if she didn't feel like one.

Meg held up a plain dark skirt. "What about this?"

Amanda had already rejected the skirt once and was about to reject it again when something occurred to her. She grabbed it out of Meg's hand and held it up to herself.

"Do you suppose Mama could turn it into a divided skirt?"

"I don't know why not," Josie said. "You know what a sewing whiz Mama is now that she has a stitching machine."

Amanda rushed to the bedroom door. "Mama!" she called, sticking her head into the hall.

Moments later, Mama came running up the stairs. "What is it?" Her gaze took in all three of her daughters as she wiped her hands on her spotless apron.

Amanda told her what she wanted done. "I need it in a hurry." Scooter had agreed to open up the office and see that their prisoner had breakfast, but she didn't feel

122

right about leaving her deputy alone for long.

"I'll have it done in no time."

"Mama . . ." Amanda's voice broke. "Is Papa . . ."

She heard Mama's intake of breath. "He's worried about you and fears for your safety. As do I."

"I'll be careful, Mama, I promise."

Mama shook her head. "Fighting crime is no job for a woman."

"Mama, please . . . I want you to be proud of me. Proud of what I'm trying to do."

"I *am* proud of you. Proud of all my daughters. But this . . ." Mama shook her head. "This is not what I raised you for." Mama looked about to say something more but instead left with the skirt flung over her arm. The door closed behind her, but not soon enough to hide her tears.

Mama's tears affected Amanda more than Papa's bluster, though both reactions rose from the same concern for her welfare.

Josie ran her hand across Amanda's back. "You can't blame Mama for being worried. Papa too. We're all worried about you. That's because we love you."

"I know." Amanda blinked back the burning in her eyes. Sheriffs don't cry.

Meg sighed in sympathy. "None of us will

think poorly of you if you resign."

"I can't do that. You know I'm not a quitter."

"We all know that," Meg said. "You faced a lynch mob and escorted a murderer to jail. That's more than most of our male sheriffs have done."

Stopping a hanging was the least of it. She also kept the prisoner from escaping, but that would only worry her family more. Best not to mention it.

"*Alleged* murderer," she said instead and pulled a plain white shirtwaist out of a drawer. Did Mr. Rennick really kill that man? He claimed he hadn't, but didn't all guilty men lie? And wouldn't a wrongly accused man want to stay and clear his name instead of trying to escape?

"Alleged or not, it was still a brave thing you did." Meg looked pale and had declined Mama's offer of coffee or tea. It sure did look like she might be having morning sickness. If Josie noticed, she didn't say anything.

"Weren't you scared?" Meg asked.

"Of course I was scared." She held up the shirtwaist. "What do you think of this?" she asked, anxious to change the subject. "All I need is a vest." A dark vest would show off her shiny badge.

Meg frowned. "Only men wear vests."

"And some believe that only men can be sheriffs. I aim to prove them wrong." She stared at herself in the cheval mirror. A hat. She needed a hat, and none of the fancy ones she'd designed would do.

With a flurry of activity, she pulled the hat boxes from atop the tall wardrobe. Where was it? She'd worn the black wide-brimmed Stetson only once. Wouldn't you know it was in the last box she checked? She placed it on her head and whirled about to face the mirror.

It was perfect . . . almost. She glanced around, and her gaze fell on her grand-mother's photograph. She plucked a red quill from a vase and stuck it in the hatband. Red was her grandmother's favorite color, and the feather once adorned the very first hat Grandmama had made for her. It was her grandmother who instilled in her the love of hat making.

She stared at herself. *A hat's like a woman,* her grandmother liked to say. *A good one gets better with age. A cheap one only gets old.*

She whirled to face her sisters. "What do you think?" she asked. "Do I or do I not look like the country's best female sheriff?"

Dressed in her newly bifurcated skirt, Amanda rode into town and tried to ignore the disapproving stares and shouted insults that greeted her at every turn.

"We don't want no female sheriff!" someone yelled as she passed a surprisingly large crowd on the corner of Main and First.

"Yeah," added another. "Go home where you belong."

"She ain't got no home. That's 'cuz no man will marry her!"

Amanda bit back the retort that flew to her lips. A graduate of Miss Brackett's Training School for Volunteer Workers of the Suffrage Campaign, she had been taught to respond to public scorn with grace and charm, but never had it been so hard to do.

A crowd of women flocked in front of the sheriff's office, blocking the boardwalk in both directions. Sighing, Amanda tugged on the reins of her pony and reminded herself of Miss Brackett's teachings. *Grace and charm, grace and charm, grace and charm . . .*

Dismounting, she tied her horse to the hitching post and stomped onto the boardwalk. The heck with grace. Charm too. Glaring at the small gathering, she braced herself for battle. Before she could speak, the women burst into applause, startling her.

The banker's wife, Mrs. Mooney, signaled for quiet. Round as a boardinghouse cat, she never missed an opportunity to mention her social position, to which she gave more credence than anyone else. On her head sat a heliotrope monstrosity with feathers sticking out like the arms of a windmill. Anyone stepping too close was liable to get poked in the eye.

"As the bank president's wife, I thought it only right that we give a proper welcome to our new sheriff," she said, fluttering her ring-laden hands.

Surprised and more than a little gratified, Amanda smiled. "Why, thank you, Mrs. Mooney. That's mighty kind of you."

The noisy welcome brought Scooter running out of the office.

"Meet my new deputy," Amanda said.

This brought another round of applause. Not used to so much attention, Scooter's face turned red as a barn.

T-Bone's wife, Claudia, checked Amanda over from head to toe. Her orange-red hair had been tortured into sausage curls and her rounded body shoehorned into a frock two sizes too small. Worse, she insisted upon wearing an unflattering pale-yellow hat tilted in such a way as to allow her curls to fall unhampered at the back of the head.

"Well, what do you know?" Claudia drawled. "If you don't look official."

Amanda smiled and turned a full circle so that they could see her entire outfit. Mama had done a bang-up job of turning the skirt into a divided one. She'd altered the tan leather vest that no longer fit Papa, and it provided a perfect finish to her uniform. With Josie's help, they had even managed to adjust the belt holding up the holster so her gun settled at her side where it belonged, rather than at her knees.

Everyone oohed and aahed. Two more ladies joined the group. One of them lifted the hem of her skirt above the six-inch limit set by town ordinance as she stepped onto the boardwalk.

"Aren't you at least a little upset that your husband lost the election to a woman?" someone asked the butcher's wife.

"Heck, no!" Claudia replied, her sausage curls shaking. "I've got no bone to pick with Amanda." Her little butcher joke brought gales of laughter from the crowd.

Ordering everyone to be quiet, Mrs. Mooney turned to Amanda. "We are here today to offer our services."

"Your services?" Amanda's mind whirled. "Oh, you mean you want to join my new women's suffragist group."

"Suffragist group?" Mrs. Mooney stared down her considerable nose. Righteous indignation was emphasized by the quivering feathers on her hat. "Certainly not. We have more important things to worry about than voting. We want to be your posse."

"My posse?" Goodness gracious, Amanda hadn't even thought about putting together her own posse. Did she need one? She hadn't a clue how to track down the bad guys and certainly would need help. Since the women looked dead serious, she studied them each in turn. They ranged in age from the early twenties to mid to late sixties.

The ever-present knitting needles sticking out of Mrs. Perl's rucksack gave Amanda pause, as did the low-cut dress and obscenely rouged face of good-time gal Goldie. If poor taste was a crime, half the women in town were deserving of arrest.

"You do know that a posse's job is to go after outlaws?" Amanda asked tactfully, not wishing to hurt their feelings. Recalling the town ordinance that forbade women of uncertain chastity from being out after dark, she added, "Sometimes even at night."

"We know what the job entails," Ellie-May

Walker said, hands on her ample hips. "And since the men of this town can't seem to do the job, it's up to us women."

"Hear, hear," Mrs. Granby said, illegally popping open her parasol and jeopardizing the well-being of the town's horse population. In less than five minutes, not one but two laws had been broken — three if blocking the boardwalk was counted. No wonder the other sheriffs didn't have time to concentrate on real crimes.

"Amen, sister," Mrs. Wellmaker said. Married to the minister of the Two-Time Community Church, her virtuous white felt hat hardly seemed to belong to the dowdy red-and-purple dress that circled her like a lampshade.

Mrs. Mooney inclined her head. "As the bank president's wife, I say we go after those bandits and show them we mean business."

Amanda wasn't sure what kind of business the motley group was ready for, but it sure didn't look like law enforcement. Some were married; some, widowed. Miss Cynthia Read had never wed, though it wasn't from lack of trying. She didn't bother with feathers. Instead, an entire stuffed dove perched atop the rounded crown of her hat — a fad Amanda utterly opposed. If the style caught on, the entire bird population would be endangered.

A retired schoolmarm, Miss Read had perfected the impressive stare that Amanda remembered from her youth and could still make grown men shake in their boots.

The youngest woman was Becky-Sue Harris, who giggled at the slightest provocation. True to form, she let out a high-pitched squeal that made Amanda flinch. A pretty girl with auburn hair and blue eyes, she looked closer to fifteen than twenty-one, and the poke bonnet tied beneath her chin was partly to blame.

"Oh, this is so exciting," she said and giggled. Next to her, Scooter got all red in the face again and laughed too.

"Do any of you know how to fire a weapon?" Amanda asked. It seemed as good a place as any to start.

The women looked at each other, but only the gun shop owner's wife, Ellie-May, raised her hand. "I've got me a shotgun, and I know how to use it."

That was music to Amanda's ears. "All right, Ellie-May, you're in. As for the rest of you, you need to get yourselves a weapon and learn how to shoot."

Ellie-May lifted her chin. "I'll see that my husband gives you all discounts."

"That would be most helpful," Amanda

said. "There's also the matter of clothes." She pointed to her own divided skirt. Strangely enough, she felt more comfortable in her new no-nonsense attire than she'd ever felt in long ruffled dresses or fashionable traveling suits.

"As my posse, you will all need to be able to move quickly and freely. You also need sturdy footwear so you can run."

Mrs. Perl gasped. A stout woman with a stack of quivering chins, she was the only one not wearing a hat. Instead, a lacy scarf was arranged over her thin brown hair like a crocheted doily on the arm of an upholstered chair. "Run? But that's so . . . unladylike."

Amanda scoffed. "We're not catching gentlemen; we're catching criminals who probably wouldn't know a lady from a mule." Had they known that she had knocked a man unconscious last night with the butt of her gun, they would no doubt be shocked. "It's hard work, and we must dress accordingly."

The women stared down at their own dainty shoes and then studied Amanda's sensible boots and split skirt.

"Soon as you're ready, I'll swear you in," Amanda said. If the need for more practical clothes didn't discourage them, perhaps the necessity of shooting lessons would.

Solemn heads bobbed up and down, but any hope of them grasping the seriousness of their undertaking was dashed the moment Becky-Sue squealed, "Oh my! This is so much fun. I can hardly wait to get started."

Mrs. Perl tittered and waved her knitting needles. "My son won't believe it. He thinks I'm a doddering old fool. Wait till he hears I'm actually working with the sheriff." She lowered her voice to a loud whisper. "Of course, when I write to him, I won't mention that it's a *woman* sheriff."

This brought appreciative laughter all around.

Mrs. Mooney, as usual, took charge. "I think we've done enough jawing for the day. I say we get started! We have much work to accomplish, and there's no time to lose."

The women departed, walking in groups of twos and threes. They headed for Walker's Gun Shop, cackling like a bunch of old hens. Watching them, Amanda's reservations increased.

Even Scooter looked worried, his usual grin replaced by a frown.

"What do you think?" she asked.

"I think Grandpappy was right. Getting a

bunch of possums up the same tree is near impossible."

FOURTEEN

Seated behind the sheriff's desk moments later, Amanda pressed her hand on the scarred wood surface and willed her stomach to stop churning. She couldn't make head or tail out of the jumble of papers the last sheriff left behind and finally ended up tossing the whole mess into the waste basket.

Upon seeing a cockroach skitter from behind the wicker basket, she shuddered. Next to Austin's new palace-like lockup and jailor's quarters, Two-Time's jailhouse was not worth a tinker's curse. Amanda had seen cleaner pigsties.

"You okay, Sheriff?"

Scooter looked so concerned about her welfare that she straightened her back and forced a reassuring smile. If only she could control her quivering nerves . . .

"I'm fine." She ran her palm over the desk. The now-cleared surface gave her a false sense of control. "I just need time to get a handle on the job."

"Like Grandpappy always said, a good leader governs a nation as he would cook fish. I guess you could say the same for a town."

Amanda pinched the spot between her eyebrows. She didn't want to discourage him by admitting she'd never cooked a fish in her life. "Any problems?" She slanted her head toward the jail cells in back to indicate the sole prisoner, Mr. Rennick.

"Nope. But he keeps asking for you."

"Guess I better see what he wants." She hesitated. "Is he all right? His head?"

"Looked all right to me," Scooter said.

"What time does he have to go before the judge?"

"Well, now, that's a problem," Scooter said. "Lynch was called out of town and doesn't know when he'll be back."

She grimaced. Rennick had already proven to be a difficult prisoner, and now she was stuck with him.

Just as she started to rise from her desk, the door flew open, and in walked Mayor Troutman. He looked even more beleaguered than he had the night before. His bow tie was askew, and his derby tipped to the side.

She lowered herself back into her seat. "What happened to you?"

"What happened?" He mopped his brow with a handkerchief. "I spent the morning defending your honor, that's what."

She blinked. "My hon——"

"The town council held an emergency meeting this morning to discuss the problem."

Scooter frowned. "What problem?"

"What problem?" Troutman thundered, his mustache quivering. "Why, the sheriff being a woman, of course."

"And did they come up with a solution?" she asked wryly.

"Unfortunately not!"

"I guess that means I'll just have to remain a woman," she said, winking at her deputy, who grinned back.

"Yes, and that's why the council decided to call for your resignation."

She leaned back in her chair. A high tolerance for criticism had served her well in the past. Bucking society required a tough exterior and a firm belief in what she was doing. But nothing she'd done prior compared to the task she'd taken on now.

"Tell them to keep calling, 'cause I'm not going anywhere. I intend to clean up this town like I was elected to do." Like Scooter's siblings and cousins elected her to do.

"The council isn't gonna like that."

Her resolve increased. "Are they aware that I saved a suspect from a lynch mob?"

"Oh, they're aware of it, ma'am. But some think you did the town no favor."

"I'm sure Mr. Rennick would disagree."

Troutman rubbed his whiskered chin, and she could almost see the wheels turning in his head. "Here's the thing," he said, abruptly changing tactics. He continued in a voice clearly meant to appeal to her more *rational* side. "No man is willing to take orders from a woman. No disrespect intended, mind you. It's the way things have been for thousands of years, and we see no reason to upset the applecart. That means you won't be able to find anyone willing to assist you. Without a deputy or even a posse to back you up, you haven't got a chance of bringing law and order to this town."

"I've already got a deputy," she said. Dressed in his usual overalls and slouch hat, Scooter looked as much a deputy sheriff as a duck resembled a dog. Better not mention her posse till she'd seen how the ladies made out.

Scooter grabbed the mayor's hand in that overzealous way of his. He jerked it up and down as if trying to squeeze the last drop of

138

water out of an old rusty pump. "Deputy Sheriff Hobson, at your service."

Looking startled, the mayor pulled his hand away and reared back as if he'd just been bitten by a rattler. "He's a baker's son and a loafer. You'd be better off hiring a goat."

Amanda's temper flared. It was bad enough that people voiced derogatory comments about her, but she wasn't about to let anyone disparage Scooter.

"My *deputy,*" she said emphatically, "was most helpful last night in facing down that lynch mob." It seemed best not to mention that the prisoner nearly escaped before they could lock him up. "I believe the two of us make a formidable team."

Scooter beamed. "I believe we do too, Sheriff."

The mayor scoffed. "A mule team, more like it."

The smile left Scooter's face. "Like Grandpappy always said, one must sometimes let turnips be pears."

Forehead furrowed, Troutman stared at Scooter for a moment before tossing a set of keys on the desk. "Those are for upstairs."

She'd forgotten that the job of sheriff included living quarters.

He then reached into his coat pocket and

pulled out a check. "That's the first and probably last month's pay." He slapped her salary onto the desk. The check was made out for forty dollars. "I'll see that a check is issued for your . . . eh . . . deputy."

"Where's the rest?" she asked. The usual pay for sheriff was two dollars a day.

"The rest?"

"I happen to know that's less than customary pay for sheriff."

"That's because you're less than a man." He whirled about and left the office, slamming the door shut behind him.

She banged the desk with her fist. "Ooh, he makes me so mad."

The mayor did, however, do her one favor. He made her more determined than ever to show him and his cronies she could do the job she'd been elected to do. Even if it killed her.

Deputy Hobson gave her a sympathetic look. "I don't think you're less than a man."

He looked and sounded so serious, she couldn't help but laugh. "Thank you, Scooter. I appreciate that."

Rick paced back and forth in his cell like a caged animal. He still couldn't believe he was behind bars. Again.

To make matters worse, he had been put

there by a lady sheriff and her overzealous sidekick. The lady's knowledge of guns would probably fit on a three-cent postage stamp with room to spare. Yet after he'd overtaken her deputy, she'd clobbered him over the head with the butt of her Colt like nobody's business.

How could such a small package be so lethal? Never had he felt more mortified — as if the egg-sized bump on the back of his head wasn't bad enough.

He still couldn't believe it. He was no lightweight. Had in fact fought off half a dozen thugs during a prison riot. Yet one pint-sized woman had gotten the best of him.

The memory made his head pound harder. Gingerly, he reached back to finger the sore lump. Cripes! Why did she have to earn her bread as a sheriff at his expense?

He turned stiffly, almost stumbling in the confines of the tiny space. He was better suited for the great outdoors than an iron cage. If he ever got out of this mess, he'd be tempted to spend the rest of his life avoiding anything with a roof over it.

He whirled about and punched the wall, but all he got for his effort was sore knuckles. Even the narrow barred window that looked out on an empty field offered no chance of escape. After spending five years in prison, he swore off confinement forever. Yet here he was less than six months later, behind bars again. And he had only himself to blame.

Of all the stupid, idiotic . . . Shaking with fury, he tried to think. He'd escaped a hanging, but no man was that lucky twice. If he didn't find a way out of this mess, he would soon be keeping company with the daisies.

His thoughts interrupted by raised voices, he turned to stare out the open door leading to the sheriff's office. All morning long, he'd watched a parade of disgruntled citizens storming in and out of the office. Now, he studied the lady sheriff seen in profile. Like it or not, she was his best chance of getting out of there alive. She might be his only chance.

He tried reconciling the woman currently holding her own against a group of combatant citizens with the one he found stranded in the middle of the Texas wilderness. He didn't want to feel sorry for her, but how could he not? It hadn't been an easy morning. Even now, he could hear a group of angry protestors outside demanding a new election.

No sooner had the mayor left than members of the town council arrived, insisting upon her resignation. She might not have the experience or knowledge required of a lawman, but she sure did know how to hold her own against those blathering council members.

No slack showed in her rope, that's for sure. Instead, she let each unwelcome visitor have his or her say before pointing them firmly to the door. In some cases, she even ordered her eager deputy to bodily escort the person out. He couldn't help but admire Miss Sheriff Lockwood.

It helped that there were no architectural nightmares on her head today. Instead, she wore a sensible high-crowned, wide-brimmed hat. The hat was bound with a band that sported a brave red feather standing as stiff and straight as the lady's back. The whimsical feather offered a strange contrast to the serious-looking Colt hanging at her side.

What she lacked in skills, she made up for in sheer determination. Or maybe it was mule-headed stubbornness. Whatever it was, he intended to use it to his own advantage . . . if only he could figure out how. Winning over a woman like that wouldn't be easy. She wasn't the kind to fall for charm or flattery. What then?

He was still considering the problem when

she appeared in front of his cell. She stood facing him, feet apart, hands at her waist, blue-green eyes focused directly on him. She looked formidable enough, but how far would that get her should she confront a real outlaw?

"You'll wear out your leather pacing back and forth," she said.

"It wouldn't be the first time."

"Deputy Hobson said you wanted to see me."

He stopped pacing and faced her square on. His gaze lingered on the red feather in her hatband before dropping down to take in the rest of her. Hard to believe that such a dainty woman could deliver such a lethal blow. His still-throbbing head might never be the same.

They measured each other like two poker players in a high stake game. "My horse . . ."

"He's at the stables," she said. "Took him there myself. I'll see that the county foots the bill."

"Here's the thing. My horse doesn't take kindly to being cooped up for long periods of time. You could say he's a restless sort."

Her eyes shimmered with light from the barred window. "Kind of like his owner," she said.

"Maybe. That's why I named him . . .

Spirit." Actually, his horse answered to the name of Killer, but that hardly seemed like a name that would win a lady's heart. "Would it be possible to arrange for him to be exercised?" It was his experience that most stable owners kept horses confined. When Rick escaped — if he escaped — he wanted his horse in tip-top condition and ready to run and run hard.

"I can ask," she said.

An idea suddenly occurred to him. "Perhaps you could ride him." Having his horse hitched in front of the sheriff's office instead of the stables would be mighty convenient when he broke out of jail.

"I don't see how." She indicated her office with a slight toss of her head. "I've got work to do."

"Most of which will probably have to be done on horseback."

Her gaze sharpened. "You want me to ride your horse in an official capacity?"

He shrugged. "That hobby horse of yours is a joke. Been my experience that two things command respect — an accurate shot and the right mount." His gaze dropped to the Colt at her waist. "Ride my horse, and you'll be halfway there. You'll also be doin' me a favor."

He could practically see the wheels turning in that pretty head of hers. "Is he easy to ride?"

"Easy as they come. Long as you keep him between you and the ground, you shouldn't have any problems."

She laughed, a sweet musical sound that made him smile. "Okay, I'll think about it."

Any hope he had scored points with her was dashed the moment her smiled faded and a scowl took its place.

"Guess you're wonderin' how a man accused of killin' could be so concerned about a horse."

"That's not what I was wondering," she said. "But now that you mention it . . ."

He arched a brow. "Like I told you before, I didn't kill nobody. And while we're here jawin' away, the real killer is on the lam."

Today, her luminous eyes were more green than blue, allowing him to clearly see the doubt in their lively depths. "You were caught at the scene of the crime going through a dead man's pockets."

"I admit things look bad. Had they shown up moments earlier, they'd have found me searchin' his room."

"For what?" she asked.

"For whatever I could find."

She frowned. "You also tried to escape. That hardly sounds like the actions of an innocent man."

"Never said I was innocent. All I said is I wasn't a killer."

She lifted her chin. "I guess we'll just have to wait and see if the bullets in the victim match your gun."

"Well, now, ma'am. That would be a trick, since the murder weapon was a knife."

Her reddening cheeks were the only hitch in her staunch demeanor. "So if you didn't kill him, then who did?"

"You're the sheriff," he said. "You tell me."

FIFTEEN

First thing the following morning, Amanda and Scooter walked the short distance to the hotel. Dressed in dark trousers, a boiled shirt, vest, and wide-brimmed hat, Scooter didn't look like a baker boy today, though he still smelled of hot cross buns.

"This is so exciting!" he exclaimed. "We're doin' real detective work. Like one of those whatcha call 'ems? Pinkertons."

She heaved a sigh. As much she appreciated her deputy's enthusiasm, she needed him to clamp a lid on it. Whooping with glee while snapping handcuffs on a prisoner was unprofessional, to say the least. But that's exactly what he'd done earlier while detaining a rowdy drunk.

"Scooter . . . I don't want you to take this the wrong way. I really like your zeal for law and order . . ."

"Why, thank you, Sheriff. That's the nicest thing anyone ever said to me."

He wasn't making it any easier for her, but still, she plunged on. "When you have a certain authority as we have, it's important to maintain a" — she searched for the right words — "respectful demeanor."

"I know what you mean," he said. "Nothing worse than disr'spectful demons."

"Demeanor," she said. "It's how we conduct ourselves."

"Don't you worry. From now on, you're gonna see all the demeanor I have."

"That's good," she said, relieved that he didn't take offense. "I'm glad we had this little talk."

"Oh, me too, me too," he said. "So what are we lookin' for at the hotel?"

"The murder weapon." The one thing that bothered her about Rennick's case was that no knife was found. She'd questioned several of the witnesses, and no one could tell her what happened to the weapon.

"Also, we're looking for anything that can tell us who the victim was. Where he came from . . . what he was doing in Two-Time." After searching the victim's room, they would check out Rennick's room.

Scooter scratched the side of his head. "Do we need to know all that stuff? I thought our job was to arrest the suspect and let the court handle the rest. Don't we have other outlaws to catch?"

"Yes, we do. But as sheriff, I will have to testify during the trial." It still galled her that she'd made a mistake regarding the murder weapon. Looking like a fool in front of a prisoner couldn't be a good thing.

Scooter accepted her explanation without comment, and they walked the rest of the way to the hotel in silence.

"Has room 108 been cleaned?" she asked the sleepy-eyed clerk behind the front desk after requesting the key to the suspect's and victim's rooms. She had sent strict orders that both rooms not be disturbed until she said so.

The man yawned, his horseshoe mustache quivering. He then unfolded himself from a chair, reached for the keys on the wallboard, and tossed them onto the counter. "Are you kiddin'? No one will touch it. Say it's haunted or somethin'."

Thanking him, she grabbed the keys and headed for the stairs, Scooter at her heels. "We'll check the victim's room first," she said.

As they approached the door at the far end of the hall, Scooter pulled out his Colt.

"Just to be on the safe side," he assured her.

A maid spotted the weapon and scampered away like a scared rabbit.

Scooter frowned. "Wonder what got into her?"

Amanda glanced at the gun in his hand but said nothing. Instead, she stooped to insert the key into the lock and turned the knob.

The room was in shambles. Turned upside down more like it — Rennick's work? Or someone else's?

Scooter holstered his gun. "Holy smokes! It looks like a cyclone hit."

Dried blood spotted the carpet, leaving a metallic scent in the air.

"Check under the mattress," she said. He hesitated, and she laughed. "You don't believe in ghosts, do you?"

"Heck, no."

While Scooter tore the bed apart, she dug through the clothes in the drawers and wardrobe. Not much there. A pair of trousers and shirts, long johns and woolen socks. Just clothes, nothing personal. No photographs or letters. That alone was odd. The man's past was as nonexistent as his future. It sure did seem that the victim was as much of a puzzle as the suspect.

She looked behind the picture frames on the wall, checked the bedside table, shook out the draperies, and peered under the chest of drawers. All she found was dust balls and a two-inch peacock feather.

She held the iridescent feather in her palm. "Find anything?" she called.

"Nope." Joining her, Scooter stared at her hand.

She rolled her eyes in jest. "Oh no. Don't tell me. Your grandfather had a saying for this too."

Scooter grinned. "One must walk a long time behind a duck before one picks up a peacock feather."

Amanda laughed. She couldn't help it. Wisdom probably lurked beneath those words somewhere, but for now, it remained a mystery.

"Are we done here?" he asked.

"Yes, we're done."

Slipping the feather in her skirt pocket, she turned slowly, scanning the room from baseboard to ceiling. What did Rennick do with the blasted knife?

The odor of hay, manure, and the warm smell of horse flesh greeted Amanda at the stables. She remembered Mr. Rennick's horse well. Next to Molly, he looked like a giant.

Normally, the horses stood quietly in their stalls, but today, restless movement greeted

152

her from all sides as she walked down the center aisle of the barn. Some horses pawed the ground. Others snorted or whickered.

Next to her, stable owner Gabby Jones shook his grizzled head. Bits of hay stuck to his shirt and trousers, making him look like he'd swapped clothes with a scarecrow. He gestured to the stall holding Rennick's black gelding.

"That dang horse is riling up the others. He won't settle down."

So Rennick spoke the truth. "His name is Spirit, and he needs exercise."

"His name is mud, and I've got a policy that goes like this — if you don't do somethin' to calm him, I'm drivin' him out of town and lettin' him go."

"You can't do that."

"Try me." The stable owner spit a stream of tobacco juice on the dirt floor and stomped off.

Amanda hadn't made up her mind whether to take her prisoner up on his offer, but now it seemed like she had no choice. A domesticated horse loose in the wilds had little if any chance of survival.

She walked to Spirit's stall and spoke softly over the half door. "It's okay, boy." Her thoughts traveled back to the day she first met Rennick. How well she remembered this horse. One moment, the steed seemed perfectly passive; the next thing she knew, he'd turned into a fiery demon with thunderous hooves that barely touched the ground.

Now, he hardly resembled that same horse. Instead, he seemed almost spiritless as he knocked against the wooden dividers, tail swishing and hay rustling beneath his hooves.

Moving slowly, she slid into the stall. The horse froze in place, facing forward, ears pinned back. For the longest while, neither of them moved. Finally, she reached up to rub her hand along his slick neck. He still didn't move his legs, but his muscles quivered beneath her tentative touch, and his ears twitched. Finally, he pressed his soft nose into the palm of her hand.

Standing two hands taller than her pony, Spirit had clear eyes and a shiny coat, both signs of good health. He also emitted an earthy smell. She fed him an apple and reached for his bridle, hanging on a nail.

"Your owner doesn't like being locked up either," she whispered. Spirit and his owner were two of a kind in that regard. How else were they alike?

"You wouldn't hurt anyone, would you?" How about his owner? Rennick continued to insist he was innocent, but was he? Had he not tried to escape, she might have given his claim of innocence more credence. Only a man with something to hide would try to run. Or at least that's what she believed.

Talking softly, she slipped the bridle over Spirit's head and led him out of the stall and into the bright sunshine. Almost immediately, Spirit perked up. His ears pricked, and he held his head high.

Around and around the building they walked. Only after making certain the horse wouldn't bolt did she saddle and mount him. The ground looked so far away. She closed her eyes. *Okay, I can do this. Just don't look down.*

Eyes open, she stared straight ahead and gently squeezed her legs against the horse's sides. Spirit moved forward, and she held onto the reins with a white-knuckled grasp.

Riding her own pony was an entirely different experience. He bounced up and down like a sewing machine needle. Spirit's longer legs provided a much more pleasant ride. If she didn't know better, she'd think someone had smoothed out the rutted road. After a few turns, she forgot her fear of heights and relaxed. Several more turns, and it felt like she and the horse were one.

"Wow!" Catching herself, she laughed.

She had spent too much time with Scooter. Now she even talked like him. If she didn't watch out, she'd soon be quoting Grandpappy.

"Come on, boy. Let's go. Whoopie!"

Spirit responded with a smooth, easy gait. Only a slight shift of weight, leg pressure, or seat motion was needed to increase speed or change directions. In no time at all, they were out of town and enjoying the open countryside.

Amanda loved her brown-and-white cow pony dearly, but my, oh my, did this horse make her feel like she could conquer the world.

Last night's windstorm had left the sky dark with dust, but the air was now still, and only Spirit's trotting hooves broke the silence. She was tempted to keep going and could have ridden forever through the wooded canyons and over dry grassy hills. But running was not the Lockwood way. Nor would it help the suffrage cause. Like it or not, she had to stay and show her naysayers that a woman was up to the task of maintaining law and order.

She was just about to turn back when she spotted smoke. She reined in Spirit and rose in the saddle for a better look. A jolt of alarm rushed through her. The black column appeared to be coming from the Freeman farm.

Clicking her tongue, she pressed her heels into the horse's flanks. Spirit took off in a gallop and raced up an incline.

At the top of the hill, the cabin came into full view, and she gasped. Dark smoke curled from the shingled roof. Oh no!

John Freeman had built that cabin with his own hands for his bride, and the couple was expecting their first child.

With rising panic, she snapped the reins, urging the horse to go even faster. Spirit's hooves pounded the ground as he carried her down the incline and toward the burning cabin. No sooner had they reached the property than she slid off the saddle and ran up the steps to the porch.

"Mary-Louise! John!"

She jiggled the doorknob, but it held tight. The recent surge in crime had everyone on edge, and doors that had never before been locked were now bolted.

Pounding on the solid wood, she screamed their names. Maybe they weren't home. Oh God, please let that be true. But since her friend was heavy with child, it seemed odd that she would have left the house.

The windows were still shuttered from last night's windstorm, and there was no way to open them from outside. Convinced the house was empty, she drew away from the window, but something made her stop in her tracks.

Was that . . . She gasped. "Oh no!" Please don't let that be a baby's thin cry. But it was; she knew it was. That meant that Mary-Louise had already given birth, and never would she leave her child alone.

She pounded the door with both fists. "Mary-Louise! Open up!"

She kicked hard, and pain shot up her leg. The door didn't budge. Having lost family members during the Indian Wars, John took no chances, and the door was strong enough to guard a fort.

She yelled and pounded, banged, and kicked. She shoved her shoulder against the door hard. Tears of pain blurred her vision as she desperately battered the door like an angry ram.

Growing more desperate by the minute, she ran around the house, checking windows, hoping to find one not shuttered. Thick smoke shot out of the eaves, and the sound of crackling flames filled her heart with terror. Frantically looking for something — anything — to use on the door, she spotted a woodpile with a hatchet sticking out of a log.

Grabbing the ax with both hands, she raced back to the porch. She raised the tool over her head and swung it with all her might. A spidery crack appeared in the wood.

"Come on, come on." Swinging the ax hard, she struck the door again and again.

Suddenly, the house's owner, John, appeared, seemingly out of nowhere.

"Step back!" he shouted.

Face grim, he heaved his shoulder against the door, but it held fast. He gave the door a mighty kick with a booted foot, and the already weakened wood splintered. Two more kicks, and the door fell inward with a bang.

She dashed inside after him. Thick smoke curled around her like a giant serpent. Orange tongues licked the wall dividing the kitchen from the parlor. Flames leaped to the ceiling, raced along a rafter, and showered bright-orange sparks across the room.

Mary-Louise was sprawled on the floor, and John dropped to her side.

Throat closing in protest, Amanda covered her mouth and nose with her hand and frantically searched the room. The baby . . . Where was the baby? She was sure she'd heard an infant's cry.

Eyes burning, she flew to the bedroom

and burst through the door. Blinking against the smoke, she quickly searched the room. No baby. She slammed the door shut. That's when she heard a soft cry.

The baby could barely be heard over the roar of flames and crackling wood. "Where are you, where are you?" she cried in both a question and a prayer.

Frantically knocking over chairs, tables, and a footstool, she finally found the child hidden beneath a cover in a basket next to the sofa. Grabbing the basket with both hands, she stumbled blindly out the front door, down the porch steps, and away from the burning house.

She set the basket ever so gently beneath the shade of a cottonwood. Coughing, she gasped for air and fell to her knees. Her eyes stung, and her raw throat felt like it was lined in acid.

The crying had stopped. Fearing the worst, she lifted a corner of what looked like a canvas flour sack. The baby — a boy — was naked and still attached to the umbilical cord. His red skin moist with birth fluids, he was unbelievably tiny — no larger than a child's doll. Eyes squeezed shut, he sucked hungrily on his hand.

She blinked back tears and gave a prayer of thanksgiving. Had the baby's basket not been on the floor below the smoke, she doubted he would have survived.

Blood dripped onto the child's rounded belly. She lowered the sack, folding the coarse fabric away from his face, and held up her sore hands. The knuckles were battered and covered with blood. Blisters had formed on her palms from gripping the hatchet.

Wiping her hands on her skirt, she noticed for the first time Mary-Louise lying nearby on a patch of grass. Fearing the worst, Amanda ran to her side. She shook her gently. Why, oh, why didn't she carry smelling salts with her like Mama always did?

"Mary-Louise." There was a strange rasping sound emerging from her parched throat. "Your baby is safe."

She pressed her ear to Mary-Louise's chest. She was still breathing, but barely. Where was John? Oh God, where was he? Had he gone back inside the burning inferno looking for his child? How did they miss each other?

She sprang to her feet and watched in horror as the entire roof of the house collapsed. Convinced John was inside, her legs folded like a fan beneath her, and she dropped to the ground, knees first, tears rolling down her cheeks.

Then she heard something. Holding her breath, she glanced to the side of the house just as a horse and wagon charged out of the barn. Driving the wagon helter-skelter, John pulled up in front of her. Looking like a wild man, he jumped from the wagon and scooped Mary-Louise off the ground. He laid her in the back of the wagon.

"The baby," Amanda rasped, handing him the basket. Face grim, John took it from her and set it next to his wife. "It's a boy, and he's fine," she said, hoping to relieve his mind, but the panic in his eyes remained.

"You better have the doctor check your throat," he shouted as he scrambled onto the driver's seat.

She said she would and told him to hurry. Between her croaking voice and the rattle of wagon wheels, she doubted he heard her. He drove away with nary a glance at his burning house, leaving a cloud of dust behind.

She turned to where she'd left Spirit, but the horse was nowhere in sight. In her haste to reach the burning house, she had neglected to tether him.

She tried calling his name, but all that emerged from her dry throat was a rough frog-like croak.

By now, even the walls of the house had

caved in. She shuddered to think what would have happened had John not arrived in time.

Worn to a frazzle, she leaned against a tree trunk before starting back to town on foot.

Sixteen

Amanda entered the sheriff's office with bandaged hands and headed straight for the bucket kept in the corner. After ladling water into a tin cup, she gulped it down. Her throat felt prickly and dry as a pinecone. Never could she remember feeling so thirsty.

Dr. Stybeck said her lungs were clear but it would take a day or two for her throat to heal. Mary-Louise and the baby were resting comfortably in the doctor's spare room. John had left to see if a hotel room was available until they could make other arrangements.

Amanda was working on a second cup of water when Mr. Rennick's voice drifted through the door. She set the half-empty cup on her desk. Who was he talking to? Had her deputy arrested someone in her absence?

Dreading having to explain Rennick's

missing horse, she walked to the door dividing the office from the cellblock. Scooter had already released the drunk, so the other cells were empty. Rennick's back was toward her, his low baritone voice directed out the window.

"Who are you talking to?" she rasped. It better not be someone planning to help him escape.

He turned, his gaze dropping to her bandaged hands. "What happened to you?"

She closed the distance between them so as not to strain her voice. "Never mind that. Who are you talking to?"

"I was talkin' to Kill . . . eh . . . Spirit."

Her mouth dropped. "Spirit is here?"

"Spirit always finds me. Eventually." He slanted a gaze at her hands. "I'd hate to see the other guy."

"Very funny," she said, and then she told him what had happened.

Concern filled his eyes, and it was all she could do keep from bursting into tears. *Grace and charm. Grace and charm. Grace and charm.* Miss Brackett insisted that those two little words would get a woman through every difficult or awkward situation. Unfortunately, her chant was better suited for withstanding censure than kindness.

"Everyone okay?" he asked.

She struggled to speak around the lump in her throat. "Yes, thank God."

She felt oddly self-conscious beneath his steady gaze. What a sight she must look. Somehow, her hair had fallen from its usual tight bun to trail down her back in a tangled mass of waves.

Seldom did she pay more than the obligatory attention to her appearance, except for when attending suffragist conventions and giving speeches. It irritated her that he always made her aware of how she looked. Or how she wished she looked.

"You should go home and get some rest," he said, and she caught a note of sympathy in his voice.

She groaned inwardly. That's all she needed: a suspected killer feeling sorry for her. "I can't. Not till Deputy Hobson returns. Do you know where he went?"

"When Spirit showed up, I got worried and sent your deputy out to search for you."

She blinked. "You sent my deputy —"

He shrugged. "Someone's gotta look after you."

Something softened in her chest for as long as it took to remember that his so-called concern was all part of his plan to con her into believing him innocent. Even if he was sincere — which he wasn't — an independent woman didn't need a man taking care of her. Certainly, Amanda didn't need him. The very idea went against everything she believed in.

"I can take care of myself," she said in a rough voice that had little to do with her sore throat.

"If that's true, then I reckon you plan on goin' home and restin' that throat." When she hesitated, he added, "I'll hold down the fort."

The idea of her prisoner taking over in her absence made her laugh, and she forgot her irritation with him. "All right, but not till I take care of Spirit. A horse smart enough to locate its owner might be smart enough to help him escape."

She turned to leave, very much aware that Mr. Rennick's gaze followed her up the steps and into the office. *Grace and charm. Grace and charm. Grace and charm . . .*

Amanda hardly slept that night. Whenever she closed her eyes, she saw the burning cabin and relived every horrifying moment. The memory of her own failed efforts to save Mary-Louise and the baby haunted her.

As sheriff, her job was to protect citizens, and she had failed her first test. Or would have had John not shown up in time.

The thought was still on her mind two days later when she met Mary-Louise for an early breakfast in the hotel dining room.

Before taking a seat opposite her friend, she peered into the wicker baby carriage. "He's beautiful," Amanda said. He had his mother's reddish-brown hair and the cutest button nose imaginable. "Have you come up with a name yet?"

"We named him Randall after John's brother." Randall had died two years earlier of consumption. John had taken his brother's death hard. "We're calling him Randy for short."

Amanda sat. "That's a fine name."

Mary-Louise had dark shadows under her eyes and seemed distracted. She hardly touched her breakfast. No doubt, more than the fire was on her mind. It was common knowledge that John's shoemaking business had been struggling in recent years. Mail-order catalogs were booming, and ready-made shoes from back east could be purchased cheaper than John could make them. The fire couldn't have come at a worse time.

Mary-Louise didn't want to talk about the fire, but she did mention that John had gone to the house that morning to see if anything could be salvaged. Their livestock was being taken care of by other farmers in the area who offered to help.

After leaving the hotel, Amanda rode out to the Freeman homestead. Sifting through ashes was never a pleasant experience, and John could probably use a friend.

John greeted her with a terse nod. In his hand was a stick that he used to poke through the ashes. His eyes were black as coal and his mouth set in a grim line.

"Find anything?" she asked.

"Nothing."

"I'm so sorry."

He threw the stick down. "Yeah, so am I."

He started to leave, but she stopped him with a hand on his arm. They'd been friends for a good many years, long before he married Mary-Louise. He liked to play practical jokes and make people laugh. That was up until two years ago when his business began to fail. That's when the laughter stopped. Mary-Louise insisted everything was fine. *He just has a lot on his mind.* Amanda felt there was something she wasn't saying and worried that perhaps their marriage was in trouble.

"What can I do to help?" she asked. Her throat felt better, but her voice was still slightly hoarse.

He shook his head. "Nothing. There's

nothing anyone can do." He turned abruptly and walked away. Head low, shoulders rounded, he looked like he carried the world on his back, and her heart went out to him.

After he left, she rounded the perimeter of the foundation. Stopping by the area that was once the kitchen, she thrust the toe of her boot through the ashes. A black fork lay next to a charred frying pan.

Sighing, Amanda turned to leave when something caught her eye. It looked like a corner of a banknote. She tried picking it up with her bandaged hand, but it crumbled at her touch.

Moments later, she sat astride Spirit and took one last look at the cast iron stove rising from the ashes like an angry fist. Dark clouds sailed across the sky. For some odd reason, a sense of foreboding washed over her, sending shivers down her spine.

Upon returning to town, Amanda found a group of agitated cattle ranchers waiting in her office. The sight made her groan. *Now what?*

"How can I help you?" she asked, taking her place behind her desk and hiding her bandaged hands on her lap.

Everyone started talking at once.

"Quiet!" yelled the man known as Tee Pee,

short for Tall Tale Pete. "We're lookin' for the sheriff."

"I *am* the sheriff."

Tee Pee pushed his hat back and regarded her with black button eyes. "When I heard 'bout a lady sheriff, I thought it was a joke."

"Sorry to disappoint you, but it's no joke."

Tee Pee's eyebrows met in a frown. "It seems like we got more troubles than we knew."

Ignoring his comment, she said, "Suppose you tell me what brought you here."

"Someone's rustlin' our cattle," one of the men said.

"Hush," Tee Pee hissed. "I'm doing the talkin'." Palms on her desk, he leaned forward. "Someone's rustlin' our cattle."

"Yeah," added the owner of the Double R Ranch. "They went and took a bunch of our calves."

That wasn't too surprising. Many ranchers waited until the calves were weaned before branding them. That made a rustler's job easier, as it allowed him to put whatever brand he wanted on calf hides.

"Any idea who the rustlers might be?" she asked.

Tee Pee straightened. "If we knew that, we wouldn't be here. We'd be stretchin' their necks from the tallest cottonwood."

"Okay, I'll check into it," she said.

Tee Pee glared at her. "Yeah, well, you do that." He turned to the others. "Come on, men. We're on our own."

Heart sinking, Amanda watched the ranchers stomp out of her office. She didn't have the first idea how to track down cattle rustlers, and even if she did, she didn't have the time. Not with the stack of criminal complaints already piled up on her desk.

No sooner had the ranchers left than Mrs. Dodson stopped by to complain about a neighbor helping himself to her vegetable garden. She was followed by Mr. Hatton, who claimed that Mrs. Berry was chasing her cheating husband down the street with her crutches.

Just as he left, in walked Mrs. Brubaker, an older woman with a perpetual scowl. She plunked a brown glass bottle on Amanda's desk. The label read *Dr. Conkey's Miracle Cure for Aging.*

"He promised me that concoction would take years off my face." She stabbed her sunken, parched cheeks with the tips of her fingers. "Do I look any younger?"

It wasn't her face but her dreadful hat that made her look older than her years, but Amanda didn't want to say as much. Why anyone would wear a hat shaped like a gigantic mushroom was beyond the pale.

"Uh . . ."

Mrs. Brubaker lifted all three of her chins. "Just as I thought. I want my money back."

"I believe Dr. Conkey has already left town." Or would have if he knew what was good for him.

"You're the sheriff. Find him!" The older woman grabbed her bottle and left.

The parade of citizens continued with no end in sight. Some of the "crimes" were almost laughable, such as the one lodged by the spinster Higgins who complained that Mr. Matthews winked at her. The woman was so unpleasant in nature, it was hard to imagine any man — even one as myopic and deaf as Mr. Matthews — flirting with her.

Miss Higgins left, and Amanda turned to the next person in line just as a loud boom shook the building and rattled the windows. The beads on the lampshade bounced like corn kernels on a hot skillet. Deputy Hobson ran into the office, hat flying off his head.

"Hurry, Sheriff," he yelled, hand on the pistol by his side. "We're under siege!"

SEVENTEEN

Grabbing her hat and leaving the still long line of complaining citizens in her office, Amanda shot out the door after Scooter.

"What do you mean under siege?" she called to her deputy. Leaping off the boardwalk, she raced to her (Rennick's) horse.

For answer, a second boom rent the air, followed by another.

Scooter's eyes widened. "Sounds like war!"

The booming sounds came from west of town. Grabbing hold of the saddle horn, she jammed her foot into the stirrup, then swung her leg over the leather. The divided skirt sure did make mounting a breeze.

Riding side by side, she and Scooter raced down Main. Thanks to her new mount, she no longer had to struggle to keep up with her deputy's horse.

The loud booms brought shopkeepers running out of stores, some brandishing shotguns. Dogs barked, horses neighed, and chicken feathers flew about like flurries in a snowstorm. Poor Mrs. Dobbins dropped her basket of groceries as she ran to safety, breaking the six-inch raised hem law.

Outside of town, blue smoke streamed toward a cloudy sky, guiding Amanda and Hobson to an old farm wagon with the words *Rain King* written on the slatted wood sides. A man wearing a top hat and long purple duster stood in the bed of the wagon next to a dusty black cannon.

"Hello there," she called, reining in her horse.

The stranger pulled a rammer rod out of the barrel of the cannon and straightened. Dark, wavy hair fell to his shoulders, and his duster reached to the toes of his dusty black boots. The patch on his eye gave him the appearance of a pirate.

"Why, hello there . . . uh . . ." Standing the metal rod on end, he stared at her badge and frowned.

She dismounted and walked up to the side of the wagon. "I'm Sheriff Lockwood."

An incredulous look crossed his face. "Well, if that don't beat all. A lady sheriff, eh? Never thought I'd see the day."

She slanted her head toward the cannon. "What's the meaning of this?"

"The meaning? Oh, you mean ol' Betsy here." He ran a hand along the cannon's black muzzle. "See those clouds up there? I aim to make it rain. That's why they call me the Rain King. Some folks have paid me good money to end the drought."

She eyed him warily. The town had no shortage of quacks who promised every cure under the sun from an ingrown toenail to baldness, but this was the first she heard of someone claiming to control the weather.

"And you think shooting off cannons is going to end the drought?"

"No question about it. Why, during the War Between the States, every major battle was followed by downpours caused by heavy artillery fire. In fact, nearly two hundred battles were followed by torrential rains, and that's no coincidence. All I'm doing is putting that phenomena to good use."

Standing by her side, Deputy Hobson's eyes were round as pie tins. "Wow! That's amazing."

"If it works," Amanda said, which she doubted.

"Oh, it works all right," the Rain King assured her. "Even Napoleon noticed that rain often followed major battles. Those clouds have the water. We just have to shake it loose. Kinda like shaking money from a miser." He laughed at his own joke and slapped his hand on the cannon. "That's ol' Betsy's job."

"Well, I'll be a donkey's uncle," Scooter exclaimed, clearly impressed. "Grandpappy was right. He who spits into the sky gets it back in his own face. Yoo-hoo!"

Amanda sighed. As much as she hated the thought of curbing her deputy's enthusiasm, it would have to be done. That is, if such a thing were possible. So far, talking to him about the problem had not worked.

For now, she concentrated on the latest charlatan to peddle his way through town. "Unfortunately, my job is to keep the peace, and you and your friend here are disturbing it."

The Rain King furrowed his brow. "It seems to me the good citizens of Two-Time must make a choice between rain and peace. Can't have both."

"As much as I would like to see an end to the drought, right now, we choose peace."

The Rain King looked insulted. "Suit yourself," he said peevishly. He climbed out of the wagon bed and, with an indignant shake of the head, heaved himself onto the driver's seat. Muttering, he shook the reins, and he and his wagon rumbled off.

"Great guns!" Scooter exclaimed. "Never

thought anyone could actually make it rain."

Amanda mounted her horse. "They can't," she said. "He's just another snake oil salesman. He could no sooner make it rain than a cat can knit a sweater."

Just as she and Hobson reached town, she was forced to eat those words. The wind grew stronger, the day grew dark, and all at once, the skies opened up, releasing a gully-washer that promised to put an end to the two-year drought and then some.

Raising his hat high over his head, Hobson lifted his face to the pounding rain. "Holy mackerel!" he yelled. "The sky is falling!"

The rain pounded the windows of the sheriff's office that night as Amanda sat at her desk going through the stack of complaints and requests for help. It seemed like everyone in town had a stranded cat, an intolerable neighbor, or an elderly relative on the loose.

Elbows on the desk, she held up her head with the palms of her hands. The magnitude of the job grew more apparent with each passing hour, and her apprehension knew no end.

Never could she remember feeling so discouraged or overwhelmed. How foolish of her to think she was up to the task.

"I can't do this!"

"Sure you can."

Dropping her hands, she spun around in her chair. She hadn't noticed that the door to the cellblock was open. She certainly didn't know she'd spoken aloud.

Instead of his usual pacing, Mr. Rennick stood watching her. In the dim lantern light, his dark eyes seemed to beckon.

"How do you know what I can or cannot do?" she snapped.

He rubbed the back of his head. "Seen you in action, that's how."

"Yeah, well, my so-called action wasn't much use during the Freeman fire when it was most needed."

"Still blamin' yourself for that, are you?"

"It's not just the fire." Though that was a big part of it. There were still unanswered questions as to how the fire started. If she couldn't even get to the bottom of a simple fire, how would she ever track down a cattle rustler or horse thief? She brushed the pile of wanted posters off her desk and onto the floor.

"I don't even know where to start."

"Been my experience that riding a new path at full trot means trouble."

Sighing, she shook her head. She was too

tired to figure out riddles. It was enough trying to make sense of Scooter's peculiar quotes. "What's that supposed to mean?"

"It means start slow. Take your time. Prioritize. Look for Cooper's killer first, and the rest will fall into place."

She rolled her eyes. There he went again. Insisting on his innocence. Instead of arguing with him as usual, she left her desk and walked to the open door separating her office from the cell block. Crossing her arms, she leaned a shoulder against the doorjamb. "You make it sound so easy."

"Nothing's easy." His dark eyes reflected glimmers of light as he studied her. "You never did say how you and Kill . . . uh . . . my horse got along?"

The question brought an unbidden smile to her face. "Like a bear to a honey tree."

He grinned. "See? Now that you have a decent mount, half your troubles are over."

"You mean you still trust me with your horse? After what happened?"

"I'm not worried about him. Like I said, he'll always find his way back to me." He tilted his head. "So what's all this talk about not doin' your job?"

"I know nothing about tracking down outlaws." She hated complaining or feeling sorry for herself — to a prisoner no less —

but once started, she couldn't seem to stop. "I don't know how to find a bunch of stolen calves or a quack doctor. I can't even fire a gun."

"Sure you can. Your hope-a-thingie will attest to that." He rubbed the back of his head. "You just have to learn to use the business side as well as the grip. As for trackin' down stolen cattle, all you need is a good pair of ears."

"Ears?"

"The problem with rustlin' longhorns is that a mama and her babe have a way of findin' their way back to each other. I had occasion to meet one longhorn who'd traveled more than five miles to find her calf."

"Are you sure Spirit's not got longhorn blood?"

He laughed. "Could be." After a moment, he added, "The only way to prevent such reunions is for rustlers to keep calves penned up. Ever hear the sound a calf makes when he's separated from his mama?"

She shook her head. "Can't say that I have."

"They bawl like all get out." He pointed to the side of his head. "That's where the ears come in."

"So you're saying I just have to ride

around listening for bawling calves." He made it sound like a piece of cake.

"Either that or follow a worried longhorn mom lookin' for her babe."

"This is Texas. There's a lot of land to cover out there."

He lifted his broad shoulders. "Sometimes, a person gets lucky."

She narrowed her eyes. "How do you know so much about cattle? Don't tell me that rustling is among your many talents."

"Sorry to disappoint you, but in my youth, I worked on a cattle ranch."

"Did you now?" She slanted her head. "Any other advice? On how to be a sheriff, I mean?" Right now, she could use all the advice she could get, even if it came from a dubious source.

"Never trust anything a prisoner says. Been my experience that most of them have no honor."

"I'll keep that in mind, Mr. Rennick."

"Call me Rick."

"I'd rather not," she said. "Getting on friendly terms with a soon to be condemned man is like naming an animal you plan on eating."

A lazy but no less suggestive grin spread across his face. "Do you plan on eatin' me?"

"Certainly not!" Of all the cheeky things

to say. Face flaming, she turned to leave. "Good night, Mr. Rennick."

"G'night, Miss Sheriff."

Rick woke to a strange smell, and his mind scrambled to make sense of his surroundings. Nightmares had marked his sleep. In his dreams, he was drowning.

A strange scraping sound sharpened his senses. Cracks in the ceiling gave him something to focus on while the fog cleared in his head.

He sniffed, and a strong tallow smell filled his nostrils.

Wide awake now, he stared at the barred window over his cot. A spider web hung in the corner. The rain was still falling, and the sky was steel gray. He was no longer dreaming, but the effects of the nightmare remained.

Each time he closed his eyes, his mind flew back to the night he was caught. The happy couple in the hall. A man exiting the room and limping down the hall. The body on the floor. A woman's screams . . .

A good-time girl had been hired by Cooper. When she entered the room, her screams brought staff and guests running. Confusion reigned, and Rick was dragged bodily from the hotel. Hands tied. Torches.

Rope . . . He was sure his time was up.

None of this explained the odor or strange scraping sound. What little hay remained in the thin mattress rustled as he sat up. Swinging his feet to the floor, he rubbed his face with both hands and then started on his sore back. For all the good the thin mattress did, he might as well sleep on a pile of rocks.

He shifted his gaze to the cell next to his and blinked. Was that really the lady sheriff on hands and knees scrubbing the brick floor? The tallow smell was actually lye soap.

He cleared his throat. The scouring stone stilled in her hand, and she looked up to meet his gaze. Just like that, he found himself drowning yet again, this time in the liquid pools of her turquoise eyes. She looked more like herself this morning than she had the night before.

She was truly a woman of contradictions, one moment all vim and vinegar like she looked today. At other times, usually when she sat at her desk and thought no one was looking, she appeared as soft and vulnerable as a kitten.

"Morning, Mr. Rennick!" she said in a cool, crisp voice.

"Morning," he muttered, pinching his forehead. How was it possible to have a hangover without touching a drop of alcohol? "Heard you say you planned on cleanin' up the town. Didn't know you meant it literally."

"This jail is in terrible condition." Her eyes flashed. "It's not a suitable place for man nor beast."

He pulled his gaze away from her and glanced around. If she thought this was bad, she should see the cells at Huntsville Penitentiary. "So which am I?"

"What?"

"Man or beast? Which am I?"

She pursed her lips. "That's to be determined," she said and went back to scrubbing.

She certainly was a sight for sore eyes, and the emptiness of his life hit him full force as he watched her. She even looked appealing on hands and knees. That crazy outfit of hers couldn't hide her feminine charms. He'd have to be blind or dead not to notice her slender waist and nicely rounded hips. And she sure did know how to wiggle that caboose of hers.

With a groan, he forced his gaze to the grimy floor beneath his feet. It had been a long time since he'd been with a woman. Hadn't even thought about it all that much. Been too busy trying to stay alive. Had almost forgotten what it meant to feel attracted to someone. To feel like a man instead of a criminal.

Not that he could ever have feelings for the female sheriff. He knew all too well the pain that came from loving an independent woman like her. Had experienced firsthand the heartbreak that such a woman could bring to those who loved her.

Irritated by the unwelcome memories, he called in a gruff voice, "What's a body have to do around here to get a cup of coffee?"

She tossed a look over her shoulder. "Your breakfast should be here at any minute."

Then she stood, picked up her bucket, and left, but only for as long as it took to return with a broom. Flinging it right and left, she swept the cobwebs from the corners of the cell next to his as if fighting off an advancing army.

Never had he seen a more gallant battle raged against dirt and grime. "Don't you have some outlaws to catch?"

"Yes, and as soon as it stops raining, I intend to do just that."

He blew out his breath and shook his head. He never did understand the inner workings of a woman's mind, and that went double for Miss Lockwood. So far, his efforts to earn her trust had gotten him nowhere. He'd tried flattery and appealing to her womanly senses. He even befriended her when her spirits lagged or she questioned her ability, though that part had been genuine.

Still, nothing he said or did persuaded her to change her mind. She was hell-bent on keeping him locked up, and time was running out fast. If he didn't convince her to set him free before the circuit judge arrived, he was bound for buzzard's bait sure as night followed day.

EIGHTEEN

It was after ten that morning by the time Mrs. Ackermann finally arrived with Rennick's breakfast. The woman had no concept of time and often smelled of alcohol.

Today, she stomped inside, dripping rain water all over the floor, and didn't even bother wiping her muddy feet on the rug Amanda had placed in front of the door.

Owner of a local boardinghouse, she had been hired by the town council to prepare meals for prisoners. She was a large-boned woman with a thick German accent. Beneath a floral bonnet, her unkempt dark hair framed a pudgy red face.

Amanda stood the broom against the wall and greeted her with a frown.

"You're late again."

The woman lifted her shoulders beneath her rain-soaked cloak with a careless shrug. "Got here soon as I could." Offering no apologies, she set the tray on the desk. She hadn't even thought to cover the plate or coffee cup, and the tray swam in rainwater.

Scooter reached for it, and Amanda stopped him with her hand. Never in all her born days had she seen a more sorrowful excuse for a meal, and her stomach turned. The coffee looked murky as dishwater, and the rubbery gray eggs drowning in water would make a chicken blush in shame. No words could adequately describe the charred strips of bacon.

"What is that?" Amanda asked.

The woman reached her hand beneath a stained apron to scratch her belly. "It's his breakfast. Whatcha think it is?"

"It doesn't look fit to feed a hog." Amanda picked up the tray and shoved it back at her. "Take it away. We no longer need your services."

The woman's face collapsed inward like a prune left in the sun too long. "Harrumph. I'd like to see you do better." She left in a huff.

Scooter shook his head. "By ginger, I guess you told her."

"Yes, well . . ." Amanda reached in the desk drawer for her purse and drew out several coins. "Go to the hotel, and purchase the breakfast special. And hurry. Poor Mr. Rennick is probably starved." Poor? She called a suspected killer poor? Fortunately, Scooter didn't seem to notice.

"Yes, sir, Sheriff!"

Thanks to the lady sheriff, Rick's meals were suddenly fit for a king. Eggs cooked to perfection, along with fluffy flapjacks and crisp bacon made up his breakfast. Savory roast beef, creamy mashed potatoes, gravy, and string beans arrived for his midday meal. Roast chicken, pork, or leg of lamb were on the menu for supper.

Never could he remember eating so well. Least not in recent years. It sure did beat the worm-infested meals served at the state pen. Mealtime was the only bright spot in an otherwise frustrating existence.

He was no closer now to proving his innocence than he was at the start. He sure wasn't making any headway with the lady. Despite his best efforts to win her over and convince her of his innocence, she refused to cooperate. Food was his only consolation. At least till he came up with another plan.

Regardless of the heavy rains, the chants continued outside calling for the lady's resignation. When she wasn't waging a war on dirt, Miss Sheriff faced her critics with composed dignity, earning his begrudging respect. Whenever someone criticized her deputy, she resorted to bluster and bravado — also earning his respect.

Only on the rarest of occasions and after the most trying of situations did he glimpse a chink in her armor. Even then, it took a sharp eye to note the droop of a shoulder, the clench of a hand, a quiver of her pretty pink lips.

After thoroughly cleaning and disinfecting one cell, she and her deputy had moved him into it so that they could clean the other two.

For the remainder of the week, she scrubbed — or rather attacked — floors, walls, and windows. Soap bubbles flurried up as years of grime vanished beneath the rough surface of her scrubbing stone. He was willing to bet it wasn't just dirt she battled, but something more personal and deeply ingrained. Fear? Self-doubt?

She made her deputy toss out the thin mattresses and stuff clean straw into new ticking. After trashing all the moth-eaten wool blankets, she replaced them with new ones. She then sprayed the place with lavender perfume.

"Smells like a bordello in here," Rick said, though he had no complaint.

"I wouldn't know," she said. She looked

at him so funny, he got a sick feeling in his gut.

"Oh, no you don't." He backed against the rough wall of his cell, palms spread outward. "Don't even think about it."

She tossed a nod at her deputy. What Deputy Hobson lacked in years, he made up for in enthusiasm and had been racing around all week eager to impress his new boss. Now he approached his cell with a bowl of soapy water and a razor.

Rick took the bowl of water but refused the razor. "I'm not shaving." He still hadn't given up hope of escaping. Until then, he didn't want anyone knowing what he looked like without his beard.

Aware suddenly that Miss Sheriff was watching him with arms folded, he shook his head. "I said I'm not shaving."

"Have it your way, Mr. Rennick, but you should know that I just got word that the circuit judge is on the way."

"So? Hasn't he ever seen a man in a beard?"

"Oh, he's seen them all right," she said. "They're always the ones he condemns to hang."

Rick took the razor.

Amanda stared out the office window onto

192

Main. The rain had stopped the day before, and rays of sunshine trickled through parted gray clouds. Steam rose from water-soaked rooftops, and ribbons of mud still ran ankle-deep through the center of town. The Rain King had made a believer of her.

For three days, the rain had kept most, but not all, disgruntled citizens from traipsing a path to her door and demanding her resignation. For that, she was grateful, but she had a feeling the reprieve was about to end.

The rain had been a boon to farmers, but the best thing it did was curb crime. Almost as soon as the rain stopped, the stage was robbed, someone stole farmer Hancock's chickens, and one of the local ranch owners complained about somebody cutting his barbed wire fence.

She walked to her desk. Scooter had left to fetch Rennick's breakfast, as was now his morning chore. As soon as he returned, they would ride out to the Wendell farm. There was still the matter of those missing horses. She planned to stop at Tee Pee's ranch on the way back. He'd threatened to pursue the rustlers himself, and she intended to make sure he stayed within the law. She also wanted to find out how Mary-Louise and her new baby were doing. Amanda still had questions about the fire before she could file away the report.

She reached for her Colt and dumped the bullets out of the chamber. She then walked to the door of the cellblock. Rennick stopped pacing, an inquisitive look on his face. He still hadn't shaved, but his hair was neatly combed and tied at the back of his neck with a piece of rawhide.

Several dime novels supplied by her deputy were stacked at the foot of Rennick's cot.

She tossed a nod toward the books. "Escapist literature?" she asked with a wry smile.

"Absolutely. Did you know that Billy the Kid escaped jail through a chimney?"

She shrugged. "Sorry we can't accommodate you, but as you see, we have no chimneys."

"What a pity."

"Yes, isn't it?" She tilted her head. "Any advice on how to find missing chickens?" Her prisoner seemed to have an answer for most everything.

"Track down the local wolf pack and smell their breaths."

"Very funny."

His gaze fell on the Colt in her hand, and he arched a dark eyebrow.

"How about helping me with my aiming problem?" she said.

"You gonna trust me with your gun?" he asked.

"It's not loaded," she said.

"Ah."

She handed it to him muzzle first.

He spun the chamber to check for bullets. "Lesson number one, never point a gun unless you mean to use it."

"I told you, it's not loaded."

"Yeah, well, the graveyards are filled with men shot by unloaded guns." He pointed the gun, sighting it on the water basin in the next cell. "Hold your gun in both hands like this. Now aim at your target, and bring your eye to the front sight. Keep your arm solid, your wrist straight."

He talked in a clear, smooth tone, taking his time. "Next, cock the hammer with your thumb. Remember to squeeze the trigger. Don't jerk it." He turned to her. "Got all that?"

"I think so."

"Good. Now you try it."

"Chow time." Scooter appeared at the doorway. Seeing Rennick with a gun, he dropped the tray. Quick as a flash, he pulled out his weapon. "Shall I shoot? Shall I shoot?"

■ ■ ■ ■

After calming her deputy, Amanda sent him back to the hotel for more food while she cleaned up the broken dishes and mopped up the coffee.

No sooner had she finished than the door flew open and in popped Mrs. Mooney, followed by several other posse members. The group crowded into the office, careful to wipe their muddied feet on the rug in the doorway. Amanda almost didn't recognize them.

Gone were the bustled frocks, fancy hats, and chatelaine purses. Instead, every last one of them had followed her example and were now appropriately dressed for the job in divided skirts, white shirtwaists, and vests. High-button boots had replaced dainty slippers, and Mother Hubbard bonnets and bird-trimmed headgear had been exchanged for sensible wide-brimmed hats, each sporting a tall red feather.

Even Becky-Sue had traded in her frilly skirts and lacy shirtwaists for a more conservative skirt and shirt. The giggles, however, remained.

Somehow, Goldie managed to make a divided skirt and plain shirtwaist look like something that should only be worn in a bawdy house.

The women all appeared to be armed. A few guns were holstered. The grip of Mrs. Perl's peacemaker stuck out of her rucksack along with her knitting needles. Other firearms were tucked into the waists of split skirts.

Her deputy returned from the hotel. He took one look at the newly clad ladies and almost dropped the breakfast tray a second time. "Gee willikers, will you look at that?"

Through the open door in back, Mr. Rennick could be seen gawking through the bars, a look of sheer disbelief on his face.

True to form, Mrs. Mooney took charge. "As the bank president's wife, I wish to inform you that we are reporting to duty."

Deputy Hobson found his voice. "By Jupiter. A real posse!"

"You better take the prisoner his breakfast," Amanda said. She was having a hard enough time dealing with Becky-Sue's giggles without Scooter adding to the confusion.

"Yes, sir, Sheriff!"

Amanda waited for him to slip through the door leading to the cellblock before facing the women. Never had she seen such an earnest-looking group, not even at the suffrage meetings. Their eagerness to please and put themselves in danger touched her deeply. She also felt responsible for their safety. If anything should happen . . .

"Do you all know how to fire your weapons?" she asked.

Ellie-May Walker seemed to regard the question as a personal affront. "My husband wouldn't sell a gun without giving proper instruction," she said with a shake of her saddlebag hips.

Mrs. Mooney lifted her head with an air of importance. "Just tell us what you want us to do, and we'll do it!"

T-Bone's wife pumped the air with a fist. Her rounded curls hung down her back like the sausages sold at her husband's butcher shop. "We'll show the men of this town how to end crime."

"You got that right," Mrs. Albright sniffed. The narrow crown of her hat rose from her head like a stove pipe. "Do you know what my Carl said when I told him what I was doing? He said this was a great day for outlaws and a bad day for the town." She placed her hands at her waist. "I intend to make him eat those words."

"Speaking of eating," Mrs. Myrtle Granby said, holding a jeweled lorgnette to her eyes. "Let's get on with it. I need to be home in time to cook supper."

Mrs. Mooney leaned sideways to whisper in Amanda's ear. "Her poor, dear husband is like a bagpipe. He never utters a sound until his stomach is full."

Every gossipy comment that fell from her lips was prefixed with the word *poor,* as if that somehow took the sting out of any unkind words.

Amanda regarded the group with misgivings. If anything should happen to any of them . . .

"Upholding law and order is dangerous work even for a man. But for us women —"

"Nonsense," Mrs. Perl said with a shake of a knitting needle. "It would have to be a pretty low man to harm a woman. That gives us the advantage."

Her remark was followed by murmurs of agreement, and Amanda's warnings fell on deaf ears.

She glanced at the stack of complaints on her desk. Somehow, she had to put her posse to work without putting them in danger — at least until she knew their full capabilities, if any.

The bank lost a large shipment of gold during a recent stage holdup. Before that, a bag of money was stolen from a bank teller. But the horses taken from the county poor farm were by far the greater loss in term of need. Mr. Wendell depended on those horses to work his fields. Then there were those missing calves . . .

"Are you ready to ride?" Amanda asked. With a group this size, they could scour the Wendell farm with a fine-tooth comb. The rain had probably washed away any clues, but it wouldn't hurt to check, and it would give her posse practice working together in a relatively safe environment.

"We're ready," Mrs. Mooney said, and for once, she didn't mention her social position. "Don't you have to swear us in or something?"

"Yes . . . yes, of course." Amanda cleared her throat. She had no idea how to swear in a posse, but the oath couldn't be much different than the one she herself took as sheriff.

"Wait," Mrs. Perl said. "I think we need a name for our posse. It would make us sound more official."

Amanda frowned. Did a sheriff's posse have a name?

Becky-Sue waved her hand. "We should call ourselves the Red Feather posse." She pointed to the feather on her black felt hat and giggled.

Mrs. Mooney nodded. "As the wife of the

bank president, I say we make it official. All in favor of calling ourselves the Red Feather posse, say aye."

Their voices rang out in unison. "Aye!"

"Okay, Red Feathers," Amanda said. "Raise your right hands."

The women repeated after her in solemn voices. Scooter returned, and after setting the empty tray on her desk, took the oath too.

After duly swearing them in, Amanda explained their first assignment. "Horses were stolen from the Wendell farm. I want you to check out the property while I question the residents. Someone might have seen or heard something. You never know."

Becky-Sue pressed her hands together. "Oh, this is so exciting!" she said and giggled.

"Yes, it is," Scooter agreed, and they both laughed.

Amanda frowned. "Just remember to stay together and wait for instructions. The bad guys have guns, and they know how to use them."

Not that she thought they would run into any outlaws at the farm, but every possibility must be considered.

Scooter gave a solemn nod. "Like Grand-

pappy always said, there's a cure for everything but stark death."

NINETEEN

The sight greeting Amanda outside the office made her stop in her tracks and do a double take.

Wagons, buggies, and buckboards were parked haphazardly in all directions. The vehicles not only created a logjam, they broke every parking law on the books and then some.

Bullwhip, the stagecoach driver, stood on the opposite side of the street shaking his fist. "Get these doggone vehicles outta my way!" he bellowed, his red beard quivering along with his low-crowned felt hat. "Or I'll be late."

Amanda glared at him. When had Bullwhip ever concerned himself with staying on schedule? She still hadn't forgiven him for leaving her stranded in the middle of nowhere. Since the stage was robbed, he did her a favor, which was the only reason she hadn't confronted him. Still, she wasn't

ready to altogether excuse him or his obnox-
ious ways.

He wasn't the only one throwing a fit. Far
from it. Traffic was stopped on Main in both
directions, and curses rent the air.

Amanda raised her hand and called, "Give
us a moment." She turned to Mrs. Mooney.
"We have a problem."

Mrs. Mooney folded her arms across her
ample chest. "I'll say. How dare they talk to
the bank president's wife in such a way!
Have they no respect? There ought to be a
law."

"You can say that again," added Mrs. Perl.
"How else could we park without getting
our wheels stuck in the mud?"

Amanda threw up her arms. "The problem
I'm talking about is that I need my posse
on horseback." Who ever heard of a posse
on wheels?

"Horses?" Mrs. Mooney's eyebrows shot
up. "You said we needed guns. You said
nothing about horses."

"I just assumed . . ."

"Oh dear." Mrs. Perl rubbed the small of
her back. "My sacroiliac won't let me ride a
horse."

Deputy Hobson commiserated with a
shake of his head. "My grandmama had the
same problem."

"I can't ride my horse either," added Mrs. Granby, eyes rounded behind the frame of her lorgnette. "He's scared of noise, and there's no telling what he'll do once we get to shooting."

The former schoolmarm tossed her head in agreement and added, "I haven't ridden horseback since I was thrown at the age of twelve and . . ."

The excuses seemed to know no end. The minister's wife spoke for several women when she explained her husband's objections. "He said it's bad enough that I'm now dressed like a man — he's not having me spread my limbs like a clothespin just to ride a horse."

Becky-Sue got all red in the face and giggled.

By now, the angry group of men had grown in number and stood on the opposite side of the street shoulder to shoulder like an army about to advance.

"If you don't move those blasted vehicles, we'll do it for you!" someone shouted and followed with enough curses to make a sailor blush.

Fearing violence was about to break out, Amanda jogged down the steps to her (Rennick's) horse. She still felt the need to remind herself that it wasn't her horse, but he felt more like her own every day.

Right now, the only way to assure a peaceful resolution was to get the ladies out of town. Fast! The transportation problem would have to wait.

She quickly untied Spirit and swung onto the saddle. "All right, Red Feathers. Time to hit the trail!"

The man introduced himself to Rick as attorney-at-law Charles Birdseye. "Time to get to work. I've been hired to represent you." He was dressed in striped, black trousers, matching frock coat, and a short, crowned hat.

"Lucky you," Rick muttered. The circuit judge was due any day, and only now did his assigned lawyer get around to meeting with him.

Birdseye set a chair in front of the cell and wiggled it back and forth as if to make certain it would hold his stout body before trusting it enough to sit. He then opened his brown leather portfolio on his lap. He cleared his throat, and his bulbous nose twitched.

"Smells like a bawdy house in here."

The perfume was a welcome change from the usual jailhouse smells. Unfortunately, it kept the lady and the garments in her hope chest very much on Rick's mind.

"Miss Sheriff has no respect for dirt," Rick said.

"Miss Lockwood has no respect for a lot of things, including a woman's rightful place in the home. It'll take a tough man to tame her, that's for sure."

Rick's eyebrows rose. Taming Miss Sheriff? Would such a thing be possible? He doubted it.

Birdseye studied him. "First thing we need to do is get you cleaned up. Hair, beard." His frown increased as his gaze traveled down the length of him. "Clothes."

"I like the way I look."

Birdseye pulled a sheet of paper from his case. "If you show up in court like that, the jury might decide to improve your appearance with a necktie."

He popped a monocle before his eye and proceeded to read. A generous mustache shadowed thick red lips that moved silently as he read. The wide mouth didn't seem to belong with his small beady eyes and narrow forehead.

"Says here that you're charged with killing one Mr. Cooper."

Rick frowned. What kind of lawyer was this? He hadn't even bothered familiarizing himself with the case prior to their meeting.

The lawyer folded the paper. "Glad to hear it. The last few cases I handled were boring land disputes. Nothing like a good murder case to liven things up."

"How many cases like mine have you handled?" Rick asked.

"Like yours? Oh, you mean murder cases. None. You're my first." He rubbed his hands together with obvious glee. "Can't wait to get started."

Rick had a bad feeling about this. A very bad feeling . . .

Amanda raced out of town with mixed feelings, her deputy by her side. They were followed by no less than a half dozen wheeled vehicles. It was hardly the kind of posse she'd imagined, but they did look impressive if not altogether intimidating.

The pounding of horses' hooves and rattling wagon wheels sent folks scurrying for cover. Twice, they had to stop to pull a vehicle out of the mud. This required everyone to scamper about collecting rocks to give the wheels traction.

Scooter, with the help of an occasional passerby, was then able to push the vehicles free with a thrust of his shoulder and several quotes from good ole Grandpappy.

Amanda shook her head in amazement.

How was it possible to know so many quotes about rocks and mud?

The moment they reached open land, Amanda urged Spirit into a full gallop. Grazing cattle looked up as they passed. Wild mustangs lifted their tails and galloped away. Prairie dogs popped head first into holes. The mother of a baby buffalo threw back her head and bellowed. A flock of blackbirds took to the sky.

The last of the clouds drifted away just as they reached the poor farm. Old Mr. Jacobs looked up from working in the field. Instead of the usual grin, a frown creased his shiny dark forehead.

Signaling her posse to halt with a raised hand, Amanda rode up to the fence and waited for him to meet her there.

"Lord have mercy, I thought the cavalry was coming," he said, resting his hoe against a fence post.

Amanda glanced back at the line of motley vehicles. Some cavalry. "We're here on business. I'm the new sheriff, and that's my posse. We're here to help track down those stolen horses."

His eyebrows disappeared beneath the brim of his floppy straw hat. "Well, shoot me a star."

Amanda knew from past conversations

that the shooting star saying grew out of Reconstruction revivals where many former slaves were converted. To test the authenticity of their religion, the newly converted lifted their arms to the heavens and asked the Lord to shoot them a star.

She and her posse were authentic, all right, at least by earthly standards, but the only star he was likely to see was the one attached to her vest.

"Did you see or hear anything suspicious the night the horses were stolen?" she asked.

"No, sir, Sheriff. None of us saw or heard nothing out of the ordinary."

Her gaze traveled the field behind him where the other workers had stopped to stare at the strange collection of vehicles strung along the roadway. "If you think of anything, let me know."

"Will do." He grabbed his hoe and walked away. "Will do."

Tugging on the reins, she turned Spirit around and galloped back to where Scooter waited with the others. "The horses were stolen from that paddock. Have everyone spread out on foot. Make them walk an arm's length away from each other."

"What are we looking for?" Scooter asked.

Good question. It was too late to look for footprints, and even if it wasn't, the rain would have washed them away. "Cigarette or stogie butts," she said, trying to sound like she knew what she was doing. "Anything out of the ordinary."

With an enthusiastic wave of his arm, he rode away to inform the ladies of their duties.

Amanda heaved a sigh. She had little hope of them finding anything, but at least that would keep them out of her hair while she questioned the farm's residents.

Amanda rode up to the farmhouse, and Mrs. Wendell waved from the porch. "Heard you're the new sheriff," she called.

Amanda dismounted. "You heard right." She felt guilty for coming empty-handed, but there hadn't been any time to shop or raid her mother's pantry. "We're checking out the scene of the crime now."

"You won't find anything. Not after all this time. 'Sides, those thieves are sneaky as a fox."

"Do you mind if I question the residents?" The pasture could be seen from the house. Older people sometimes had trouble sleeping. It was possible that one of them might have seen or heard something.

It didn't take long to find that someone did — the old Welshman, Mr. El.

"How are you today, Mr. El?" she asked.

"Do you mind if I ask you some questions?"

Interpreting his grunt as a yes, she sat in a chair opposite him.

He pulled out his gold watch, thumbed the case open, and checked the time before answering her questions. For a man living in a county poor farm, he sure did carry an expensive-looking watch. Probably a family heirloom. It bothered her that he never looked directly at her. Rather, his eyes focused on his watch, the window, the floor.

He claimed he looked outside sometime after midnight the night the horses vanished and saw moving lights in the direction of the pasture.

"How many lights did you see?" she asked.

Eyes lowered, he adjusted the steel frame of his spectacles. "Six," he muttered in a low, croaky voice. "I saw six lights. Or maybe it was eight."

The number surprised her. Why were so many men needed to steal three horses? Unless, of course, someone or something interrupted them from stealing the rest. "Why didn't you wake Mr. Wendell or Mr. Jacobs?"

"By the time I found my specs, the lights were gone." He stopped to cough. "Thought maybe I was imagining things."

"I see." Amanda thanked him. None of

the other residents had anything to add, and she wasn't even sure what, if anything, Mr. El actually did witness. He seemed a bit weak north of the ears, so maybe he only imagined seeing lights.

She descended the stairs to the ground floor. Mrs. Wendell was nowhere in sight, but voices drew her into the kitchen.

Miss Read was sitting at the table teaching Charley his numbers. The boy looked up as she entered and grinned.

"Oh, sorry," she said. "I didn't mean to disturb your lesson."

"No problem," Miss Read said. "We're just about finished."

As Amanda turned to leave, something caught her eye. The pantry door was open, and the normally empty shelves were packed with canned goods. Sacks of flour, sugar, and rice were stacked on the floor, along with a toe sack of pecans. A whole ham hung from the ceiling.

What little money the county provided the poor farm was hardly enough to cover expenses. The Wendells depended on donations to feed and clothe their indigent residents. Judging by the well-stocked shelves, a recent donor had been especially generous. Maybe the church had run one of its fund-raisers, which it did from time to time.

Whoever was responsible for the windfall earned her gratitude. Now she didn't feel so bad for coming empty-handed.

"Amanda!" Mrs. Wendell motioned to her frantically from the doorway. "Hurry! Trouble's a-brewing outside!"

TWENTY

Amanda sprinted out of the kitchen so fast, she almost slipped on the polished wood floor. Once outside, it didn't take but a second to spot the trouble.

Her posse was chasing a lone man across an empty field and yelling at him to stop. Divided skirts yanked up to unprecedented heights, the women were gaining fast.

"What in the world —"

She dashed down the porch steps, waving her arms over her head. "Wait!" Quickly untying Spirit, she slammed a foot into the stirrups and swung a leg over the saddle.

By the time she reached the other side of the paddock and slid from her mount, the women had already tackled the man to the muddy ground and were piled on top of him like a stack of tossed books.

A shocking display of flailing legs greeted Amanda's startled eyes. Buried beneath the pile of squirming female bodies came the man's cries for help.

"Stop!" Amanda grabbed the hand of the preacher's wife and yanked her off the heap. Slipping and sliding in the mud, she pulled each of the women away from the hapless man.

Their victim lay facedown in the muck. He didn't move. Fearing the worst, Amanda shook him on the shoulder. "Sir? Are you all right?"

Moaning, he stirred. Guns drawn, the women stood in a circle around him, dripping with mud. For good measure, Mrs. Perl even whipped out her knitting needles and pointed them in a threatening way.

Boots sinking in the sludge, Amanda managed to help the man to his feet. He swayed slightly, and she slid an arm around his waist to steady him. Either he was dazed or drunk. Hard to tell. Maybe he was just in shock. His frock coat sleeve was torn and covered in mud. His black hat was squashed flat as a flapjack.

Was he a stranger? Hard to know what he looked like beneath the dark ooze. Right now, he resembled some sort of swamp monster.

Mrs. Mooney stepped forward. Unlike the others, she wore the gooey mess well and managed to look unbearably important despite being covered from head to toe. "As the bank president's wife, I wish to inform you that you are under arrest."

"You can't arrest him," Amanda said. "That's my job." Wiping her soiled hands against her skirt, she asked, "Who are you, and what are you doing here?"

For answer, the man stooped to retrieve something from a mud puddle, and the gun triggers clicked like so many snapping fingers.

Mrs. Perl held her gun in one hand and her knitting needles in the other. It was hard to know if she intended to shoot him or knit him a sweater. The jewels on Mrs. Granby's lorgnette winked in the sun as she lifted it to her eyes with a filthy hand. The school-marm's expression would have given even the unruliest schoolboy nightmares.

Becky-Sue giggled. "Oh, this is so much fun."

Amanda signaled for them to lower their weapons. Being accidentally shot by her own posse was a possibility she didn't want to contemplate. Surrounded by a group of ready-to-attack women, the man wasn't going anywhere. It didn't even look like he was armed.

He straightened and attempted to brush the wet soil off what looked like a book. His face plastered with mud, only the whites of his eyes were visible. He wiped the leather cover with his handkerchief, and Amanda suddenly realized he was holding a Bible.

"I'm Reverend Thomas Maine and these . . . these . . . heathens attacked me for no reason."

Amanda gasped. "You're a minister?"

The pastor's wife looked him up and down as if she alone could determine the validity of his statement. Mrs. Granby peered at him intently through her folding spectacles.

As if in reminder of his standing in society, he bowed slightly. "At your service. I've been riding since dawn and stopped to rest my horse when these . . . these . . ." He shuddered. "Never have I been treated in such a despicable manner, not even when I accidentally married a bride to the wrong man."

"I'm so sorry." Amanda felt terrible. "I'm the sheriff and take full responsibility." She motioned the others to put away their guns. "We're on the lookout for horse thieves, and I'm afraid my . . . posse got carried away."

Scooter came galloping up to them, his horse's hooves splashing mud everywhere.

"Is he the horse thief?" he sang out, hardly able to contain his excitement as he practically leaped off the saddle, gun in hand. "Shall I shoot? Shall I shoot?"

"Absolutely not," Amanda said, pushing the barrel of his gun aside.

Reverend Maine gave his head an indignant toss. "I'll have you know, young man, I am *not* a horse thief."

Scooter holstered his gun. "You aren't?" He looked dubious. "Are you sure?"

"Of course I'm sure."

"What a pity," Becky-Sue said, and for once, she didn't giggle.

Mrs. Perl stuck her knitting needles into her rucksack. "Well, you sure look like it to me. Why'd you take off like that?"

Mrs. Mooney scoffed. "We begged you to stop. Why didn't you?"

"I'm a preacher, ma'am, and was practicing my sermon out loud when you called to me. I'm used to people begging me to stop preaching, and that's what I did. Never occurred to me you wanted me to stop walking."

Scooter regarded the man with a solemn expression. "Like Grandpappy always said, 'Crab walk too much, he get in crab soup.' "

Worried about how she would explain this to the town council members, Amanda muttered beneath her breath, "Or mud stew."

■ ■ ■ ■

Later that afternoon, a group of disgruntled men stormed into the sheriff's office, led by Mr. Mooney.

Amanda looked up from her desk, and her heart sank. What got the town riled up this time? The fiasco with the preacher, no doubt. Just don't let it be another bank holdup. She hadn't even had time to track down the last robbers.

Glaring at her from beneath his black derby, Mooney pounded his fist on her desk, startling her. "As the bank president, I demand to know what right you have turning our wives into a bunch of gun-toting, hysterical maniacs!"

Next to him, T-Bone wiped his hands on his meat-stained apron. The pockmarks on his face stood out like red polka dots. "If that ain't bad enough, my wife came home covered in mud. She said she chased down a suspected horse thief."

"I can explain —" Amanda began.

Mooney cut her off with a wave of his hand. "Explain, my foot! I won't have my wife brawling like a common thug."

Amanda folded her arms across her chest. As unfortunate as the situation was, it hardly qualified as a brawl. "I'll have you know that my posse —"

"Wives!" Mr. Granby exclaimed with an emphatic toss of his head. "We're talking about our wives! I won't have you turning mine into a raving lunatic!"

"According to *your* constitution" — she would never consider it hers until it recognized women as full-fledged citizens — "we women are already considered lunatics."

T-Bone glared at her. "That's why you need to stay at home where you belong and can't get into trouble."

She seethed with mounting rage. *Grace and charm, grace and charm, grace and charm . . .*

"The world would be a better place if men stayed at home," she said. Thanks to Miss Brackett's tutoring, she managed to sound amazingly calm despite the boiling pot inside. "At least there'd be less crime." Some female outlaws did exist, but very few by comparison to men.

T-Bone's face turned as red as the uncooked meat in his shop. "Look who's calling the kettle black. You've been arrested more times than the rest of us here put together. You're nothing but a crazy, hare-brained, cockamamie . . ." On and on he ranted, exhibiting a vocabulary that would impress even Webster.

Her mouth dropped open. Never had she been so insulted in her life. Glaring at him, she rose slowly out of her chair. "And you," she said, managing to maintain grace if not charm, "are nothing but a misogynistic . . ."

Alarm crossed Mr. Mooney's face. "Gentlemen and . . . eh . . ." He seemed at a loss as to how to address her. "I'm sure we can voice our grievances without resorting to name calling. Mr. Perl . . . I believe you wished to say something."

"I sure as heck do." Mr. Perl tugged on the knitted scarf around his neck so hard, he looked like he was trying to hang himself. "I walked into the house for my noontime meal, and what did I find? Nothing but an empty table!" Blue veins pulsated in his forehead. "Is it too much to ask that a man expect his meals on time?"

"That's nothing," Mr. Walker said, giving his balding head a shake. "When I asked my wife to fetch my pipe, she told me to get it myself. Said she had better things to do with her time." He sniffed and wrinkled his thick, cone-shaped nose.

Reverend Wellmaker discounted Walker's complaint with a wave of his hand. "You think that's bad?" A wide-eyed look of righteous indignation filled the frames of his spectacles. "I'll tell you what's bad. My wife leaving the house wearing trousers!" He made it sound like she'd broken all Ten Commandments and was working on an eleventh. "It's unbiblical."

Amanda didn't like arguing with the minister, but she couldn't let such a statement go unchallenged. "Actually, she was wearing a split skirt, and I don't believe those are mentioned in the —"

"I don't care what you call it," Mrs. Albright's husband, Carl, said through clenched teeth. "It's indecent for a woman to suggest she has . . . has . . ."

"I think the word you're looking for is *legs*," Amanda said.

The men's mouths dropped.

Reverend Wellmaker cleared his throat, recovering first. "To make matters worse, my wife helped beat up a man of God." He shuddered.

"Yes, that was most unfortunate," Amanda agreed.

Mr. Mooney took charge again. "As the bank president, I insist that you disband your posse at once."

Amanda fought for control. It was bad enough the mayor tried telling her what to do, but the bank president? "Gentlemen, if you object to your wives assisting me, you'll

have to take the matter up with *them.*
Meanwhile, I have work to do. So if you
would kindly leave . . ."

Mr. Mooney leaned over the desk. "You
know what you are? You're a . . . a . . . a
home wrecker, that's what!"

He swung his bulky body around, and he
and the others stomped out of the office.
The slammed door rattled the windows.
Amanda threw up her hands. She'd been
called a lot of things in her life, but home
wrecker? That was a new one. No sooner
had the last man left than Rennick's laughter rolled into her office like a tumbleweed
in the wind. It was a nice laugh. A warm
laugh that drew her to the open door separating his cell from the office.

That's when she got the surprise of her
life. At last, he had put the razor to good
use, and the difference was astonishing.
Never would she have guessed that such a
handsome square face was hidden behind
that ragged beard and scruffy mustache.

"Why are you laughing?" she asked curtly
to hide her quickening pulse.

"You being a home wrecker."

"Not funny," she said.

"Sure it is."

He was always on the move, and today
was no different. Holding on to the bars

with both hands, he squatted up and down. She tried her best not to notice the muscles of his arms and chest rippling beneath his shirt.

He grinned at her as if reading her mind, and a warm feeling crept up her neck.

"I must say, there's never a dull moment around here," he said, bending his knees. "What's that about your powder puff posse attacking a preacher?"

"They want to be called the Red Feather posse, and the preacher part was a mistake." She sighed. "They mistook him for a horse thief."

He straightened, and his mouth quirked with humor. "An easy mistake to make, I'm sure." He squatted again. "Is it true what they said? Have you been arrested?"

Her cheeks flared. "I'm afraid so. But it was always for a good cause."

He arched an eyebrow. "That's good to hear. Nothin' worse than going to jail for a bad cause."

"Speaking from experience?"

He shrugged.

As usual, he made it extremely difficult to keep her emotions under control. Every sympathetic look, engaging smile, and encouraging word was feigned for the sole purpose of manipulating her. But even knowing the name of his game, she found herself liking him more each day. It was the oddest thing, and she was at a loss to explain it.

Cheeks flaming beneath his measured gaze, she lowered her lashes, and that's when she noticed the loose brick at the bottom of his cell. It hadn't been there when she scrubbed the floor. "You weren't trying to escape, were you?"

"Be a little hard to do, since this cell is built tighter than a spinster's corset."

Refusing to let his choice of words distract her, she said, "Only a guilty man would try to escape."

Hs straightened. "Is that what you think?"

"It's what I know. So save your energy." Unlike many jails in the west, which were flimsy at best, this one was well-built. "No prisoner has managed to leave before his time, and I mean to keep it that way."

His devastating grin almost took her breath away. Glowering at him, she turned to leave. If he thought he could charm her with his crooked smile . . . he was right, and she'd better watch her step.

"Always a first time," he called after her.

TWENTY-ONE

Mary-Louise had agreed to meet Amanda for lunch and was waiting for her at a corner table in the hotel dining room. They hugged before Amanda bent down to peer at the infant asleep in the wicker baby carriage.

Mary-Louise's pale face and dark shadows indicated a lack of sleep. Her normally well-groomed red hair hung limply down her back, and her gingham dress was wrinkled.

"Are you okay?" Amanda asked. It couldn't be easy taking care of a newborn while dealing with the aftermath of a fire.

Mary-Louise looked like she was battling tears. "Everyone has been so kind and generous. The hotel isn't even charging us for staying here. And the church ladies donated all sorts of things for the baby." She moistened her lips before adding, "John is hoping to sell our livestock so we can start rebuilding soon."

It was the opening Amanda had hoped for.

"That's wonderful news. Do you have fire insurance?" It was unlikely, as most insurance companies refused to insure wooden structures, but she had to ask.

"Insurance? No."

"What a pity, but thank God everything is working out. Is there anything else you need? Clothes?"

"We're fine for now."

Amanda moistened her lips. "I need to ask you a few questions about the fire for my report. I'm still not clear on how it started."

Mary-Louise's expression darkened. "I told you. A piece of burning paper fell out of the stove. Why do you keep hounding me?"

Surprised by her friend's sharp tone, Amanda sat back in her chair. "I'm not hounding you. As sheriff, I'm required to investigate all fires and —"

"You keep harping on this. It's like you think I started the fire on purpose."

Amanda reached for Mary-Louise's hand. "I'm sorry if that's how I make you feel. I certainly don't mean to —"

"I told you what happened." Mary-Louise pulled her hand away. "I have nothing more to say." She shot up from her chair. Without another word, she reached for the handle of the baby carriage and wheeled it away.

"Mary-Louise, please —"

Watching her friend storm out of the dining room, Amanda felt a sinking feeling. It seemed there was more to the fire than Mary-Louise was willing to admit. A lot more. The question was what?

That night, Rick paced the cell, waiting for the deputy sheriff to return. Gunfire had sent Hobson racing out of the office more than an hour ago. Like it or not, the kid was the only chance he had of saving his neck.

Despite his best efforts, he'd gotten nowhere with the lady sheriff. She still didn't believe in his innocence.

Did Hobson? Hard to know. But that's what he intended to find out. If there was a weak link in the Lady Sheriff Lockwood's armor, it was her overenthusiastic deputy.

Rick sure in blazes couldn't depend on his lawyer. What was his name? Birdseye, that's it. Bird *shit,* more like it.

He seemed more interested in making a name for himself than proving Rick's innocence. His advice? Plead guilty and throw himself on the mercy of the court. What kind of hogwash was that?

It was after eleven by the time Hobson arrived, this time, with two prisoners in tow.

Rick waited for him to shove the men into the cell next to his. No sooner did the one — a heavyset man with a sweeping mustache — hit the cot than he started sawing wood. The other one didn't look that far behind.

"Got a minute?" Rick asked, motioning Hobson closer.

Hobson approached his cell with obvious curiosity. "I guess so. Why?"

Though both men in the next cell were passed out cold, he lowered his voice. "I'm concerned about your boss."

"You are?"

"Yes. She seems terribly overworked. I don't know what she'd do if she didn't have you."

Hobson's face turned a vivid shade of pink. "I do what I can."

"You kind of remind me of . . ." He glanced at the dime novel sticking out of Hobson's vest pocket for the name of the latest hero. "Buffalo Bill."

"Oh, wow!"

Rick cleared his throat. "That's why I'm asking for your help. I don't want to put any more on the sheriff's shoulders."

Hobson looked interested. "What kind of help?"

"The night Cooper was murdered . . . I saw someone leave his room. Find that man, and you'll find the killer. More than that, you'll be a hero. Just like in a dime novel."

"You think so?" Hobson looked as bright-eyed as a child on Christmas morn. "Wow." He thought for a moment. "What did he look like?"

Rick described him the best he could. Unfortunately, the man had no distinguishing features, and the dimly lit hall allowed only a quick glance. "He was about your height. Light hair. Smoked a cigarette."

Hobson hung his thumbs from his belt. "You just described half the men in this town."

"He walked funny. Like one leg was longer than the other."

Hobson frowned. "Lot of cowpunchers walk funny. Like I said, you just described half the men in this town."

"That's why I need your help. I'll recognize him on sight." At least he hoped he would.

"That's kind of a problem. Being that you're in jail and all."

Rick rubbed his whiskered chin. "Yeah, that is a problem. What do you think Buffalo Bill would do?"

A slow grin spread across Hobson's face. "I think he'd put on a really good show."

Rick grinned back. "I think you're right."

He then explained what he wanted Hobson to do.

"Oh, wow!"

Rick shot his hand through the bars. "We got a deal?"

Hobson grabbed Rick's hand and practically shook his arm out of its socket. "Deal."

Amanda spent very little time at home since taking over as sheriff. She was too busy stopping brawls, hauling drunks to jail, or tracking down Old Man Pendergrass. The former Confederate soldier had the disturbing habit of wandering about town in an advanced state of undress.

The last time he roamed the streets buck naked, three members of the Tuesday Afternoon Quilting Bee broke a city ordinance by fainting dead away and blocking the boardwalk.

Amanda was lucky if she got five or six hours of sleep on any given night. Mama, as always, was worried about her and made her promise to come home that Friday night for supper. Since she was already late, she left Scooter in charge of the daily task of chasing down Pendergrass. Her deputy took it in his usual philosophical way.

"Like Grandpappy always said, a thousand men can't undress a naked man." With that, he ran out the door, giving chase.

Smiling to herself, she gathered her belongings and, after locking the office, started for home.

Surprised to find her two sisters and brothers-in-law seated around the dining room table, she kissed her mother on the cheek and apologized profusely for being late.

"What's the special occasion?" she asked, taking her place next to Meg. Papa looked up briefly from cutting the roast beef on his plate but remained silent.

Mama smiled, her soft-eyed gaze traveling the length of the table. Having her family together made her look as contented as a hen on a nest. "No special occasion. It's been a while since we all sat down together, and I thought it time."

Her mother didn't fool Amanda one whit. She hadn't spoken to Papa since putting on the sheriff's badge. What would be the point? She knew where he stood, and they would only argue.

Mama's answer to everything, even family friction, was to break bread together.

Good try, Mama. Unfortunately, it would take a lot more than Mama's delicious roast beef and blueberry pie to smooth Papa's feathers.

"Yes, it has been a while," Meg was saying.

Meg's husband, Grant, raised his glass to Amanda. "And it's not every day that I get to dine with a lady sheriff."

A tall, clean-shaven man, Grant was born and raised in Boston. Though he'd picked up a slight Texas drawl, he still called the parlor the *pahlah.* A lawyer by trade and graduate of Harvard, he met Meg when she was the plaintiff in a breach-of-promise lawsuit. Since he was the lawyer for the defense, it was a miracle they ever got together.

"Time goes so fast," Meg rushed to say, with a slight shake of her head at Grant. "I can't believe we'll soon be celebrating our first wedding anniversary."

Amanda placed her napkin on her lap and said nothing. Apparently, any discussion of her job had been deemed off-limits. Mama's idea, no doubt, to keep peace in the family.

Across the table, Ralph reached for Josie's hand. A pale-faced man with a concave chest, he wheezed with each breath. "And we'll soon be going on our sixth."

Josie seemed especially quiet, but it was the bags under her eyes that worried Amanda. Did she know Meg was expecting? Or was something else going on?

"Pass the salad, will you?" Meg asked.

Mama handed the salad across the table. "Speaking of which, has anyone seen my good salad bowl? I've searched high and low for it. You girls didn't borrow it, did you?"

"Not I," Josie said.

Meg helped herself to salad and passed the bowl to Amanda. "Nor me."

"I'm sure it will turn up," Papa said, relieving Amanda of having to confess that the salad bowl in question was still molding felt for a hat she had started to make before taking over as sheriff. Now, she didn't know when or even if she would have time to finish it. Her dream of opening a hat shop seemed far away.

"Are you feeling all right, Meg?" Mama asked, seeming to have forgotten her salad bowl. "You've hardly touched your food."

"I'm fine," Meg said, making an effort to chew.

Grant rubbed his wife's back. "I think we should tell them."

"Tell us what?" Ralph asked, helping himself to another roll.

Meg bit her lower lip and cast a glance at Josie. "We're going to have a baby."

Mama's face lit up. "Oh, Meg!" She clasped her hands to her chest. "That's the best news ever!"

"Spectacular," Papa agreed, holding his water glass aloft. "This calls for a real celebration."

Josie looked no less delighted. "I'm so happy for you, Meg," she said, then promptly burst into tears.

Alarmed, Meg dropped her fork. "Oh, Josie, I didn't want to tell you . . . I'm so sorry."

"What?" Josie dabbed her eyes with her husband's handkerchief. "Sorry? What are you talking about? I'm your sister. Why wouldn't you want to tell me?"

Meg inhaled and swiped a blond strand away from her face. "I just thought —"

Josie brushed away her concerns with a shake of her hand. "This is great news. I'm going to be an aunt."

Amanda frowned. She was just as confused at the others. "Then why are you crying?"

"Oh, this —" Josie palmed away the last of the tears and struggled for control. "I'm just sorry that I w-won't b-be around to see the b-baby grow up."

A stunned silence followed, punctuated by Josie's sobs.

Papa set his glass down. "What do you mean, you won't be around? What nonsense is this?"

Josie turned to her husband. "You t-tell them."

Before he had a chance, all twenty-two clocks adorning the dining room walls struck the hour of seven p.m. Chimes, bongs, and cuckoos filled the air but did nothing to snap the waiting tension that stretched across the table.

Sensing bad news ahead, Amanda set her fork down and reached for her napkin.

Papa, as usual, pulled out his watch to check that it was accurate. Seemingly satisfied, he slipped the watch into his vest pocket without making any adjustments.

Josie was visibly upset, but Amanda was more concerned about her brother-in-law. Tonight, he looked especially pale and appeared to have lost weight. Even more worrisome, his lips were tinged blue.

Ralph tugged on the collar of his shirt and took a swallow of water. The moment the last of the clock chimes faded away, he began. "As you know, I have a lung problem."

Fearing the worst, Amanda dug her fingers into her palms. She had grown so used to his heavy breathing that she'd hardly noticed it in recent months. Now that attention had been drawn to his condition, his breathing problems appeared to have gotten worse. A whole lot worse.

"I'm sorry to say my lungs aren't getting any better." He glanced at Josie, and she squeezed his hand.

Amanda held her breath. Surely, Ralph wasn't going to . . .

As if to guess her thoughts, Ralph pulled his gaze away from Josie. "The doctor advised me to move to a climate with less humidity."

Amanda's breath caught in her throat. Relief was immediately followed by dismay. "You're leaving?"

Josie took a sip of water before answering. "Yes. We're moving to Arizona Territory where the air is dry. The Texas humidity is only making his condition worse."

Meg looked stricken, and Mama gasped. Papa said nothing. He just stood and left the room. His actions came as no surprise to Amanda. There was nothing he hated more than his daughters leaving home to make lives of their own. But to actually leave Two-Time — to altogether leave the state — in his mind, that was unthinkable.

Mama drew her gaze from Papa's retreating back. "That's . . . that's so far away."

"I know, Mama," Josie said. "But they say the dry climate does wonders for the health, and Ralph has an uncle who lives there in

Tucson. He promised Ralph a job in his general store, and . . . and I'll write every day. I promise." She made a gallant attempt to pull herself together and even managed a wan smile. "Once the railroad reaches Tucson, you can all come and visit."

Amanda swallowed the lump forming in her throat. "But that will take too long."

"Not that long," Ralph said. "The Southern Pacific has already reached Phoenix, and there're plans to connect."

Next to him, Josie dabbed at her eyes with a handkerchief. Ralph covered her hand with his own. "We might not have to stay there permanently," he added with a look of apology.

Amanda sympathized with him. With Josie too. But she also felt bad for Meg, whose happy news got lost in the gloom that followed Josie's announcement. No one felt much like eating, and the evening ended abruptly with hugs and tears all around.

Twenty-Two

The following night, Amanda sat in her office and stared at the items found at the Wendell farm.

Not much there. A bullet casing, several cigarette butts, a length of string, a piece of leather, and a tin can. Normal trash that might be found on any piece of property. Nothing that spelled out the identity of the horse thieves.

Despite questioning farmers, ranchers, and railroad workers, she still didn't have a clue as to who stole the Wendell horses. She'd sifted through the ashes left from the Freeman fire, and that still remained a puzzle too. There had to be a reason why Mary-Louise had stormed out of the hotel dining room and seemed to be avoiding her. There was nothing on the cattle thieves either. Or the chickens or the bank robbers or . . .

Elbows on her desk, she buried her head

in her hands. She should go home. Get some sleep. She'd allowed Deputy Hobson to take the upstairs apartment. She wasn't ready to live by herself. Not yet . . . But if Papa continued to act like he was ready to disown her, she might well change her mind.

Papa was the least of her problems. She still didn't have the slightest idea what to do about the town's crime wave. Didn't even know where to start. With the thought came the tears.

"You crying?"

Rennick's voice startled her. Embarrassed to be found feeling sorry for herself, she quickly reached for the handkerchief in her sleeve. She'd not noticed that the door leading to the cellblock was open. Again. Scooter must have forgotten to shut it.

"No."

"Sure sounds like it to me."

"Sheriffs don't cry."

"Sure they do. Everyone cries."

She dabbed at tears streaming down her cheeks. "Including you, Mr. Rennick?" she called.

"I've done my share."

"Not many men would admit to such a thing," she said.

"Been my experience that neither will some women."

For several moments, neither of them spoke. Nevertheless, something like a magnet pulled her to the door separating her office from the cellblock. The gas lantern Scooter lit earlier was still burning, casting shadows on the shabby walls and floor.

She hardly recognized the man on the cot. For once, he wasn't pacing. Nor did he look like he was ready to spring up. He sat with his knees spread, arms folded across his chest, gaze boldly raking her over. On his lap was a notebook. On the floor by his foot, a bottle of ink.

He sure did look different without his beard and his hair trimmed to just above his collar. Younger, even. He'd also put on some much-needed weight. He was attractive before, but now he was just plain handsome.

Pushing a stray strand of hair behind her ear, she leaned against the threshold. "All right, I admit it. I was having a weak moment."

She hoped he'd give her one of those derisive looks she knew so well. Those, she could handle. Instead, his eyes filled with sympathy, and she struggled not to burst into tears again.

"You're not still beating yourself up for that fire, are you?"

"Maybe a little." The fire bothered her on several levels, but she didn't want to talk about it.

He regarded her from beneath a furrowed brow. "How come you're into all that women's rights stuff?"

The question surprised her, coming as it seemed from out of nowhere. "Why shouldn't I be?"

He shrugged. "I could understand it if you lived in a big city. But here in this one-horse town . . ."

"I'll have you know we have a lot more than one horse." Though that might not be true in the near future if the horse thieves continued to decimate the area.

"You know what I mean."

In the golden glow cast by the lantern, he looked sincerely interested in what she had to say. But he wasn't, of course. It was all an act. Engaging her in a conversation was just his way of trying to win her over and earn her trust. Still, she was in no mood to fight him. She'd been fighting all day. All week. Now she just wanted to enjoy a quiet moment before the saloon rowdies started shooting up the town again as they did every Saturday night.

"I guess you could say I was influenced by my grandmother." For some reason,

Grandmama had been very much on her mind of late. "When I was ten, I spent a whole summer with her. I'd been sent to her as punishment."

"Punishment for what?" he asked.

"For defacing property."

His eyebrows rose. "Defacing?"

"I tore down all the 'say no to women's rights' signs posted in town."

"At ten?"

She smiled. Now that she thought about it, it did seem like a strange thing for one so young to concern herself with, but then, she had always been a serious-minded child.

"Papa said I was born fighting for equality."

"Did the punishment do any good?" he asked.

The question made her laugh. "Absolutely not. Grandmama lived in Austin, and the town always held a foot race for the Fourth of July." Her mind traveled back to that hot, sticky summer. She often wondered how such a forward-thinking woman raised someone as old-fashioned as her father.

"I wanted so much to enter but couldn't because I was a girl. Grandmama came to the rescue." Amanda had no idea why she was telling him this, but she couldn't seem to stop herself. "She altered a pair of trousers to fit me and pinned my hair beneath a boy's cap. I entered the race in my disguise, and no one clapped louder from the sidelines than she did."

He chuckled, bringing her back to the present. "Did you win?"

"Came in third," she said, surprised at the note of pride still in her voice. She came in mere seconds behind the first- and second-place winners. "But I won first in the armadillo racing contest."

His eyes opened wider. "Armadillo?" He laughed. "Wish I could have seen that."

She laughed too. Sometime during the fifties, the animals migrated to Texas from Central America, though no one knew what brought them so far north. Never had she seen such a strange creature. Despite her fear, she bravely picked one up by the tail, something some of the boys refused to do.

"The secret is to blow on them like crazy to make them run."

Even though she'd lost the foot race, she could still recall the thrill of being judged by ability rather than gender. A person could accomplish a lot with ability and skills. Skills were something a person could work at. Something that could be controlled. Improved. It was a heady moment and one that changed her forever.

This is just the beginning, Amanda, her grandmother had said. *You'll see.*

"I promised Grandmama a blue ribbon for running the next time, but unfortunately, that was the last summer we spent together." She'd sobbed for a week upon hearing the news of her grandmother's death.

"I bet your grandmother is still rooting for you," he said.

Something stirred inside — some emotion that surprised her with its power. It felt as if someone had reached into her chest and gently squeezed her heart. Refusing to succumb to more tears, she swallowed the lump in her throat. Did Lucy Stone ever cry? Probably not.

Blast him anyway. He always knew how to disarm her, even when he didn't mean what he said. This was all part of his plan to charm her into believing his innocence. But for an instant — a split second in time — she imagined he meant what he said.

She studied him. Even in the dim light, his haunted look was evident. That part *was* real. She'd noticed it the first day they'd met, but it was even more noticeable now that he was clean-shaven. Every plane of his face, every line, seemed to point to a deep sadness. Suddenly, she wanted to know more about him. A lot more.

"If you weren't here, what would you be doing?" she asked.

"Doing?"

"Your profession."

"Horses," he said. "I once owned a horse ranch."

That didn't surprise her. Spirit was no ordinary horse. He had been well cared for, trained. "What happened?"

He clenched his jaw and looked away. "Long story."

"Long night," she said.

His gaze met hers, and she got the strangest sense that he wanted to tell her. Instead, he shook his head. "You better get some shut-eye. You look beat."

She sagged against the doorframe. She *was* beat. Still, she wanted to know more about him. Peeling herself away from the doorjamb, she moved closer to his cell and whispered a plea. "Talk to me."

"Why?"

"Right now, I'm the only friend you have."

She didn't want to tell him the real reason — that she needed someone to talk to. Whenever things had gone wrong in the past, she'd depended on her sisters. But now, they were both happily married, and she felt more like an outsider than ever. Rennick was a surprising but strangely adequate substitute.

"Been my experience that sheriffs are more apt to make enemies than friends," he said. "You and me aren't even on borrowin' terms."

She smiled. "Case you haven't noticed, I'm not like most sheriffs."

"Oh, I've noticed all right. But long as you refuse to believe I didn't kill nobody, I don't see much chance of us bein' what you call friends."

"It's not my job to decide your guilt."

"But you have. Admit it."

"What do you expect? You tried to escape."

"And that makes me guilty?" He flashed an appealing smile that threatened to melt her defenses. So now they were back to the usual cat-and-mouse games. "What do I have to do to convince you of my innocence?"

"Nothing. Only a court of law can do that."

He splayed his hands. "Why not save the court trouble? If you let me out now, we can look for the real killer together."

She laughed. She couldn't help herself. The man could charm the hide off a steer if he had the mind to do so.

He arched an eyebrow. "What's so funny?"

"You," she said. She'd taken an oath to protect and serve, and by George, that's what she intended to do. No handsome, charming, smooth-talking man could make her derelict in her duties.

"You just never give up." She tilted her head. "So why are you so against independent women?" she asked, steering the conversation away from the subject of his guilt.

She heard his intake of breath. "When I was two, my mother left me and my sister to pursue a singin' career. She billed herself as America's answer to Jenny Lind."

"She left you?" Amanda couldn't imagine a mother leaving her children. "But she came back, right?"

He shook his head. "Nope. Never did. She left my pa to raise us. We never heard from her again."

Was that the source of his sadness? Or was it something else, something more recent? "I'm so sorry. I could never do that to a child," she said softly. "Leave him, I mean. That's why I've chosen to remain single."

Few suffragists were married, which allowed them to travel at will. Elizabeth Cady Stanton was one of the few exceptions; she had several children but primarily stayed home and scripted speeches.

"You better not fall in love then," he said.

"Some people say the only cure for love is marriage."

She thought about her parents' devotion to each other. Marriage sure hadn't cured them of their love for each other; it only enhanced it. Papa's eyes still lit up when Mama came into view, but such a love was rare.

"I have no intention of falling in love," she said, blushing. What a thing to be talking about — to a man, no less. A man accused of murder . . . "I have neither the time nor inclination for such nonsense. I see how marriage has changed my sisters. A woman having to please a husband and run a household can no longer pursue her dreams."

Certainly, a married woman had no time for important stuff like making the world a better place to live. What little time Mama had left after catering to her family's needs was devoted to the church and a small circle of friends.

"My hat's off to you," he said. "You're savin' some poor man a life of misery."

"As well as myself," she said, stifling a yawn. Never could she remember feeling so exhausted.

"You better get some sleep," he said.

Nodding, she started for the door. "Good

night, Mr. Rennick."

"Turn off the light on your way out."

She turned and reached for the hanging lantern.

"Miss Sheriff."

Her hand froze. "Yes?"

"Just so you know, your grandmother's not the only one rootin' for you."

She turned off the light just in time to hide her tears.

Twenty-Three

The sound of her footsteps fading away nearly tore Rick apart. He wanted her to come back in the worst possible way. The memory of hearing her cry awakened a part of him he'd long thought dead — the part that felt for another.

Still, he was surprised he'd told her about his mother. It wasn't like him to talk about his past. He couldn't remember when he last spoke of his mother's desertion. He thought he was over it, but the reopening of old wounds made a lie out of that.

Why would he reveal something so gut-wrenchingly personal to someone he knew only under the most trying of circumstances? He'd known Christy a year before the subject of his mother came up. Yes, he'd wanted to win the sheriff's trust and help, but not like that. Never like that.

He sucked in his breath. The damage was done. Nothing to do about it now except to wait till the open wounds healed, allowing him to rebury the past.

As for the lady sheriff . . .

She sure hadn't struck him as one of those independent suffering women tonight, and that surprised him. Usually, she had the single-minded purpose of a thrown dagger.

Odd as it seemed, he wanted to take care of her and tell her detractors where to go. The thought made him grimace. As if he could take care of anyone. Hadn't even been able to take care of his wife.

Fortunately, Hobson arrived with the latest roundup of suspects, saving him from his thoughts. This group of six men were almost exact copies of the others the deputy had hauled in front of Rick's cell.

Some were indignant at being brought in for questioning for some imagined offense. Others were too drunk to care.

Hobson issued orders like a general. "All right, men, stand straight and face the cells."

This command brought more grumbling, but Hobson did some fancy maneuverings with his gun that convinced the suspects he meant business. Feet shuffled as the men turned toward Rick's cell.

Rick's gaze lit upon each one in turn, mentally comparing him with the man seen leaving Cooper's room. How was it possible that so many in town fit the description of the suspected killer? It seemed like half the population stood five foot eight or there about. And who would have ever thought there were so many men with light-colored hair?

Rick signaled to Hobson to make the suspects walk back and forth in front of his cell. Some shuffled their feet, and others couldn't walk a straight line, but none appeared to have an unequal-sized leg.

He'd only got a quick glance at the man leaving Cooper's room, but it was enough to know that they'd hit another dead end.

Frustration rose inside like steam from a kettle. This was taking too long. There had to be another way.

He caught Hobson's eye and shook his head.

Hobson took the night's disappointment in his usual stride. "All right," he said. "You're free to go."

The men filed out of the cell room, muttering among themselves.

"I'll check out the Golden Spur," Hobson said. "Maybe your guy is there."

Rick rubbed the back of his neck. "Let me go with you. It'll save time."

Hobson's eyebrows shot up. "Not a good idea. You might get the itch to run."

Rick thrust his hands through the bars. "Then handcuff me!"

"Your hands were tied the last time you tried to escape."

Rick pulled his hands in and dropped them to his side. "Then forget about dragging anyone else in here. It's a waste of time."

Hobson shrugged. "We can't stop. No, sirree. Can't do that."

Rick narrowed his eyes. "Why not?"

"Grandpappy said you should never blow out the match until you see the light."

"Is that so, eh?" Rick managed a half grin. The more he got to know this kid, the more he liked him.

Amanda rode her horse home to Peaceful Lane. She no longer thought of Spirit as Rennick's horse, and that could be a problem if she ever had to give him back. But she was too tired to worry about it now.

After settling the steed in the barn in back, she walked into the house. Mama and Papa had already retired, but the walls were alive with the sound of Papa's clocks; twenty-two in the dining room, twenty-two in the parlor — all keeping the same perfect time.

Her sisters held conflicting emotions about the constant chimes that marked each passing moment. Oddly enough, Amanda found the timepieces comforting. As a child, she liked to stand on a soapbox and pretend she was a public speaker decrying the latest social injustice. The wall of clocks served as her approving audience, bursting into applause every quarter of an hour.

Tonight, the measured *ticktocks* reminded her of a bunch of old ladies clicking their tongues in disapproval. *Making nice with a suspected killer, were you? Tsk, tsk, tsk . . .*

The brisk night air had failed to cool her hot brow. A strange and unfamiliar heat flowed through her limbs, seeming to hold her in its grip.

Just so you know, your grandmother's not the only one rooting for you.

She drew in her breath. Nothing Rennick said was worth beans. Not a word. It was all part of his ongoing attempt to win her over. Even that story about his mother was probably a bald-faced lie.

So why did his words keep repeating in her head? Why did his resonant voice still echo inside? *Your grandmother's not the only one rooting for you.*

He was a prime murder suspect. He claimed he was innocent but failed to give an adequate explanation for his presence at the scene of the crime. It was also hard to ignore that he tried to escape. Wouldn't an innocent man want to stay and clear his name?

Twisting her hands together, she paced back and forth in the dark parlor. It was no concern of hers. Innocent or guilty — made no difference. It wasn't her job to decide. Still, there was the puzzle of the missing knife and . . .

Catching herself, she pounded her fist into the palm of her hand. *Oh no, you don't, Mr. R. B. Rennick. You're not drawing me into your little game.* He played on her inexperience and charitable heart. Worse, he'd used her grandmother for his own purposes.

Lies, all of it. He didn't mean a word he said, and she hated — utterly hated — that she wished with all her heart that he did.

Amanda arrived at the office the following morning to find the cells packed and the place smelling like a bootlegger's still. Scooter had arrested seven men during the night for drunk and disorderly conduct.

Rennick didn't seem to mind the company. Instead, he was enjoying a rowdy game of cards with two of the prisoners. She pointedly ignored him. After a sleepless night, she was in no mood for his tricks. If he ever mentioned her grandmother again, she would slug him.

Some of his cellmates were local shop owners and farmers. Most were even family men. One was the mayor's son.

"How did you manage to handle all those arrests by yourself?" she asked her deputy.

Scooter grinned. "They were too far gone to give me any trouble," he explained. "So I just pulled out old Pete here" — he patted the firearm at his side — "and marched them to jail like a herd of cattle heading for water."

"Fine them each five dollars and let them go." She wanted the cells empty to make room for real outlaws, if she were ever lucky enough to catch one.

Scooter hesitated. "I'm afraid that's gonna be a problem."

She frowned. "What do you mean?"

"Between the clean cells, comfortable cots, and tasty grub, they said they've never had it so good, and they ain't leaving."

Amanda sank into her chair. "Oh, for crying out loud." She didn't have time for such nonsense. "If they won't leave of their own accord, then force them to leave."

"Yes, sir, Sheriff!" Scooter did an about-face, pulled out his Colt, and marched to the back as if on the way to war.

Moments later, all seven men, motivated

by the muzzle of Scooter's gun, moved past her desk, hands held shoulder high.

"This ain't fair," muttered one. "A man has the right to stay in jail if he wants. I demand a lawyer."

No sooner had Scooter and the prisoners left than the door swung open and Mayor Troutman barreled in, looking fit to be tied. He came to a skidding stop in front of her desk, his mouth moving like a fish gasping for air.

He stabbed the floor with his cane. "What's the meaning of arresting my son?" he sputtered.

She sat back in her chair. "He was disturbing the peace."

"He was letting off steam. That's what kids his age do."

She leaned forward. "That kid, as you call him," she said, emphasizing every word, "is forty years old. He should know better."

The mayor got all red in the face. Blue veins thick as rope stood out on his neck. "You've overstepped your boundaries this time, Miss Lockwood." He continued to rant and threatened to have her head.

With a sigh, she let her gaze wander through the open door to her lone prisoner. Instead of his usual pacing, Mr. Rennick

259

stood still and was soundlessly clapping his hands.

Just so you know, your grandmother's not the only one rooting for you.

She quickly averted her gaze. Rennick's show of support was all part of an elaborate scheme to win her over. Yet knowing it was a ruse did nothing to temper the effects. Already, she felt her defenses subside and confidence begin to build. It had been a long time since anyone applauded her or even approved of anything she did. Mama and Papa tried. Still, they couldn't help but be perplexed by a daughter who shunned marriage and the possibility of a normal life.

With a jerk, she turned her attention back to the mayor, standing so abruptly that he stepped back.

"That's *Sheriff* Lockwood," she said, leaving no room for argument. "And as long as I'm wearing this badge, I'll step over what boundaries I please." She couldn't believe the words spouting out of her mouth. And she'd said them with such authority. *Sorry, Miss Brackett, but sometimes grace and charm don't work.*

"You can leave now. In fact, I insist." *Oh my.*

The mayor looked momentarily rebuffed but soon recovered. "Not till you explain this!" He slapped a paper onto her desk. A quick glance confirmed that it was a bill she had turned in.

"You expect the town to pay for a frock coat and Bible?" he sputtered. "Your job is to arrest criminals, not convert them!"

"I know what my job is," she retorted. Before she had a chance to explain the bill and further exercise her newfound confidence, the mayor spun around and stormed out of the office.

No sooner did the mayor leave than Mr. Woodman arrived with the newly repaired hope chest. She hurried to hold the door open for him. A wiry man of undetermined race and age, his skin was the color of honey oak.

"Whew! What's got the mayor riled up this time?" he asked, his face damp from exertion.

"We arrested his son."

"If you ask me, that was long overdue." He lowered his chin to indicate the chest in his arms. "Where do you want this?"

"Put it over there against that wall."

She waited for him to set the chest down before checking out the side that had been damaged by a bullet.

"The repair is hardly noticeable," she

exclaimed, running her finger along the smooth wood. If she didn't know better, she would think the slight indentation was part of the carving. Woodman always did good work, but this time, he had far exceeded her expectations. "How much do I owe you?"

He handed her a bill, and she reached for her purse to carefully count out the right amount.

"The missus put some women's clothes and stuff inside for the poor farm," he said, mopping his forehead with a handkerchief.

"Tell her thanks. I'm sure the Wendells will put the items to good use." She paid him, and he left.

She stooped to take another look at Woodman's expert work. Wouldn't it be great if all problems could be so easily resolved?

"What do you plan on doing with your hope-a-thingie?" Rennick called from his cell.

She straightened with a sigh. "I don't know." The hope chest served as yet another reminder of how she had fallen short of her parents' hopes and dreams for her.

"Bring it here. I could use a footstool."

"Certainly not," she said. The very idea. Just because she had no use for it didn't mean she would allow it to share a cell with a prisoner. "As I told you, it's a family heirloom."

"I kinda think of us as family. Look at all the time we spend together."

"Not by choice, believe me."

As for the hope chest . . . She had no need for it, and neither sister wanted it. Meg had no room in her tiny house, and Josie insisted that Amanda keep it. The tradition was to pass it along to the next unmarried woman in line. Like it or not, that was her.

The thing would just have to stay where it was till she figured out what to do with it.

TWENTY-FOUR

Each morning, Amanda arrived at the office to find the jail cells packed, along with a daily dispatch citing yet another judicial delay. Not only did this affect the start of Rennick's trial, but also land disputes and other court cases, including dissolution of marriages and custody battles.

The town's lack of its own sitting judge was only part of the problem. Scooter enthusiastically arrested anyone who as much as thought about breaking the law. Vagrants, drunkards, rabble-rousers, and other social misfits or morally depleted citizens were all marched to jail at gunpoint.

The fact that some lawbreakers also happened to be businessmen created an unforeseen problem. For that meant that shops and other establishments were closed while their owners cooled their heels behind bars. It got so bad that the town council toyed with the idea of limiting the number of arrests that could be made on any given day in order to keep the town running smoothly.

Amanda had arranged for extra cots, stored at the now-deserted fort outside of town, to be brought to the jailhouse. As long as she was in charge, no man would sleep on the floor or have to share a cot with another.

Prisoners were fed well, made to wash, given a change of clothes if necessary, and treated with respect. So much so that the only way to get some inmates to pay their bail and leave was the same way they came in — at gunpoint.

Bail money more than paid for prisoner meals and other necessities, and soon, the town coffers began to swell. But did that satisfy the town council? It did not!

The mayor was constantly harping on her to quit and let a man take over the job. The husbands of her posse accused her of being a poor influence on their wives. One woman's husband, Mr. Granby, managed to get himself arrested just so he could enjoy a decent meal while "his wife was out gallivanting with outlaws."

The *Two-Time Gazette* ran numerous editorials blaming her for dragging women off the path of righteousness and encouraging them to "play in the Devil's playground." Her name was even uttered from the pulpit in the same critical tone afforded the fall of mankind.

The criticism and complaints weren't without merit. Some Red Feather members took a liking to Mr. Rennick and were constantly stopping by to ply him with baked goods, even when not working. Mrs. Perl knitted him a special red scarf, and Miss Read kept him supplied with his favorite peppermint candy. This raised more than a few eyebrows around town. It was bad enough that good-time gal Goldie was seen leaving the jailhouse with suspicious regularity, but visits from the minister's wife really got tongues wagging.

If wasn't just the Red Feather posse that had taken a liking to the Rennick — so had Scooter. He and Rennick were often seen with their heads together. But whenever Amanda questioned her deputy, he would shrug and act all innocent-like.

That morning when she walked in and caught Scooter coming out of the jail block with a guilty look on his face, her suspicions grew.

"What's going on?" she asked.

"Nothing," he said, ducking behind his new camera. It was a large mahogany box with maroon bellows balanced upon a tripod. "Say cabbage."

Amanda frowned. "I hate cabbage."

"Yeah, but the word relaxes the mouth so that it photographs better."

"Nothing like a relaxed mouth," she said. "Cabbage, cabbage, cabbage."

"Hold it!" He squeezed the rubber ball in his hand. A bright light flashed from the magnesium lamp, followed by gray smoke and a shower of white powder.

It seemed like forever before he yelled, "You can move now." His head popped up from beneath a black cloth, and he patted the camera like a parent patting the head of a child.

"Very impressive," she said.

He reached into a leather portfolio. "Here's the first photo I took," he said, laying a photograph on the desk in front of her. "It takes clearer pictures than my old camera."

The unexpected image of Rick took her by surprise, and her breath caught in her lungs.

Half his face was in shadows, but even so, the camera had captured the inherit strength she had come to know so well. Now she studied the high cheekbones, strong square jaw, and chiseled nose at her leisure — a luxury normally denied her.

Whereas the light side illuminated him, the dark side only added to the mystery. The burning question of his guilt or innocence remained. "So that's what you were doing when I arrived."

"If you don't like it, I can take another," Scooter said, looking uncertain.

"What? Oh, no, I think it's . . . a great likeness."

He looked pleased. "I'm starting a criminal file, just like the Pinkerton Detective Agency." He explained that the agency was creating a library to be used by lawmen across the country. "Just think, we could be the only sheriff's office with its own criminal library."

"Sounds like a great idea," she said.

The door opened, and Rennick's lawyer popped his head into the office.

"Got a minute?" he asked, indicating with a toss of his head that he wanted to talk to her in private.

Exchanging a look with Scooter, she shrugged before joining Birdseye outside.

"Miss . . . uh . . ." Mr. Birdseye removed his hat upon addressing her but seemed at a loss as to how to proceed from there.

"You can call me Sheriff," she said briskly. "What can I do for you?"

He cleared his throat. "I've met with your

prisoner many times, as you know. I'm afraid none of our meetings have been productive. The man's as close-mouthed as a clam."

What he said came as no surprise, but she wasn't sure why he was telling her this.

"I wonder," he continued, "if you could tell me anything about him."

Oh yes, she could tell him plenty. She could tell him that Rick was the most stubborn, arrogant, and annoying man she'd ever met.

But of course, she wouldn't.

When she hesitated, Birdseye added, "His background. History? Anything would help."

"I know he once owned a horse ranch. That's all I can tell you."

Birdseye grimaced. "I've never had a more difficult client. He refuses to talk about himself. He claims he's innocent but won't explain why he was in Cooper's room. He refuses to plead guilty, self-defense, or even insanity."

"What about the missing murder weapon?" she asked. "He had no time to hide it. Someone must have walked out of that room with it, and we know it wasn't Rick."

"That's the one and only thing in his favor," he said.

Since he didn't sound all that confident, she asked, "And if the jurors don't buy that argument?"

"Let me put it this way. If I was the prosecutor, I'd be jumping for joy about now."

Rick looked up from the newspaper as Miss Sheriff stormed into the cell room. One look at her face told him she was loaded to the muzzle.

Standing, he gaped at her. Never had he seen her horns in such a tangle. "What's got you so riled this time?"

She glared at him, eyes flashing blue fire. "I told you once, and I'll tell you again!" The red feather on her hat shook as she spoke. "I am not letting you go. So you can just get that out of your head."

He rubbed the back of his neck. "All right."

She narrowed her eyes. "I mean it."

"I heard you."

Her eyes blazed with doubt. "Whether you like it or not, you're standing trial. Your lawyer —"

"So that's what this is about. Birdsh . . . uh . . . talked to you."

"He's trying to save your neck."

"By having me admit to somethin' I didn't do!"

She blew out her breath. "If you work with him, justice —"

"Justice? Justice! I spent five years in prison for a crime I didn't commit. Five years! That's what justice did to me."

She gasped as if someone had just punched her in the stomach, and he immediately regretted his hastily spoken words.

"I-I didn't know," she stammered.

There was no way she could know. His breath whooshed out of him. He hated arguing with her. She wasn't to blame for any of this. The endless court delays and failed efforts to find the real killer frustrated him, but it wasn't fair to take it out on her. He sensed that she truly cared about and wanted to help him — or was that just wishful thinking on his part? All he really knew for sure was that he needed someone to believe in him, and he wanted that person to be Amanda.

"They thought I killed my wife," he said quietly, the previously unspoken words sounding strange even to his own ears.

Her lips parted and eyes widened, but otherwise, she didn't move. "Go on," she said as he struggled to continue.

And so, at last, he told her the whole ugly story. Each word weighed heavy, like it carried a piece of his heart with it. How he found his wife dead. The long, drawn-out trial. The fact that it took five years before a witness came forward. He told her everything except perhaps the most important thing of all — that the man he was now accused of killing was his wife's real killer.

The eyes that had moments earlier blazed with blue fire now softened with sympathy and compassion. "I'm so sorry."

Something snapped inside him. He didn't want her feeling sorry for him. Memories of the past had stirred up the anger he'd thought had been long buried.

"So what do you want me to do? Stand by and let justice fail again?" He didn't know he'd raised his voice until he saw her flinch.

"You can do that!" she shouted back. "Or you can stand up and fight like a man."

"I *am* fightin'. The only way I know how. By tryin' to find the real killer." He picked up a stack of photographs from his cot and waved them at her. "Given enough time and with Hobson's help, I'll find him. I swear to God I will."

Her eyes widened. "Hobson took those?"

He tossed the photographs onto the cot.

"I gave him the description of the man seen leaving Cooper's room. He hauled in every man he could find fittin' that description, but it took too much time. We figured that photographs would be quicker." He frowned. "I don't want the kid gettin' into trouble for this."

He heard her intake of breath. "I-I don't know what to say."

"Say you believe me. Say you believe I'm innocent. Say —" Surprised that he'd almost asked her to say that she cared, he clamped down on his jaw. "Th-that's all I want."

"I —" She shook her head. "I want to . . ."

He didn't mean to make her feel bad. She had enough on her shoulders. Enough to worry about. Guilt washed over him. He'd tried to take advantage of her inexperience and yes, even her good heart. For that, he felt ashamed.

"I won't ask you to help me escape. Never again." His voice hardened. "Just don't ask me to put my faith in the justice system."

Amanda left her office in a state of confusion and rode straight to her sister's house. She couldn't shake the feeling that some insidious and nameless something had simmered beneath her angry exchange with

Rennick. It was as if they were both fighting an invisible foe that neither one of them wanted to acknowledge.

But that wasn't the only thing that bothered her. Despite Rick's harrowing story, she still didn't know if he was guilty or innocent of killing Michael Cooper. Rick didn't strike her as a killer, but spending five years in prison for a crime he didn't commit could do strange things to a man.

The light was still shining in Meg's front window. Even so, Amanda hesitated knocking at such a late hour. She was still debating when the door flew open.

Meg's husband Grant filled the doorway, his large frame blocking out the light from behind. "Amanda? I thought I heard something. Are you all right? Your father —"

"He's fine. Is Meg still up?"

"I'm here," Meg said, squeezing next to her husband. "What's wrong?"

"Do you have a moment to talk?"

"Of course."

"I'll let you two go at it," Grant said, backing away from the door.

Meg smiled after him. Reaching for her shawl, she stepped onto the tiny porch, closing the door behind her. A dog's bark was followed by a cat's snarl. Loud voices drifted from a neighboring house. Mr.

McGinnis was playing his bagpipes to the tune of his neighbor's curses.

It was life as usual on Peaceful Lane.

Gunfire coming from the direction of Main Street meant things were normal in town as well. Scooter was no doubt filling the jail cells again and relishing every moment.

Meg pulled the shawl tight around her shoulders. "What's wrong, Mandy?"

"The day after tomorrow, Rick's . . . Mr. Rennick's trial will begin." Instead of feeling relief at receiving the news, she felt worried. Scared, even.

Meg frowned. "Is that a problem? I mean you're not required to do anything, are you?"

"I'm expected to take the stand for the state and talk about the crime scene." Amanda inhaled. "The problem is . . . what if he's not guilty?"

It wasn't the first time the question of his guilt had crossed her mind, but it was getting harder to discount. If only he hadn't tried to escape. Still, if he was truly guilty, why waste time looking for a killer who didn't exist? Or was he just trying to confuse her?

Meg looked surprised. "What makes you think he's not guilty?"

Amanda lifted her gaze to the starry sky, but before she could answer, Meg let out a gasp, and her eyes widened in alarm.

"Oh, Amanda. Don't tell me you have . . . feelings for this man."

"What?" Amanda stared at her. "Certainly not." The very idea . . . "I don't want to see an innocent man hang. That's all. And you know the town has made up its mind as to his guilt. The trial is just a formality."

"Are you sure that's all there is to it?"

"Of course I'm sure."

Meg looked unconvinced. "From what I heard from some of the women in town, not only is Mr. Rennick handsome, he's also very charming."

"Who told you that?"

"Miss Read for one. It seems likes she's taken quite a fancy to him."

"Miss Read is hardly an expert on men," Amanda said, feeling even more out of sorts than before. She should never have come here. Trust Meg to jump to all the wrong conclusions.

"And neither are you," Meg reminded her gently. "You've never had a beau. Nor have you ever before shown interest in the opposite sex. Some men will say anything to get what they want. It takes experience to separate the wheat from the chaff."

Amanda resented Meg throwing her inexperience with men in her face. In any case, it wasn't entirely accurate. There had been someone, years ago, when she was sixteen. His name was Jonathan Campbell, and he was the handsomest man in town. When he'd invited her to the annual Christmas ball, she couldn't believe her good fortune. She even stood still long enough for Mama to measure for a new dress. But after she picketed his father's business for mistreating a Chinese worker, Jonathan refused to be her escort and took Mary Hopkins to the dance instead.

"Don't be angry, Amanda," Meg was saying. "I'm only pointing out the facts. I don't believe you've even been kissed."

Amanda scoffed. Of course she'd been kissed. Why, she'd once kissed Johnny Fletcher behind the church organ. It wasn't much, but it was enough to know that kissing was overrated. She could happily live the rest of her life without repeating the experience.

"This has nothing to do with the opposite sex. Or with Mr. Rennick's good looks and charm. I'd have the same doubts about his guilt if he had two heads and the appeal of a rattler."

Meg looked unconvinced but let the statement pass without comment. "So what do you plan on doing?"

Amanda let out a long, harrowing sigh before answering. "I have no idea."

TWENTY-FIVE

Rennick shoved his hands through the cell opening. "That time already?"

Amanda's breath caught as their gazes clashed. He looked especially handsome today in his new plaid shirt and trousers, hair neatly trimmed. Scooter had done a good job making him presentable for court.

"Sure enough is," Scooter said, snapping handcuffs around Rennick's wrists. "We don't want to be late. Makes the judge mad."

"Wouldn't want to do that," Rennick said. "Not that the judge hasn't kept us waiting."

Amanda unlocked the cell door without comment, her conversation with Meg very much on her mind. *Are you sure you don't have feelings for him?* What a ridiculous notion. Crazy. Absolutely insane.

To think that she would fall for . . . have feelings for . . . It was too ridiculous for words. Meg's pregnancy had certainly clouded her thinking.

Scooter pulled out his gun. "Just in case you get a notion to escape."

"Don't worry," Rennick said with a meaningful look at Amanda. "I've heard tell that only the guilty run."

"Is that so? That's good to know. But as Grandpappy always said, he who is not dead is not yet clear of defects."

"Wise man, your grandpappy."

Amanda bit her lower lip. His calm demeanor didn't fool her. She'd heard him moan in his sleep, heard him cry out not just once but several times.

With a sigh, she turned and led the way outside. His guilt or innocence was now up to the court. He was no longer her responsibility. She should be happy to have one less thing to worry about. She *was* happy. Or would be once this whole thing was over.

Together, Amanda and Scooter walked Rennick to the old schoolhouse that served as the courthouse. People lined both sides of the street as they walked the short distance down Main. Since she'd taken over as sheriff, everything that happened in and around the sheriff's office had become of prime interest to the citizens of Two-Time.

Seeing today's crowd, Scooter practically crowed. "This is so exciting! It's like we're on stage or somethin'."

In no mood for her deputy's enthusiasm, she snapped, "Make them back away." She didn't want anyone close to her prisoner.

"Will do, Sheriff." Scooter walked ahead of them, waving his gun and yelling, "Move it. Move it."

Rennick's stoic expression made her heart ache. No doubt he was thinking about his first trial and how that turned out. She didn't want to feel sorry for him. She didn't want to feel anything at all for him, but she couldn't help herself.

Pulling her gaze away, she stared straight ahead. Unfortunately, blocking him from view only increased her awareness of him in other ways. She could still feel the power coiled inside him, smell the fresh fragrance of soap on warm skin, the spicy fragrance of Bay Rum hair tonic.

"Birdseye is a good lawyer," she said, uttering those words for her own sake as well as his. "Long as you work with him."

"I'd have a better chance if you'd just let me go," he said, his voice barely loud enough to be heard over the buzzing crowd.

"You said you wouldn't ask that of me again," she whispered.

"That was on the condition you didn't ask me to believe in justice."

"If you're as innocent as you claim . . . you have nothing to worry about."

"We both know that's not true."

She felt a squeezing pain inside. He was right. The jury would look at the evidence and come to only one conclusion: guilty as charged. Public opinion was already against him. That very morning, an editorial in the newspaper called for swift justice.

But that didn't mean she could release him. How could she? She took an oath to uphold the law, and she was bound by honor to do just that.

Fortunately, he didn't pursue the conversation, and they continued the rest of the way in silence.

At one point, Rennick stopped and exchanged a glance with a cowpuncher standing on the sidelines rolling a cigarette. Amanda had seen the man around town but didn't know his name. He worked at the Circle K Ranch. Did the two know each other?

Nerves taut, she rested her hand on the grip of her gun and urged Rennick to walk faster. She liked Rick a whole lot more than she wanted to admit, but that didn't mean she would take a chance on him escaping.

The courtroom was empty except for Rennick's lawyer. To appease those who believed that crosslighting was harmful to the eyes, the old schoolhouse was built with windows on only the one side. This lopsided lighting turned out to be a boon to the state on the sunny side and a detriment to the defense in the shadows.

Mr. Birdseye greeted his client with a nod.

She waited for Scooter to attach the floor chain to Rennick's ankle before turning to Rennick's lawyer. "Do you have a moment?"

For answer, he followed her to the back of the room where they could talk in private.

She indicated Rennick with a slight nod. "Have you worked out a defense?" A word of encouragement was all that she needed.

Birdseye rubbed his chin and grimaced. "None that the prosecutor won't blow away. Since he refuses to plead guilty, I'd say his chances are good as a snowflake in you know where."

She inhaled. "He still claims his innocence."

"They all do. No criminal I ever heard of admitted to guilt."

She frowned. "We still haven't found the weapon."

"Well, now, that's the problem."

Her spine stiffened. "How do you mean?"

"A maid cleaning Cooper's room found

the knife. Said she found it under the chest of drawers."

Amanda was barely able to control her gasp of surprise. She'd searched under that bureau herself. "That's not possible. We turned that room upside down. There was no knife. I'll stake my life on it."

Birdseye splayed his hands. "What can I say? The maid claims she found it in the room and is prepared to testify to that in court."

Amanda stared at him. "When? When did she find it?"

"Couple of days ago."

Amanda's mind whirled. Someone must have put that knife in the room after she and Scooter had searched it. It was the only thing that made sense. But not just someone — the *real* killer.

This was the first tangible proof of Rick's innocence, but rather than relieve her mind, it only worried her more. The missing weapon was the one thing that worked in Rick's favor; the argument that he had no time to get rid of it was no longer valid.

The sound of gunfire coming from somewhere outside made her practically leap to the schoolhouse window. In a town like Two-Time, such a sound was not all that uncommon. But now that law and order was her responsibility, it felt like a call to action.

"Sounds like trouble. I better go."

"You do that, Sheriff," Birdseye said. "We'll still be here when you get back."

She motioned to her deputy sheriff to stay with Rennick and dashed out the door.

Moments later, Amanda spotted a chair flying out of the batwing doors of the Golden Spur Saloon, giving a pretty good indication where the shot originated. From inside came the sound of a scuffle punctuated with loud thuds and shouts.

Hand on her holstered Colt, Amanda ran the distance to the saloon. Without hesitating, she dashed through the doors, ducking to avoid a tossed whiskey bottle.

A crowd of onlookers gathered around two men battling on the sawdust floor. Contorted faces mere inches apart, the men hammered each other tooth and nail. She recognized one as Gopher. She'd not set eyes on him since the night she stopped Rick's hanging.

The second man — a stranger — looked like he was on the losing end.

Gopher and his brothers, Blade and Buster, had caused trouble in the town for as long as she could remember.

She pulled out her Colt. "Okay, you two.

That's enough!"

No one paid her any heed, least of all the battling duo.

She raised her arm and pulled the trigger. The bullet ricocheted off the tin ceiling and hit the steer horn gas light fixture. Bone pieces flew in every direction. The two men broke apart, the stranger holding his bloodied nose.

The saloon owner, Pepper, glared at her from behind the polished bar. "Hey, this ain't a proper place for no lady!"

"No place for anyone," she said. "What's going on?"

Gopher staggered to his feet, picked up his hat, and slapped it against his leg. "He's a cheat."

His opponent sat up and dabbed at his nose with a red kerchief. "He's a blasted liar." If his short-brimmed, short-crowned hat didn't peg him as a northerner, his clipped speech did.

"Yeah, well, you both better leave now, or I'll arrest the two of you for disturbing the peace."

The stranger climbed to his feet, and the spectators backed away to give him room. Without another word, he swayed once, twice, and finally stumbled outside through the swinging doors.

Amanda kept her gun pointed at Gopher. "You too, Coldwell."

His eyes glittered like two pieces of coal, his mouth as straight and sharp as the blade of a knife. "I ain't finished my game."

"Yeah, you have," she said.

His lip lifted in an ugly smirk. "What do you think, men? Did I or did I not finish my game?"

"You sure enough didn't," his brother Buster said, and Blade backed him up. A chorus of voices raised in agreement.

A tense silence followed, broken only by Keith Watson's mouth organ, which he played with great diligence. All eyes remained on Amanda.

She was in a terrible bind and had no idea how to get out of it. Let Gopher have his way, and she would lose what little credibility she had. On the other hand, she was outnumbered thirty to one, and only a fool would stand up against such odds.

Gopher glared at her with a knowing expression. "I think it would be a good idea for you to leave now." He tossed a nod at the game table. "Me and the boys have a game to finish."

She made a quick if not altogether wise decision. "The only thing you're going to do is walk out that door."

He laughed without mirth, sending chills down her spine. Next to him, Blade's mustache twitched above a smile that turned her blood cold.

"You always were a feisty one," Gopher said. "What you need is a good man to tame you." He turned to the crowd. "What do you think, men? Shall I show the lady here who's running this town?"

His question was answered with approving hoots and hollers. The mouth organ kept playing. Gopher started toward her, his hands curled into fists by his side.

She gripped the gun tight, but they both knew she didn't have the heart to shoot a man point blank.

Just as he reached out to grab her, the batwing doors burst inward, and in walked the Red Feather posse. Suddenly, all hell broke loose. Chairs crashed against walls. Overturned tables scattered coins and faro chips across the floor. Playing cards flew up in the air.

Mrs. Perl held a man at bay with her knitting needles pointed at his jugular.

Holding her lorgnette in one hand, Mrs. Granby used the well-aimed fist of the other hand to punch a man in the mouth.

Good-time gal Goldie jumped on Gopher's back. He spun around, trying to shake her off.

"What the —"

The preacher's wife baptized Buster with a whiskey bottle, and Becky-Sue bopped Blade over the head with her parasol.

Mrs. Mooney, using her position as the bank president's wife and without benefit of respectability, punched Harvey Harper square in the nasal promontory with her well-placed, ring-laden knuckles.

One man grabbed hold of the butcher's wife, but her husband came to her rescue. "Hey, that's my wife!" With that, T-Bone swung his fist and knocked the man out cold.

A cowpuncher dived for the retired schoolmarm, and she used her knowledge of male anatomy to great advantage. His friend lifted his fist to punch her back. Losing all manner of restraint, Amanda hit him over the head with the grip of her gun. The man teetered back and forth, spun like a slow-moving whirligig, and finally collapsed out cold on the floor.

As a whole, the men seemed at a loss as to how to handle a bunch of kicking, screaming, clawing females. Some couldn't bring themselves to hit a woman, much to their detriment. Others, whose principles were dulled by whiskey, soon learned the folly of their ways, and prone bodies began stacking up like haphazard logs.

The blacksmith finally restored order. "Okay, men, that's enough." Wiping his bloodied lip with his shirt-sleeve, he pointed a grimy finger at Gopher. "You're leaving now, just like the lady said."

Gopher's face turned a vivid red, and the veins of his neck stood out. His shirt was torn, and blood trickled from his nose. He looked about to argue, but seeing how his own men had turned against him, he thought better of it.

He picked his hat off the floor and shuffled toward the door, but not before impaling Amanda with malice-filled eyes. "You'll be sorry."

Breathing hard, Amanda retrieved her own hat from under an overturned table. Just before she followed her posse outside, something caught her eye, and she stooped to pick it up. It was a feather. A peacock feather, just like the one found in Cooper's hotel room. She slipped it into her vest pocket and elbowed her way out the swinging doors.

TWENTY-SIX

The Red Feather posse followed Amanda away from the saloon, boasting like a bunch of old soldiers reminiscing about the past. To hear them tell it, no battle was more gallantly fought or so bravely won.

No one was seriously hurt, but Goldie's already skimpy shirtwaist was missing a bit of vital fabric, and Becky-Sue's parasol was bashed beyond repair. Mrs. Perl's hair had unraveled from its bun like gray yarn. Hats were flattened or squashed, and some were missing red feathers. Mrs. Granby's bowed plume dangled in front of her face like a swinging pendulum.

The pastor's wife reeked of whiskey. Lord only knows what her husband would say about that!

"Did you see Blade's expression when I punched him?" Ellie-Mae Walker said, swinging her saddlebag hips from side to side.

Becky-Sue giggled. "I guess we showed them."

"We sure did," Miss Read said with a toss of her head. The schoolmarm sported a black eye, but never was a shiner worn with such pride.

Amanda laughed. She had a feeling that she hadn't heard the last of Gopher, but for now, victory felt good. "How'd you all know I needed help?"

"We went to the courthouse for Mr. Rennick's trial, and Deputy Hobson told us you might need us," Mrs. Perl explained.

"Yes," Mrs. Mooney interjected, "and he told us to make haste."

Amanda smiled. Hiring Scooter was a brilliant move, if she did say so herself.

"As the bank president's wife, I say we celebrate," Mrs. Mooney said. "Meet at my house in an hour, and I'll fix us something to eat. You too, Sheriff."

"I'd love to celebrate with you all, but duty calls. I'm needed in court."

"Oh yes, of course." Mrs. Mooney lowered her voice. "Poor, poor Mr. Rennick. Such a nice man. So handsome," she said, as if that had a bearing on the case.

Goldie adjusted her plunging neckline. "Most handsome men can't be trusted, but Mr. Rennick isn't like most." She lowered her voice as well. "I have a good instinct about men. My job requires it, and I'm telling you" — she patted her hair and tucked her shirt into the waist of her divided skirt — "I would trust Mr. Rennick with my life."

Amanda decided to stop at the office and freshen up before heading to the courthouse and was surprised to find the cowpuncher seen earlier on the street waiting for her.

He pulled off his Stetson. "Name's Larsen, but everyone calls me Kansas Pete. Got a minute?" Eyes the color of full-grain leather peered at her from beneath a mop of curly brown hair.

She didn't really have time to spare, but something about the man piqued her curiosity. Shoving the door shut, she turned. "What's this about?"

"Your prisoner."

Her gaze sharpened. "You know him?" Her instincts had been right.

He nodded. "Used to work for him. On his horse ranch in the Panhandle."

"Go on."

"He didn't do the things they say he did. He didn't kill no one." He spoke in earnest and sounded sincere.

"How do you know he didn't?"

"I know him, that's how. I know the kind

of man he is. Once, me and the other wranglers came down with an awful fever. You know what he did? He took care of us. Brought food and medicine to the bunkhouse and made sure we had everything we needed. The foreman wanted to dock our pay, but he wouldn't allow it. He insisted we get full pay even though some of us couldn't do a lick of work for weeks. That's the kind of man he is." He paused for a moment before adding, "Thought nothing 'bout staying up all night with a sick horse. Never knew him to even exaggerate a horse's good qualities to make a sale."

"Did you know Mr. Cooper?"

"Yeah, I knew him. He worked on the horse ranch. He was the foreman I mentioned earlier. Didn't much care for him."

So Cooper and Rennick had a history together. She could well imagine what the prosecutor would do with that information. "How did he and Rennick get along?"

Kansas Pete frowned. "Who's Rennick?"

Just as she suspected — Rennick was an assumed name. Knowing this didn't make her feel any better, and her spirits dropped. If he lied about his name, what else did he lie about?

"He claims his name is Rick Rennick. What name did you know him as?"

"Barrett. Rick Barrett."

"How did Barrett and Cooper get along?"

"Far as I knew, they got along just fine. But then, I didn't hang around all that long."

"So you have no way of knowing what happened after you left the horse ranch."

"No, but that don't change my opinion. Barrett is tough and expects a lot from his employees, but he would never do anyone harm."

Amanda's mind raced. "It's been years since you knew him. A lot can happen to a man in all that time. People change."

"Yeah, but Rick ain't like most people."

The man meant well, but he could offer no real proof of Rick's innocence, only opinion. That wasn't worth a wooden nickel in a court of law. An idea occurred to her, and she brightened. "You could testify as a character witness."

He made a face. "Well, here's the thing. I ain't exactly been workin' in the Lord's vineyards, if you know what I mean. My talking about character is like a politician talking about honesty. Who's gonna believe me?"

"So why are you telling me this?" she asked.

"I feel partly to blame for the trouble he's in."

"Oh? How's that?"

"I took me a trip to San Antone and happened to bump into his sister. That was the first I knew Barrett's wife had died and he no longer owned the horse ranch."

"So you knew his wife."

"Yeah. Her name was Christy. A sweet little thing. His sister didn't say how she died, and I didn't ask. We got to talking about the good old days and some of the men who worked on the ranch when I did. I happened to mention I was now working at a ranch in Two-Time and spotted Cooper."

"And you think she told Ren . . . Barrett?"

"Don't know. But there's got to be a reason Barrett turns up in the same town as Cooper. Maybe that's a coincidence. Maybe not. But I still stand by what I said: Barrett's no killer. And I'll tell you something else. After what I heard people say today, he's as good as dead."

The office door cracked open, and Meg's head appeared. "Got a minute?"

Amanda beckoned her sister in with a wave of her hand. The court was in midday recess, and she was anxious to get back, but she didn't want to send her sister away. It was obvious she had something on her mind.

"I always have time for you." Amanda motioned to the chair in front of her desk and waited for Meg to sit. Her sister didn't show weight-wise, but her cheeks were rosy, and her eyes sparkled with a warm inner glow. "What brings you to town?"

"I came to purchase fabric. Mama and I are working on baby clothes. It's so much easier now that she has a machine that does the work."

"Remember how long it took you and Josie to sew your wedding trousseau?" Amanda said and immediately regretted her words. That bridal wardrobe had been sewn when Meg was betrothed to another man. "Oh, I'm sorry, Meg. I didn't mean to . . ."

"It's all right," Meg said. "Just think. If things hadn't turned out the way they did, I wouldn't have met and fallen in love with Grant."

"I'm just glad that everything worked out as well as it did."

"It has for you too. I mean . . ." Meg gazed around the office. "Look at you. I still can't believe you're the sheriff."

"And that's not all." Amanda reached for the letter on her desk. "As soon as Lucy

Stone heard I was sheriff, she invited me to give the opening speech at the next suffragist meeting."

"Oh, Mandy, that's such a great honor. I'm so happy for you."

Amanda smiled. "Life sure does have a way of surprising us, doesn't it?" Never in a million years would she have guessed the strange sequence of events that brought her to this place. Nor did it ever occur to her that Josie would leave Two-Time.

"It sure does." Meg absentmindedly rubbed her stomach with protective hands. "I also wanted to tell you that we bought Josie's house."

"What?" Amanda blinked. "But why?"

"It just seemed like the right thing to do. They're in a hurry to leave, and with the baby coming . . . We can hardly turn around in our small house as it is."

"I'm glad you did that," Amanda said. Josie's two-story house and neat little yard would make the perfect home for Meg's growing family. "I'm sure you and Grant will be very happy there."

Meg's smile died. "The other night . . . I didn't mean to suggest that you had feelings for . . ." She glanced toward the cells in back.

"A man on trial for murder?" Amanda asked.

Meg bit her lip. "It was just . . . there was something about you I had never noticed before. You looked miserable enough to be in love."

Amanda laughed. "What a thing to say. I thought love was supposed to make a person happy."

"It can." Meg regarded her with probing eyes. "If you're in love with the right man. I just wish you could be as happy as I am. If only you could find a good man like Grant to love."

Normally, such a sentiment would put Amanda on the defensive, but today, she accepted it with good humor. "And who, pray tell, would want to set his cap for a woman sheriff?"

Meg laughed. "Who indeed?"

The conversation with Meg was very much on Amanda's mind that night as she readied for bed. She brushed her hair for the required hundred strokes before setting her hairbrush on the dressing table. She turned up the flame on the kerosene lamp and reached for her grandmother's daguerreotype.

The clock by the side of her bed ticked,

and the lamp sputtered, but otherwise, all was quiet. Even the voices of the past — her grandmother's voice — failed to fill in the emptiness of Amanda's heart.

Meg was no doubt sharing the day's joys and sorrows with her husband, and here Amanda was, staring at her grandmother's image.

Sighing, she set the picture frame next to the milliner's pliers and tailor chalk on the dresser. The peacock feather placed there days earlier drifted lazily to the floor. Stooping, she picked it up and remembered something.

She reached for the vest tossed on the back of a chair. The first pocket was empty, but the second one revealed the feather found on the floor of the Golden Spur. She arranged the feathers side by side and moved the lamp closer. The feathers were close to identical.

She reached into a dresser drawer for the packet of peacock feathers used for making hats. Pulling one out, she compared it with the others. They all looked similar, but of course, that didn't mean they came from the same bird or even the same peacock farm.

Chicken and peacock feathers were the only ones she would ever use for her hats.

Chicken feathers were easy to work with and could be dyed. Better yet, chicken feathers were cheap, easily obtainable, and a food by-product. Her second choice was peacock feathers. The magnificent birds shed their feathers naturally, so no bird was needlessly destroyed. She abhorred the practice of killing wild birds for the sole purpose of decorating hats. The demand for feathers had put some of the most beautiful species, including the snowy egret, on the brink of extinction.

She gnawed on a fingernail as she studied the feathers. One was found in Cooper's hotel room and the other at Pepper's saloon. Coincidence? Maybe. Peacock feathers symbolized many things to many people. Some thought peacock feathers represented the "evil eye" and brought bad luck or death. That's why some cowboys refused to wear them on a hat.

Others, including many Indian tribes, believed the opposite — that peacock feathers brought serenity and good fortune. One gambler drifting through town wore a peacock feather in his hat. He claimed that the eye intimidated his opponents, thus bringing him good luck.

Did other gamblers hold on to feathers for good luck? Did Cooper? There had to be a reason why a peacock feather was found in his room. What if it was left there by his killer?

Or maybe it had been there by chance. A feather could attach itself to shoes or clothing and be carried inside by an unsuspecting host.

She tried to think of any locals raising peacocks, and the only one who came to mind was Mr. Steckle. Was it possible to determine if the feathers came from his birds? Probably not. Still . . . She held her breath. Was she on to something or simply grasping at straws?

TWENTY-SEVEN

The trial moved swiftly — too swiftly for Amanda's peace of mind — and attracted an astounding amount of community interest. The courtroom was packed, but so were the grounds outside.

Witnesses for the prosecution included the young woman who found the body and the maid who discovered the knife.

Pepper, Gopher, and their cronies also testified to finding the suspect bent over the body. Birdseye's objections were as regular as clockwork, but he was soundly overruled each and every time.

Amanda and Hobson told the court how they'd searched the room and found no weapon, but their testimony hardly made a dent in the prosecutor's case. Things couldn't look worse for Rick.

That night, she heard Birdseye and Rick arguing. The door was closed between her office and the cellblock, so she couldn't make out the words, but there was no mistaking the angry voices.

Finally, Birdseye stormed through her office, his face a mask of fury.

"You can't save him, can you?" she asked.

Birdseye shook his head. "He refuses to say or do anything in his own defense. I can only save those who want to save themselves." Without another word, he stomped out of the office, slamming the door behind him.

Long after Birdseye left, Amanda sat staring into space. Her faith in Rick's innocence teetered back and forth. One minute, she was convinced he didn't kill Cooper. But then little niggling doubts crept into her head. Was it possible she had missed seeing the knife under the bureau? Was Rick playing her for a fool?

Oh, how she wanted to believe him innocent, but he sure wasn't acting like it. So far, he'd done none of the things she expected an innocent man to do. Certainly, a man with nothing to hide wouldn't try to escape like he did the night he was arrested. Was all the talk about finding the real killer a ploy designed to confuse her?

Oh, Rick . . . Why did her heart tell her one thing and her head another? Which one to believe? She had to know, and as much as she hated the thought, there was only one way to find out.

Trembling, she rose from her desk and reached for the keys on the wall. She swallowed hard and inhaled.

Moments later, she inserted a key into the lock of Rick's cell and swung the door open. She stepped aside and waited. She had done many things in her life, all in the name of justice. But this . . . this was the boldest, bravest, and maybe even dumbest thing she'd ever done. But she had to know . . .

Rick stared at the open door before meeting her eyes. "What are you doing?"

"You keep saying you're innocent. I'm giving you a chance to prove it."

He frowned. "Prove it how?"

"If you're guilty, then go — walk out of here and don't look back. If you're innocent, then stay and fight for justice. Those are your choices."

He stared at the open door, and the shadow at his forehead suggested some sort of inner battle. "You fool woman!" he snapped at last. "Don't you know what this town would do to you if I escaped?"

His concern for her seemed genuine, and that was a surprise. "Why do you care?" she cried. "You don't even care about yourself! If you did, you'd work with your lawyer. So go! Get out of here. Spend the rest of your life a wanted man. It's what you want."

The eyes that met hers flashed with sudden anger. "What I want is to find the real killer."

"Then work with Bird —"

"Work with him? He wants me to plead guilty and ask for leniency. Do you know where that would get me?" He sliced his hand across his neck.

Her heart squeezed in anguish. She felt partly responsible for his plight. A better, more knowledgeable sheriff might have done a better job investigating.

"I'm innocent." His eyes, his voice, beseeched her. "Believe it or not. That's the God's honest truth."

"Then prove it!"

He frowned. "How?"

"Tell us what you were doing in Cooper's room that night. Don't tell us you're innocent. Tell us *why* we should believe you."

He stared at the open cell door, and she held her breath. His gaze sought hers and then returned to the gaping door. A shadow winged across his forehead like a raven looking for a place to land.

Finally, he grabbed hold of a bar and slammed the steel door shut, locking himself inside. The resounding bang was all the proof her heart needed.

Palm pressed against her chest, her shoulders sagged in relief. "A guilty man would have walked out of here and never looked back," she whispered.

"I've got news for you," he said, his voice gruff. "So would an innocent man if he knew what was good for him."

Rick paced his cell into the wee hours of the morning. He still couldn't believe it. Amanda had offered him a way out of this nightmare, and like a fool, he had declined.

He had to be out of his cotton-picking mind. Any sane man in his position would have walked out of that open cell and not looked back.

Why didn't he?

He never intended to go to trial. Find the killer or escape. Those were his two choices. Sitting through another miscarriage of justice was not an option. One such trial was enough. More than enough. That's why he worked so hard to win the sheriff's reprieve.

He rested his forehead against a cold steel bar. Amanda gave him a chance to escape, and he turned it down. Why didn't he walk out of that cell and forget everything he left behind?

He knew why. Oh God. He knew why. His walking away would be a confession of guilt. At least that's how Amanda would see it.

It had been a long time since anyone believed in him. Believed in his honor and goodness. If he was doomed to hang from the gallows, he wanted to know that one person believed in him. Not just any person: *Amanda.*

There was another reason he refused to leave that cell. He knew what the town would do to her if he vanished. She was strong, tough even, but nothing she'd undergone so far could compare to what would have lain ahead had he taken her up on her offer.

So there it was. The unmitigated truth. He didn't care a hill of beans what happened to him. But he sure in blazes cared about what happened to her, and that was the shocker.

Twenty-Eight

A hushed silence fell across the courtroom as Rick took the witness stand.

He searched the faces of the spectators as he had the waiting crowd. He thought he saw the man who killed Cooper outside, but maybe not. If only he could remember what made a man with no distinguishing features so memorable. Something . . .

His gaze returned to Amanda, and his heart fairly leaped. Her face, her eyes told him she was rooting for him all the way. Today, the doubts that had darkened those gorgeous eyes of hers in the past were now gone.

He tried to recall how long it had been since someone truly trusted and believed in him. Years. The last time he saw his father alive, Rick swore up and down that he didn't kill Christy. But doubt remained in his father's eyes, and that look would haunt Rick till the day he died.

Rick was in many ways his mother's son and had her restless spirit. While his father was perfectly content with his small farm, Rick wanted more. Much more. He wanted to raise horses and had even considered raising thoroughbreds.

Such a lofty goal had made his father wary of him. His mother had big dreams too, and look what happened. She deserted the family. That made his father suspicious of all ambitious people, Rick included.

Even his sister had her doubts about his innocence, though she stuck with him through thick and thin. He'd almost forgotten how it felt to have someone honestly believe in him, no matter how tenuous. It made him feel human again. More than that, it made him want to fight for his life like he'd never fought before.

He prolonged the moment a tad longer than necessary before pulling his gaze away from Amanda and turning to his lawyer. By George, if Amanda believed him innocent, surely he could make someone else believe him — someone like a juror.

With a new sense of determination, he answered his lawyer's questions in a clear, strong voice.

Yes, he knew Cooper. The man worked for him. No, he didn't kill him. He went on to describe his surprise at finding Cooper dead. He answered honestly, truthfully, with no hesitation. He stared straight at the six-man jury who would decide his fate. Did they believe him? Hard to tell anything from the granitelike faces turned toward the witness box.

Birdseye walked him through everything that happened the night of Cooper's death. Rick described his near lynching, and all eyes turned to Amanda as he explained how she had saved him.

At last, Birdseye stepped away from the witness stand and turned to the prosecutor. "Your witness."

Sensing trouble ahead, Amanda sat forward, her back so rigid and straight, it could have been laced with steel. Though the room was stiflingly hot, a cold chill streaked down her spine, leaving a trail of gooseflesh in its wake.

The prosecutor stood, straightened his bow tie, and buttoned his frock coat before walking to the witness stand. His name was Joseph Hampton, but everyone called him the Hammer, a name that reflected his method of questioning. He looked too self-assured for Amanda's peace of mind, like a dog about to tackle a bone.

"Mr. Rennick is it? Or is it Mr. Barrett?"

Rick looked momentarily taken by surprise but quickly recovered. "My name is Rick Barrett, but I go by Rennick."

"Would that be the same Rick Barrett who owned the J. Barrett horse ranch in the Panhandle?"

Rick stared at him, his face drained of color.

"Shall I repeat the question?"

"That won't be necessary. Yes, I once owned a horse ranch."

"And are you the same Rick Barrett who was once married to Christy Ann Rennick."

"Yes."

Judge Lynch leaned toward the witness stand with the hearing horn at his ear. "What did you say?"

"I said *yes!*"

The Hammer faced the jurors and asked, "Could you please tell the court what happened to Mrs. Barrett?"

"She was shot dead."

Gaze riveted to the stand, Amanda didn't realize she held her breath until her lungs began burning.

"I mean prior to her death." When Rick failed to respond, the prosecutor continued. "Isn't it true that Mr. Cooper had his way with your wife?"

A collective gasp rose from the spectators, and Amanda pressed her fingers to her mouth.

Rick moved uncomfortably in his seat. "Yes, that's true."

"And isn't it also true that you were tried and convicted of her death?"

"Yes."

A buzz of shocked voices rose from the spectators. Judge Lynch let his gavel drop. "Order!"

The prosecutor fired questions in rapid succession, but Rick didn't waver or look away. Instead, he quietly answered — repeating his answers on occasion for the judge's benefit. Loud or soft, every word he uttered added yet another nail to his coffin.

Nails digging into her palms, Amanda listened to Rick's testimony, and her heart sank.

The prosecutor's eyes fairly gleamed as he regarded the six-man jury. "And isn't it true that you spent five years in prison, convicted of your wife's death?"

"That's correct."

"Would you please tell the court how you happen to be walking around free?"

"A witness came forward with information proving Cooper killed my wife."

The wind rushed from Amanda's lungs.

Spending time in jail for a crime he didn't commit was bound to earn the jurors' sympathies. It had certainly earned hers.

The prosecutor stepped back and could barely control his excitement. "So what you're saying is that Cooper killed your wife, and you went to prison."

"That's correct."

The hammering continued, each question more incriminatory than the one before it. "Would it be safe to assume that you hated the man?" He ran a finger the length of his mustache, and his chest puffed out — an unmistakable sign of triumph.

Amanda felt her insides turn over.

This time, Rick did hesitate, and three jurors jotted something into a notebook. "You could say that."

"Would it also be accurate to say you hated him enough to kill him?"

Birdseye jumped to his feet and voiced his objection, shouting to be heard over the buzzing crowd, but he was too late. Rick's motivation for killing Cooper was no longer in question. The damage was done, and by the end of the day, the case was in the hands of the jury.

Amanda hardly slept that night and jumped out of bed before dawn. At nine o'clock that morning, the jury was scheduled to deliberate, but that wasn't the only thing on her mind. Today, Josie and Ralph were leaving for Arizona Territory.

She was also anxious to check out the Steckle farm peacocks. Tom Steckle had been there the night Pepper and his gang tried to lynch Rick. Was Steckle at the Golden Spur Saloon when she found the second feather? She didn't remember seeing him in all the confusion, but that didn't mean he wasn't there. Maybe one of her posse members could answer her question.

She arrived at the train depot with no time to spare and immediately spotted Mama, Papa, Meg, Grant, Josie, and Ralph huddled together like frozen sheep. Dismounting her horse, she wrapped the reins around a ring on a post and hurried to join them. Everyone made an effort to maintain a cheery demeanor, but it didn't take long before they were all in tears, even Papa.

Amanda threw her arms around Josie. "Oh, I wish you didn't have to leave." Arizona Territory seemed so far away. Amanda couldn't help but worry.

The house sale — everything — had happened quickly thanks to Meg and her husband. The newspaper editor had no trouble finding someone to replace Josie. The popular Miss Lonely Hearts column would live on in her absence, but nothing would be the same.

"It won't be forever," Josie said cheerfully. "Once Ralph's lungs are strong again, we'll come back."

Amanda knew it was a lie even before she saw the shadow cross Ralph's face. Lungs got weaker over time, not stronger. Nevertheless, she forced a smile. Right now, she needed to believe anything was possible. They all did.

Josie pushed a strand of hair away from Amanda's face. "Take care of yourself. I worry about you."

Amanda looked up at her sister with tear-filled eyes. "Please don't worry. You need to concentrate on that handsome husband of yours."

"You know I will. Meanwhile, promise me you'll stay out of trouble."

Amanda shrugged. "You know me. Trouble is my middle name."

"That's what worries me." Josie turned to Meg. "I wish I could be here to help with the baby."

"Oh, Josie . . ." Fresh tears rolled down Meg's cheeks.

Grant put his arm around his wife. "Maybe when the baby's old enough to travel, we'll come and visit."

Josie brightened. "Oh, you must. You simply must!"

Ralph picked up the tapestry carpetbag by his side. Their furniture and other belongings had already been packed into one of the boxcars. "It's time."

"Promise you'll write every day." Mama dabbed her eyes with a handkerchief.

"Of course I will," Josie said.

"And be sure to keep your hat on straight," Amanda said. If a woman's hat was arranged properly, she could handle anything. Or almost anything . . .

"Ah, yes, the hat." Josie flashed the hoped-for smile before turning to Papa.

A suspicious gleam in his eyes, Papa wrapped an arm around Josie and shook Ralph's free hand. "You take care of my girl, you hear?"

Ralph's eyes were shiny too. "You know I will."

A uniformed conductor called, "All aboard!"

His cry started a flurry of activity around them as other passengers bade good-bye to loved ones and hurried across the platform toward the train, some dragging small children by the hand.

Following another round of hugs and

tears, Ralph helped Josie onto the train before boarding himself. Almost as soon as they vanished from sight, the door whooshed shut, and the whistle blew. Steam hissed from the engine; couplings clanked, and wheels began to turn. The train moved slowly at first along the steel rails and gradually picked up speed.

Soon, all that was left was a dot on the horizon, no bigger than a period at the end of a sentence. Amanda turned to find her father still gazing at the now-deserted tracks as if willing the train to come back.

She knew what it had cost him to come today. After last year's near-fatal train accident, her father had avoided the station. The town's two time zones had caused one train to leave too late and the other to arrive too early. Though he never spoke of it, Amanda knew he blamed himself for not allowing the town to adapt sooner to standard time.

"Papa!" she cried and rushed into his arms.

He held her close, his tears mingling with her own. "Don't ever leave," he said.

She looked up at him. "I have no intention of leaving, Papa." At least not permanently. Two-Time, with all its faults, was and always would be her home.

"There are many ways of leaving," he said, and she realized he wasn't talking about moving away. He was afraid for her life. "If I lost you . . ."

He dropped his arms to his sides and walked away, looking older than his years. Amanda started to follow, but then thought better of it. Knowing her father, he would rather be alone.

She was the last to leave the train depot. Her vision blurred by tears, she rode away with a heavy heart. Crazy as it seemed, she already missed Josie. Her oldest sister had stood up for her through the years. More than once, she had saved Amanda's skin following one of her many rebellious escapades. They'd had their fair share of arguments, as all sisters did, but their devotion to each other never wavered.

Blinking away tears, she started toward the Steckle farm. There was still work to do, and if she hurried, she could make it there and back before the jury arrived at a decision. She wasn't sure why she felt compelled to check out the farm. Even if she could prove the feathers came from Steckle's peacocks, how would that help Rick?

Such were her thoughts that she didn't notice the crowd of people outside the courthouse until she heard Scooter call to her.

She reined in her horse and shaded her eyes against the sun. What the —

Scooter waved his hat. "The jury has a verdict."

"So soon?" But it was only — what? A little after nine. How could they decide a man's fate so quickly? Scooter waited for her to tether her horse, and together, they hurried inside. Her heart pounded, and she could hardly breathe. Her legs threatened to give out.

The jury was already seated, and so was the judge. As was his habit, he turned over his collection of hourglasses on his bench before proceeding. "Have you reached a verdict?"

The foreman stood, pushed his spectacles up his nose. "We have, Your Honor," he said, remembering to speak in a strong, clear voice.

The bailiff took the written verdict from him and handed it to the judge. Judge Lynch showed no expression as he unfolded the paper. He blinked and read the penned words.

Taking what seemed to Amanda forever, he refolded the paper. "Would the defendant please stand?"

Rick and his lawyer rose to their feet.

At the back of the courtroom, Amanda waited with clenched fists. *Please, please, please let the verdict be not guilty.*

"Well, what is it?" the judge demanded, jamming his hearing horn to his ear.

"We, the jury, in the case of *Texas versus Richard Brandon Rennick,* also known as Barrett, find the defendant guilty of first-degree murder." The last word was barely out of the foreman's mouth before the courtroom erupted in bedlam.

Rooted to the spot, Amanda felt like the world had come to an end.

TWENTY-NINE

Amanda found Tom Steckle greasing his windmill on top of a tall wooden tower. Still in shock from the verdict, she was more determined than ever to follow every lead, no matter how insignificant it might seem. If only she had more time. If she didn't find something in the next couple of days, it would be too late to save Rick.

Perched on a high platform, a piece of straw in his mouth, Steckle looked like a scrawny bird building a nest.

No sooner had the thought crossed her mind than a crested head popped up from behind a bush. A peacock strutted toward three peahens. He fanned his tail to its full four-foot height, revealing a spectacular display of iridescent blue, green, and purple feathers. With an unpleasant honk, the male strutted about the yard. If his intention was to gain the peahens' attention, he failed miserably. The females were more interested in pecking at the dirt than their swaggering suitor.

Drawing her gaze away from the array of bright colors, Amanda tilted her head back and shaded her eyes against the sun. "I need to talk to you," she called up to the farm's owner.

Steckle peered down at her. "Well, talk."

"What do you know about Cooper?"

"Cooper? You mean the dead man Cooper?"

"That's the one."

Steckle denied knowing Cooper personally. "All I knows is that the Rennick fella killed him."

She persisted in her questioning, and he claimed he hadn't stepped foot into the Golden Spur saloon for a month of Sundays.

"Why would I?" he asked, rubbing beads of sweat off his forehead with the back of his hand. "Pepper waters down the whiskey. I get better stuff at Murray's place." He looked down on her and frowned. "Why you askin', anyhow?"

"I found a peacock feather at the scene of the crime. I also found one at the Golden Spur."

"You don't say?"

"You seem to be the only one in the area

raising peacocks."

"Yeah, well, I had to do somethin' 'bout the rattlers 'round here. So far, those birds have done a good job ridding us of snakes, but they ain't done nothing about those pesky possums on the half shell."

What he called *possums* were actually armadillos. The strange animals dug up crops and stank to high heaven.

Steckle spit out a wad of tobacco. "The trouble with peacocks is, they're noisy as all get out. Keep me up all night with their cries. Sounds like some female yelling 'help me, help me.' If you want to take 'em off my hands, you're welcome to them. Just be sure to stuff your ears with cotton if you want to catch any shut-eye."

She adjusted her hat to better shade her face. "I have no room for peacocks, but I do have a question. Like I said, seems like you're the only one around raising peacocks."

"Yeah, so?"

"So how do you suppose their feathers ended up at both the murder victim's hotel room and Pepper's saloon?"

"Beats me." He continued greasing the windmill's moving parts. "Maybe the wind blew them there."

She left the Steckle farm knowing no more

than she did when she arrived. She doubted the wind could blow feathers five miles to town. But as she raced back to court, something suddenly occurred to her — a more reasonable and compelling explanation. Now why didn't she think of that before?

She rode into town in a hurry, frowning with annoyance when the mayor flagged her down.

"*Miss* Lockwood."

In no mood to deal with him, she reined in her horse. She was anxious to get to the courthouse for the sentencing. Get to Rick . . .

The mayor stepped off the boardwalk.

"*Mr.* Troutman," she said, giving him a bit of his own medicine.

He leaned on his cane with both hands, the gilded handle gleaming in the sunlight. "I just came from the courthouse. I think you should know that Judge Lynch has imposed the death penalty."

His words hit her like a punch in the stomach. She drew in her breath. Knowing Judge Lynch, it came as no surprise. Still, she'd hoped and prayed for a different outcome.

"The hanging takes place next Friday at noon," the mayor continued as matter-offactly as if discussing something as benign as the weather. "That gives us a week to prepare."

She wasn't sure what the mayor meant by that, and she didn't care. A squeezing pain in her chest almost took her breath away, and she felt sick to her stomach. He was still talking when she rode away.

Rick didn't speak a word when Amanda and Scooter escorted him back to jail. Nor did he acknowledge the crowds lining the street.

The Red Feather posse followed behind, many of the women weeping. Miss Read embarrassed herself by bawling out loud, handkerchief fluttering in her hand. She was a far cry from the schoolmarm who could control a misbehaving pupil with a mere scowl.

Next to her, Mrs. Mooney wrung her hands in despair and murmured, "Oh, the poor, poor man."

Mrs. Perl was so upset that for once, her knitting needles remained idle in her knapsack. She didn't even sneak in a couple of stitches when they stopped to wait for a wagon to pass before crossing the street.

Even Scooter was unusually somber. "I never knew anyone who hanged," he said.

Becky-Sue commiserated with a sigh and

didn't giggle.

Later that day, after everyone including Scooter had left the office, Amanda walked into the cell room and found Rick sitting on the edge of his cot, holding his head in his hands.

"Rick," she whispered from in front of his cell. She'd encouraged him to fight, and look what it got him. She'd always believed that the truth never stayed hidden for long, that it always came out in the end. How naive of her. How foolish. He had every right to hate her. "I'm so very, very sorry."

He lifted his head but said nothing, his eyes remote.

Moistening her lips, she tried to swallow past the lump in her throat. Never could she remember feeling so utterly miserable or helpless.

How she longed to open the cell door and go to him. Touch him. Hold him . . . The need to comfort him was so strong, she could hardly stand it.

Meg had planted a seed in her head, and Amanda had been able to think of little else since. Did she have feelings for him beyond the normal concern one human had for another? Is that why she felt all confused and twisted inside? Why Rick commanded her thoughts, her dreams, her very breath?

That would certainly explain the trembling limbs, pounding heart, and quickening pulse whenever he came into view. Still, her feelings for him were too new and tender to label. It could simply be compassion she felt. Or maybe even sympathy and sorrow. Not love. *Please don't let it be love . . .*

Shaken by the possibility, she tried to think of something that would break the unbearable silence between them. "Do you remember the day we first met?"

His hands fell to his lap, and a shadow of a smile touched his lips. "Oh, I remember all right." His eyes had a faraway look in them. "I couldn't believe it when I saw you standin' in the middle of nowhere dressed to the hilt in a blue suit and wearin' a silly hat. I thought you were the most . . . beautiful woman I ever saw."

Her cheeks flared. No man had ever called her beautiful. Not the way Rick did. "And I thought you were . . . rude," she said, hoping her flippant air would break the sudden tension between them.

His eyes brimmed with something she couldn't define. "I was wrong about the hat. That wild bunch of feathers did indeed suit you. I just didn't know it at the time."

She sucked in her breath and looked away.

It was the only way she could gather her thoughts. In actuality, she'd thought him handsome and the most masculine man she'd ever met. But admitting that out loud would take her perilously close to admitting more. Much more.

"Speaking of my . . . hat . . ." She turned her gaze back to him. "I found a feather in Cooper's room. A peacock feather, just like the ones on the hat I lost that day."

He frowned. "Don't tell me Cooper liked crazy hats too."

"No, but . . . What if he was one of the men who tried to rob us that day?"

He narrowed his eyes. "That's a mighty big if."

"Maybe. Maybe not. Cooper was known to drop big bucks on faro, women, and whiskey, yet he had no visible means of support. He had to get his money from somewhere."

"And you think it was from robbing stages?"

"And banks."

He looked at her, incredulous. "And you based this theory on a feather?"

"Not just any feather. A *peacock* feather. Some people think they are good luck. What if Cooper was one of them? What if he or someone he knew kept the feathers from

329

the hat that blew off my head that day?"

Rick rubbed his chin. "Seems far-fetched. Even if it's true, it won't be easy to prove. Not with Cooper dead."

"No, but that does give us more suspects to consider. What if he was killed by one of his partners in crime? Someone planted the murder weapon in Cooper's room after we searched. Who else would have done that but the real killer?"

Rick studied her. "You're scaring me. You're starting to sound like a real sheriff."

"Is that so bad?"

"It could be. Especially if the killer gets wind that you're on to something."

She drew in her breath. She was so focused on Rick, she hadn't considered the danger to herself. "Right now, all I have are a couple of peacock feathers. The killer has nothing to worry about."

Rick paced his cell into the wee hours of the morning. If Amanda's peacock theory was right, it could take weeks — maybe months — to prove it. Even if such a thing were possible, he didn't have that kind of time. Even if he did, he didn't want her putting herself in danger. Whoever killed Cooper would have no qualms about killing again.

He thought back to the night of Cooper's murder and the man he saw leaving his room. Everything about that night was clear as crystal in his mind. Everything, that is, except the one thing that could save him — a full description of the killer.

The gnawing feeling that he had forgotten something — some telling detail — persisted. No matter how often he revisited that moment in time outside of Cooper's room, the memory continued to hover out of reach.

Maybe he tried too hard to remember. Perhaps if he cleared his mind. Thought of something else. The problem was that whenever he tried to think of something other than that night, Amanda came to mind.

He never thought to love another woman. He certainly never thought to fall for a female sheriff, of all things. But it was becoming more and more apparent that's exactly what he'd done, crazy as it seemed.

She was everything he loathed in a woman.

His father had married an independent woman, and Rick swore never to make the same mistake. He recalled little about his mother, only her unhappiness, which hung over his early childhood like a dark cloud.

The one thing he did remember was his mother's eyes. They never focused on him; rather, they looked past him or through him as if he were invisible. He now knew her dream had been so real and all-encompassing that it had blinded her to everything else. Even her own child.

The cloud of sadness hung over the family long after she'd left to make a life for herself on the stage.

He swore that no child of his would ever know the stigma of abandonment. In that regard, Christy was the perfect wife. Her only ambition was to make a home and raise a family. It was what he wanted, what they both wanted. But after little more than three months of wedded bliss, that dream died with her, along with a dream of any sort of meaningful future.

What would he have done had he found Cooper alive? That was the thing that weighed most heavily on his conscience. Would he have killed the killer? God forgive him, but he sure had wanted to.

As for Amanda . . .

He grimaced. What a mess. He had intended to win her support but never her heart — and he sure in blazes never meant to lose his own.

THIRTY

The bell over the Lockwood Watch and Clockworks shop rang out the hour precisely at noon. Like a scolding parent, the carefully spaced gongs made people scurry past Amanda's office window to complete errands, hurry to appointments, or rush home for a midday meal.

Seated at her desk, Amanda checked her pendant watch.

No sooner had the bell stopped ringing than the hammering began. Friday was still three days away, and already they were putting up the gallows in the empty field behind the jail. Each strike of the hammer was like a blow to her heart.

She covered her face with her hands. Her brother-in-law Grant agreed to go over the trial transcripts and look for grounds for appeal. But what if he failed to find anything? The thought made her sick to her stomach.

The door swung open, and Mayor Troutman barged in. Amanda's already low spirits dropped another notch. Could the day get any worse?

He dropped a stack of cards on her desk. Picking one off the top of the pile, she frowned. "What are these?"

"Why, invitations to the hanging, of course."

Her mouth dropped open. "Invitations?"

"Don't look so worried. They've already been delivered to all the important people," he said, his stogie bobbing up and down in his mouth. "Those are the extras. Thought you might want to invite friends or family."

She stared at the black-trimmed paper in disbelief. The invitation read:

Honored Guest:
With feelings of profound sorrow and regret, I hereby invite you to attend and witness the private, decent, and humane execution of R. B. Rennick, a.k.a. Barrett, guilty of murder in the first degree. We ask that all guests deport themselves in a respectful manner. Your help in making this a pleasant affair will be greatly appreciated.

It was signed *Sheriff Amanda Lockwood.*

Upon seeing her name in flowery script, her jaw dropped. The mayor couldn't bring himself to call her sheriff to her face but saw fit to sneak behind her back and include it on the invitation that she wanted no part of.

She tossed the card stock on her desk. "You had no right putting my name on this!"

The mayor jerked back with a look of surprise, stogie clamped between his teeth. "No right?" He jabbed the floor with his cane. "As much as it wounds me to say this, you are the sheriff. As such, you're in charge of the day."

Her heart practically stopped. "What do you mean, *in charge*?"

He looked surprised by the question. "Why, it's your job to see that the execution goes smoothly and in accordance with the law."

A horrible realization came over her, and her mouth ran dry. "What . . . what does that mean exactly?"

"It means, of course, that you'll escort the prisoner to the gallows and read the death warrant. The prisoner will be given a chance to say a few words before you blindfold him and . . ."

Shock waves rushed through her, and she

could hardly find her voice. "Isn't that the hangman's job?"

"The town no longer hires a hangman. We had to fire the last one so as to afford a dogcatcher."

She gripped the edge of her desk. "Does that mean I also have to —" The words stuck in her throat.

"Either you or your deputy."

He said more, a lot more. Something about a doctor and undertaker, but she was in such a stunned state of shock, she could hardly make sense of it all.

Rapping his knuckles on her desk, he flipped the butt of his cigar into the wicker wastebasket and started for the door, cane in hand. "I'll let you get back to work."

After he'd left, she picked up the invitations and tossed them into the trash. The walls, the ceiling — everything — were closing in and forcing her to battle for every breath of air.

Hands on her head, she rocked back and forth. *Fool, fool, fool!* Whatever made her think she could do this job? The very thought of having to put Rick to death — of pulling the lever to the trapdoor with her very own hand — filled her with such anguish and despair, she thought she would die.

The office door flew open, and Scooter skidded inside, his face white as a ghost. "Holy smokes!"

Jerked out of her reverie, she followed his gaze. The wastepaper basket was on fire, and bright-orange flames shot up the wall.

"Oh no!" Gasping, she jumped to her feet. "Quick, sound the alarm!"

Scooter ran outside to summon the volunteer fire brigade, but already, tongues of fire had reached a second wall. Stomping the sparks on the floor with the soles of her boots, she looked around for something to fight the fast-spreading blaze.

"Here!" yelled Rennick from his cell. He pushed a woolen blanket between the bars.

She stumbled down the steps to grab it out of his hand and sped back to the office. Swatting at the flames with the blanket, she raced from one hot spot to the next.

Wanted posters caught on fire and fell from the wall, covering her hope chest with red-hot cinders. With a gasp of alarm, she quickly extinguished the sparks with the blanket but not soon enough to prevent the lid of the wooden heirloom from scorching.

Containing the fire seemed as hopeless as saving Rick.

By the time the volunteer fire brigade

stormed inside to toss bucket after bucket of water on the blaze, not a salvageable piece of paper was left. The walls were scorched black and wanted posters burned to a crisp. An acrid smell hung in the air, stinging the eyes and nose. Soot carpeted the wood floor.

"I have to say there's never a dull moment around here," Rick called after everyone had left. He laughed.

She leaned the broom against her desk. "It's not funny," she said.

"Sure it is." His eyes fairly danced as he gazed through the open door. It was his first laugh since the trial started, and she suddenly realized how much she'd missed it. Missed the way his laugh made her feel all warm and giddy inside.

"I consider a horse broken after three rides," he said. "If the same holds true for a sheriff, I'd say you've earned the right to wear that badge."

A couple of weeks ago, she might have appreciated the compliment, but right now, she would give anything to free herself from the shiny tin star.

He watched her drag her hope chest away from the charred wall. "I see your hope-a-thingie survived."

"Just a little damage." Tomorrow, she'd

ask Mr. Woodman to look at it — again.

He chuckled. "I hate to tell you this, but I don't have much hope for that old thing. Maybe someone should take it off your hands while it's still in one piece."

She fanned the smoke with her hand, but the blue haze continued to hang ghostlike in the air. She swept up the ashes that had drifted into the cellblock.

"Sorry about the smoke. It reeks like the inside of a chimney."

His nose puckered. "I've smelled worse."

A serious look replaced his earlier smile, and she desperately wanted to say something to cheer him. "I asked my brother-in-law to look into your case. He's a lawyer."

His face closed like a slamming door. "Why?"

"I'm hoping he finds grounds for appeal. That would give us more time to get to the truth."

His eyes darkened with emotion. "I didn't know it was your job to . . . uh . . . carry out the task." He shook his head and looked away.

Her breath caught in her chest. "I didn't know it either."

All her life, she'd struggled with society's stringent rules for women. Everything from the way a woman walked and talked to the way she wore her hair and clothes and spent her free time was dictated from cradle to grave.

Women had the same capabilities as men and deserved the same opportunities. But this . . . this taking of a life was more than she'd bargained for.

"There's still time," she whispered. "I haven't given up hope."

He moved closer to the cell and held out his hand. "Amanda . . ."

She leaned the broom against the wall and lifted her hand to his. "Don't fight me on this, Rick. It's the only way."

She heard his intake of breath. "What you're tryin' to do . . . I'm much obliged. I am."

"I know what you're thinking. I haven't got a chance of proving your innocence. A woman is better suited to making a cake than taking on the role of sheriff."

He regarded her with eyes too dark to read. "What I was thinking is that I'm glad I'm not in your shoes."

"Are you saying that you wouldn't be able to . . ." She couldn't bring herself to finish the sentence. The very thought of pulling a lever and watching a man — Rick — drop to his death made her feel physically ill.

"Make a cake?" he asked, deftly lightening the mood. "Not in a million years."

During the next two days, Amanda was driven like a gale-force wind. Any new evidence casting doubt on Rick's guilt would postpone, if not altogether cancel, the hanging.

Where to begin? Where bad men gathered, of course. Saloons. Not places with which she was familiar, but desperate times called for desperate measures. With her posse and deputy stationed nearby, she squared her shoulders, lifted her chin, and walked into the first of the many town saloons.

Soon, she had her approach down pat: she'd walk inside, rap the bar for attention, then lift her voice to ask if anyone had known the deceased man, Cooper. That was how Scooter said it was done in dime novels.

Few admitted to knowing the man and then only from the faro tables. Cooper was a high-rolling gambler who lost bundles on the tables. So where did the money come from? Nothing found on his person or in his room provided a clue. Nor did the bank have a record of an account or safe deposit box in his name.

While she and Scooter were at the bank questioning the clerks, Bullwhip, the stage-coach driver, walked in carrying two canvas bags of money, an armed guard by his side. She stopped to stare. Something about the bags triggered the start of a distant memory, but she couldn't think what it was.

"Wow!" Scooter said as they left the bank. "You sure do make one heck of a sheriff."

"Doesn't she though?" Becky-Sue said and giggled.

Scooter got all red in the face as he tended to do whenever Becky-Sue was around.

Amanda turned to her posse and sighed. The women meant well, but canvassing businesses with such a large group turned out to be more of a hindrance than help. "We need to split up."

A mariachi band headed their way, forcing her to lift her voice to be heard above the music.

She sliced her hand through the air to indicate an even division. "This group takes this side of the street, the rest of you the other side. Question every shop owner, every customer, every person you meet." The man had to have done more than play faro and enjoy an occasional rendezvous with a good-time gal.

"I want to know who Cooper talked to, who his friends and enemies were, and his every movement leading up to time of death." Oh my! She was beginning to sound like an honest-to-goodness lawman.

About time.

"Deputy Hobson and I will take the barbershop and bordello."

"We will?" Scooter asked, turning beet red. "I mean, we will!"

THIRTY-ONE

Madame Bubbles owned the only bordello in town. It was a two-story brick building sedately trimmed in green. Other than the red light that shone in the window at night, the house looked prim as an old maid.

Amanda regarded the establishment with misgivings. She and her posse had combed the town, and still Cooper remained a mystery.

She glanced at Scooter. "Ready?"

"A-are w-we going in there?" he stammered.

She drew in her breath and reached for the doorknocker. "You bet we are."

They were ushered inside by a young corseted woman in a bright-red dress who told them to wait in the parlor. "Madame Bubbles will be right with you."

Nothing prim about the scarlet wallpaper decorating the interior. The heavy velvet draperies, sofas, large paintings, and ornately carved tables added to the oppressive feel of the room, along with the stale smell of perfume and cigar smoke.

Scooter looked up at the painting of an unclad woman over the fireplace, and his already red face turned purple. "Oh, wow!"

Amanda hushed him with a finger to her mouth. "Watch your demeanor."

"Right!" Stepping back, he saluted her and practically knocked over a statue of a naked lady. Fortunately, he caught it before it hit the floor, but he was still wrestling with the female form when Madame Bubbles arrived.

Even the madam's painted face couldn't hide her shock at seeing the partially unclad effigy in Scooter's arms. Unfortunately, Scooter's face was buried against the dummy's bare bosom, which sported two strategically placed jewels.

Amanda stepped in front of her deputy in an effort to distract the madam and held out her hand. "I'm Sheriff Lockwood." Though she'd seen Madame Bubbles in town on many occasions, they hadn't previously spoken. No respectable woman would be caught dead in the madam's company. "This is Deputy Hobson."

Having rid himself of the statue, Scooter whipped off his hat. "Pleased to meet you, ma'am," he said, unaware of the shiny paste stone on the tip of his nose.

While Madame Bubbles seated herself on a red velvet sofa, Amanda motioned to Scooter to rub the glittering stone off his nose and turned to the madam.

Madame Bubbles smoothed the skirt of her purple taffeta dress. "How can I help you?"

"As you probably heard, one of your . . . clients had an unfortunate encounter with a knife."

"You must be referring to Mr. Cooper."

"Yes, and I would like to speak to the person who discovered his body."

Madame Bubbles summoned the young woman who greeted them at the door with a snap of her fingers. "Send Charity in."

The young woman dropped a curtsy. "Yes, ma'am."

While waiting for Charity, Amanda caught Scooter's attention and rubbed her nose. It took several tries before he finally got the message.

Moments later, Charity entered the room dressed in a housecoat. Her flaming red hair trailed down her back. Without her face paint, she appeared years younger than she'd looked on the witness stand, no more than eighteen or nineteen.

She seemed surprised to find Madame Bubbles had guests, and her hand flew to her bare face in a self-conscious manner.

Madame Bubbles didn't seem to notice the girl's discomfort. "The sheriff wishes to ask you questions about that unfortunate incident involving Mr. Cooper."

Charity dropped her gaze to the floor and twisted her hands by her side. "I told them everything I know when I testified in court."

"I know that," Amanda said, keeping her voice and manner relaxed and friendly. "But if you could go over it one more time, Deputy Hobson and I would appreciate it." There was always the possibility she'd forgotten some small detail. "First, could you tell us when you last saw Mr. Cooper alive?"

The girl thought a moment. "Sometime before he was killed."

"Could you be more specific?"

"I think it was the Monday before. Maybe Tuesday. Coulda been Wednesday."

"Are you sure?" Deputy Hobson asked, trying to be helpful.

Charity nodded. "Yeah, I'm sure."

"What happened the night you found Mr. Cooper dead?" Amanda asked.

"The door was ajar when I got there. I called out, but when the client didn't answer, I pushed the door all the way open." The girl shuddered. "That's when I saw Mr. Cooper dead on the floor and the killer standing over him with a knife."

"Is there any chance you could be mistaken?" Amanda asked. "About the knife, I mean."

"Oh, no, ma'am. I know what I saw. Just like I said in court. It was a knife."

Rick was so wrapped up in his troubled thoughts, he didn't hear the door to the cell room open. Instead, he sensed Amanda's presence. Putting pen and paper aside, he rose from the cot, and a shiver of awareness rushed though him.

Standing in the circle of yellow light cast by the gas lantern, she acknowledged his greeting with a weary nod. She looked serious as a banker, her solemn demeanor hardly seeming to fit her small frame.

"I'm sorry," he said, his voice hoarse.

Her gaze searched his. "For what?"

"Putting you through this."

She moistened her lips and lowered her lashes. "I've hit a dead end. Grant, my brother-in-law, found nothing in the transcripts we could use." After a moment, she lifted her gaze, and he almost drowned in the liquid pools of despair in her eyes.

"We've questioned everyone in town about Cooper and . . ." She shook her head. "I even questioned the girl Charity, and she insists she saw you with a knife."

He rubbed his forehead and forced himself to recall the details of a night he'd gone over hundreds of time in his head. "The light was bad." What could the girl have seen? The silver money clip he pulled out of Cooper's pocket? Was that it?

He ran his fingers through his hair. "I reckon it's the first time a condemned man felt worse for the hangman than himself."

She looked away, and he sensed her struggle for composure. Finally, she turned her gaze back to him. The light caught the golden tips of her lush lashes, and the desperation in the depths of her eyes near broke his heart.

"Is there anyone you want me to contact?" she asked, her voice uncommonly husky.

So they really had come to the end of the line. He turned to the cot and reached for the letter he'd struggled for hours to write. He folded the letter in fourths. "Would you mail this to my sister after . . ."

She took the letter from him and slipped it into her divided skirt pocket. "Of course . . ."

Now they were talking in half sentences.

"Her name is Deborah Bradford. You can mail it general delivery to her in San Antone."

"I'll take care of it," she said. "What do you want me to do with your horse? I can arrange to have him sent to your sister, if you like."

"I want you to have him."

Her eyes widened. "Oh, I couldn't —"

"My sister doesn't need it, and there's no one else."

An agonized look washed over her face. "I'll . . . I'll take good care of him," she said.

"I expect nothin' less."

Their gazes locked for a moment before she looked away. "You're entitled to a special . . . last supper. Do you have any preferences?"

Food was the last thing on his mind, but if this really was his last meal, he might as well make the most of it. "Maybe some of Mrs. Mooney's biscuits," he said. They were the best he'd ever tasted. "And Mrs. Walker's blueberry pie."

Her eyebrows rose as he continued. "Mrs. Granby's fudge and her special corn bread would be great. And maybe Miss Read's almond cookies. That is if we can keep them away from your deputy." He paused for a moment. "Speaking of Hobson, have him bring me some of those hot cross buns."

She tilted her head sideways. "Anything else?"

He gazed into her eyes. Oh yes, there was something else. Before he died, he longed — ached — to take her in his arms and taste those pretty pink lips of hers.

"There's just one more thing . . ." He hesitated. "Would you have the last dance with me?"

Amanda stared at him in confusion. "What?"

He pushed both arms through the bars and silently beckoned her to come to him.

A surge of excitement rushed through her, followed by warm shivers that reached all the way to her toes. Even so, she didn't want to go to him, touch him, feel his breath in her hair. It would only bring them closer together and deepen the pain. But even as she fought it, the temptation proved too great, and she moved toward him as if drawn by an invisible rope.

Taking her hand in his, he pulled her as near as the steel door allowed and slid an arm around her waist. His manly smell filled her head, and the gentleness of his touch sent a flood of heat spiraling through her.

She lifted her hand to his shoulder, silently cursing the bars that separated them.

"Ready?" he asked, his voice husky. He was so close, she could see the gold flecks in his eyes.

"I'm not much of a dancer," she whispered.

"Somethin' else we have in common." He assessed her openly, as if he could see into the depths of her heart. The smoldering flames in his eyes took her breath away.

"Dare I ask if you're wearin' red beneath your sheriff attire?" he asked.

"You may not," she said, blushing. Never had she imagined discussing such an intimate topic with a man.

He feigned a look of disappointment. "Would you deny a condemned man this one small pleasure?"

Heart pounding, she felt her cheeks blaze. "I'm wearing red," she said with unaccustomed shyness.

Her reluctant admission was met with an appreciative grin. "That's my girl."

"I'm not your —"

"Shh," he said, touching a finger to her lips and all but setting her mouth on fire. "Tonight, it's just the two of us. Nothin' else exists." His hand returned to her waist. "We're on one of those — what do you call them? — tropical isles."

He rocked her gently to the rhythm of a soundless tune. Their feet didn't move, but their bodies swayed in perfect harmony.

"There's a big full moon overhead," he murmured in her ear, his warm breath on her neck.

His smooth, soft voice lulled her into believing she actually saw the things he described. Like an artist, he painted a vivid picture in her mind. As if by some magic, the bars seemed to melt away, and she almost imagined her head on his chest, the sound of his beating heart in her ear, the surf curling around their ankles.

"Over there," he murmured softly, "is the Big Dipper."

In her mind, she saw the sky, and never had the stars looked so bright. And the ocean! She swore she could hear the gentle lap of waves rolling past them onto a sandy beach. Great guns, she could almost feel the soft tropical breeze brush against her flushed body.

Oh God. If this wasn't love . . .

How long they danced, she didn't know. Time and place held no meaning. But eventually, the vision he created in her head faded away, and stark reality took its place. Swallowing a sob, she stared up at him. Day after tomorrow, this man would hang, and he would be lost to her forever.

A pain shot through her and lodged in her throat. She felt as if her heart had broken, filling her chest with a thousand little pieces. Tears filled her eyes.

"Don't cry," he whispered. "Please, don't cry." He wiped a tear from her cheek with his thumb, and his gaze fell on her trembling lips. "None of this is your fault," he murmured.

She reached through the bars to press her hand against his cheek. "I can't —"

Tenderness lit his eyes. "The last time I was locked up, something unexpected happened. A witness confessed on his deathbed."

"And you think something like that will happen again?"

He smoothed a strand of hair away from her face, his knuckle brushing her damp cheek. "Lookin' at you makes me believe anythin's possible."

She wanted so much to believe that too. Believe in a miracle. Believe that her prayers would be answered. Instead, an anguished cry rose from her depths, shattering what little control remained. Pulling out of his arms, she turned and ran.

"Amanda, wait!"

His voice ringing in her ears, she fled from her office, but this time, there was no escaping reality.

Her hands shook so hard, it took several tries before she could turn the key and lock the door.

She shivered, but not from the cold night air. Hugging herself, she looked up and down Main. The yellow glow of gas street-lights barely penetrated the thick veil of night. A crescent moon floated high above, curling like a pale-yellow feather.

The wooden scaffold couldn't be seen, but its skeletal frame cast a gloomy shadow over the town. She couldn't think of any other explanation for the unusual quiet. No gunfire rent the air. Only the thin sound of a fiddle wafted from a distant saloon, but even the music lacked the usual verve.

Spirit, tied to the rail in front, swished his tail and scraped the ground with a hoof as if to say *Let's go.*

The upstairs windows were dark, so even Scooter had retired.

If only she could talk to her sisters, but Josie was gone, and Meg needed her rest. Mama and Papa wouldn't understand, and most of her friends had drifted away since she took over as sheriff. Never had Amanda felt so utterly alone.

She pressed her forehead against the door, eyes shut. How was it possible to feel both hot and cold at the same time? *Oh, Rick . . .*

Her body swayed from side to side as if unwilling to give up the memory of dancing in his arms. He made her aware of an inner part she never knew existed. A part that liked being held by him, touched by him, teased by him. Despite her protests, she even liked that he approved of her choice of undergarments. How was such a thing possible?

Her eyes flew open. Oh no! Now she sounded like her sisters. She was never one for silly schoolgirl crushes. Not like Meg and Josie who, in their younger days, had fallen in and out of love as easily as birds taking flight. But not her. She was too busy saving orphans, helping war veterans, supporting the poor, and marching for women's rights.

How she'd hated the way her sisters carried on about their beaus and, later, the men they eventually wed. It was Grant this and Ralph that until, at times, she thought she would scream.

Now at long last, she understood. Loving someone changed the way the world looked. It changed priorities. It changed the depth and width and very shape of the heart.

Meg and Josie were contentedly married, but there would be no happily ever after for her. Where her sisters had fallen for respectable men, *she* was in love with a condemned killer scheduled to die.

She stared at the hand that would pull the lever and shuddered in horror. Had she known what her duties as a sheriff entailed, she would not have accepted the post.

Never had she felt so utterly miserable. So unbelievably bereft. She had no idea that pain could cut so deep without drawing blood. Her misery was so acute, she could barely manage to throw herself into the saddle. Once mounted, she looked up at the starlit sky, and the full realization hit her.

She'd been so busy learning to be sheriff that she'd forgotten to do one essential thing — she'd forgotten to safeguard her heart. Now it was too late.

THIRTY-TWO

Amanda didn't sleep that night. It was as if the night were alive with echoes from the past. But there was another voice, a stronger voice, a voice that could only come from the deepest regions of her heart. *You, Amanda Lockwood, are in love with Rick Barrett, and there is no way you will participate in his death.*

Every time the voice cut through her, she sat upright in her bed and whispered denials that were swallowed up by the dark of night. No, no, it can't be. What she felt was pity, sorrow. She would feel the same for any man sent to his death.

It seemed foolish to deny what she knew in her heart was true, but old habits die hard. After vowing all these years to be her own woman and not depend on a man, it was hard to admit that she needed Rick. Needed to be held by him, loved by him. Needed him in her life.

She twisted and turned until the first glimmer of dawn crept though her bedroom window. Somewhere around three a.m., she had made her decision. She would hand in her resignation effective immediately.

Maybe that would postpone Rick's hanging. Maybe it wouldn't. Either way, his blood would not be on her hands.

She rose and quickly completed her morning ablutions, then dressed. After brushing her hair and pinning it into a bun, she attached the sheriff badge to her chest for what she supposed would be the very last time.

Lifting the picture frame from the dressing table, she ran her finger over the glass. "Sorry, Grandmama, but I can't do it. I just can't."

She replaced the daguerreotype and left the room. Tiptoeing in the hall so as not to wake her parents, she descended the stairs.

A movement in front of the parlor window startled her. "Papa?"

He turned, his bulk outlined against the breaking dawn. "You're up early," he said.

"I couldn't sleep."

"Coffee's ready."

He followed her into the kitchen and watched as she poured herself a cup, a stream of sunlight capturing them in its path.

"Amanda —"

"Don't say it, Papa. I know how much you disapprove of my being sheriff, and you are right. I should have listened to you." She blew on the hot brew and took a sip. The coffee tasted as bitter as her words. "I'm handing in my resignation first thing this morning."

He studied her from beneath a craggy brow. "Because of the hanging?"

"What they ask of me . . ." A pain unlike any she had ever known shot through her. "Could . . . could you put a man to death, Papa?"

"I don't know. Maybe. If I thought he would bring harm to my family."

She set her cup on the counter. "What if there was no danger to you personally? What if you thought he had been wrongly accused?" *What if it was someone you loved?*

He raised an eyebrow. "You think this man innocent?"

She drew in her breath. "He is, Papa. I know he is."

He set his empty cup on the counter, and his thick eyebrows twitched. "Are you sure that's not just wishful thinking on your part?"

She considered the question long and hard before answering. Love was supposedly blind. If that was true, then maybe she was just fooling herself. But was it really blind? Or did it open the eyes, allowing them to see what others could not?

"Yes," she said finally. "I'm sure."

"Based on what evidence?"

She told him about the knife and how it had suddenly appeared. "Someone wanted him to take the blame. It's the only thing that makes sense."

His forehead creased, and he looked at her so strangely, she feared she'd given too much away. Had he guessed her true feelings?

"Have you done everything in your power to help him?" he asked. "As sheriff."

It seemed like a strange question. "Yes. I think so," she said.

What would Papa think if he knew that she'd gone as far as offering Rick a chance to escape? No doubt Papa would be furious. Appalled. Shocked, even. As much as he disapproved of her being the sheriff, he would never forgive her for doing something so lawless.

"Do you know who you were named after?" he asked, filling in the sudden silence.

Papa had a habit of abruptly changing the subject whenever it veered off in an awkward direction, but she refused to fall for that old trick.

"Did you hear what I said, Papa? I think Rick — the prisoner — is innocent."

If he noticed her slip of tongue, he gave no indication. "I heard," he said and after a moment added, "You were named after my sister."

"I know." Her namesake had drowned as a child, but that's all she really knew. No one, not even Grandmama, had talked about her much except in general terms or hushed whispers.

Still, the deceased child haunted the family like a ghost refusing to be exorcised. Amanda's earliest memory was of her father dragging her and her two sisters down to the river's edge and making them swim back and forth until their bellies hurt and their little legs and arms ached. He was determined that no other family member would ever drown.

"She was only seven when she died." Papa heaved a sigh and added in a faraway voice, "We were having such a good time that day."

Amanda bit her lower lip. She knew about the drowning but hadn't known her father had been present. Did he blame himself?

"I tried to save her," he said, as if to read her mind. "And failed."

His admission surprised her. Never had she heard Papa admit failure. "You were only a child."

"Ten. I was ten. Old enough to take care of her." His voice drifted away. From the adjoining dining room came the sound of all twenty-two clocks, marking the startling revelations of the past with a cacophony of chimes.

Did this explain why he was so protective of his daughters? To the point of even keeping suitors away? It was only by sheer determination and Mama's intervention that her brothers-in-law managed to court and marry her sisters.

"It was my idea to tie a rope to a tree so we could swing out over the water." His voice broke. "When it was my sister's turn, she dropped into the river smooth as a mermaid. I didn't know she was in trouble. Not at first. She didn't make a sound. Not a sound. Never did I know that death could be so silent."

"Oh, Papa." Moving to his side, she threw her arms around him. She hadn't known the full story of his sister's death, only the pain left behind and the constant fear that history would repeat itself.

They clung to each other, his voice rumbling up from his chest. "Silence always reminds me of her death."

She pulled away to study his face. "Is that why you collect all those clocks, Papa?" Twenty-two in the dining room, twenty-two in the parlor. Heaven only knew how many in his shop. The constant ticks of clocks allowed for no silence, thus drowning out the memories of soundless screams.

"Maybe," he said. "Maybe."

She never really thought much about clocks or the passing of time until her grandmother died. Somehow, the constant *ticks* and *tocks* widened the gap between life and death. The more time that passed, the further away her grandmother had seemed and the more her happy childhood memories faded.

"Why are you telling me this, Papa? Why now after so many years?"

"I'm still haunted by the thought that I didn't do enough to save her. Had I realized sooner she was in trouble . . . In the end, that's what we judge ourselves on. Whether or not we did enough."

With that, he turned and left the kitchen.

Later that morning, Amanda sat Scooter down. Papa had asked her if she'd done everything in her power to save Rick, and it was a question very much on her mind.

She'd scoured the town, questioned tens of dozens if not hundreds of people, and found nothing to support Rick's innocence. Not a thing. Still, she couldn't shake the feeling that somewhere, a stone was left unturned. For that reason, she couldn't bring herself to resign as sheriff. Not yet . . .

She leaned toward her deputy and lowered her voice. "What I'm about to say is between you and me. It must not leave this office."

Scooter's eyes grew round as pie plates. "Oh, wow, it sounds serious."

"Shh." She glanced at the closed door leading to the cells. "It is serious." Of all the things she'd done in the past — all the trouble she'd caused her parents, her teachers, the town — never had she tackled anything as crucial.

"I'm going to ask you to do something for me. If you don't feel right about it, that's okay. You don't have to do it. Just let me know."

Curiosity suffused Scooter's face. "Does this have something to do with tomorrow's hanging?"

"Yes," she whispered, swallowing hard. Just the sight of the gallows looming out back made her feel ill. "Like I said, you don't have to do it."

"What is it?" he asked without hesitation. "What do you want me to do?"

As quickly as she could, she explained her daring plan. As she spoke, his eyebrows kept inching upward, and his face turned red as if he was holding his breath.

"Gee willikers," he said when she finished. "That's some plan."

No cause she'd ever worked for was as urgent and important as this one. "You don't have to do it, Scooter," she assured him once again. "It's not required by your job, and I don't want you getting in trouble."

His eyes flashed with excitement. "I'll do it!"

She sat back with a frown. "You need to think about it."

"I did think about it."

"What? For five seconds?" She sighed. "You do understand what's at stake, right? If something goes wrong, you could go to jail. We all could."

"I said I'll do it, and I will."

Fear for his safety almost made her change her mind, but then her father's words repeated themselves in her head as they had dozens of times since their early morning talk. *In the end, that's always what we judge*

ourselves on. Whether or not we did enough.
Papa still obsessed over the question after all these years. Rick too was haunted and continued to blame himself for not better protecting his wife.

Whatever happened, she wanted to know in her heart she'd done everything possible to save Rick. The hardest part would be getting him to cooperate.

"Okay, but if anything happens and we get caught . . ."

He grinned. "I'll say I know nothing and you'd lost your mind."

Despite her depression, she laughed. "I don't want you getting in trouble."

"What about you?" he asked. "You could go to jail."

His concern touched her. "If it comes to that . . . well . . . let's not cross that bridge till we get to it."

"Wow. You really are somethin', Sheriff."

She smiled. "I don't know about that." She checked the time on her pendant watch and went over everything again, step by step. "When our red-feathered friends deliver Rick's last . . ." She cleared her voice. "The food he requested. Tell them to return at eight o'clock tonight sharp. I'll be waiting."

Scooter glanced at the door leading to the

cells. "Does he know?"

"Not yet," she whispered. "Not yet. Now go . . ."

The mayor arrived at the office that afternoon with last-minute details on how the hanging was to proceed. He paced back and forth, stopping from time to time to stare at the charred hope chest that now resembled a burnt loaf of bread beneath the blackened walls.

"We pride ourselves on putting on a decent and humane hanging," he said magnanimously, his thick stogie clamped in the corner of his mouth. "I trust you will continue our fine tradition even though you are a —"

"Woman," she said.

Turning to face her, he pulled the cigar away from his mouth and flicked an ash on her floor. "You know what I mean." His eyebrows drew together. "Some people think it's unseemly for a woman to . . . uh . . ."

"Conduct a decent and humane hanging?"

"Exactly!"

She gritted her teeth. "Rest assured that I'm fully prepared to see that justice is served."

"With no hysterics," he said. "I wouldn't want our out-of-town guests made to feel uncomfortable. I plan to run for governor of this fine state, so my political future hangs in the balance."

Seething inwardly, she stood in an effort to encourage him to leave. It sickened her that he would use a hanging for political gain. On the other hand, it didn't surprise her. "Then we'll all just have to hang together, won't we?"

Had he understood the irony of her words, he might have looked less pleased. "Glad you see it my way." With another glance at the fire-damaged walls, he left her office humming beneath his breath.

At exactly seven thirty that night, Amanda kneeled in front of the hope chest and ran her hand over the charred surface. She had yet to ask carpenter Woodman to take a look. She'd had too many other things on her mind, but if anyone could repair the damage, he could.

The old chest had never much interested her, but now she studied it with new eyes. Originally, it had been her maternal grandfather's betrothal gift to her grandmother. Why had she never before noticed the intricate carvings? The details were astonishing. According to family history, the carvings represented everything his future bride had loved. Horses, birds, and flowers graced all sides. The splendor of the magnificent sailing ship that eventually brought the couple to America had not been diminished by the fire.

Amanda traced first her Irish grandmother's initials, then her mother's. Her finger paused on *J. L.* for Josie. How she missed her oldest sister. Would Josie approve of what she was about to do? Probably not. Next, she ran a finger over *M. L.* for Meg, pausing when she reached the empty space beneath.

That's where her own initials were meant to go. But unlike her sisters who dreamed of carving a part of themselves into the fine oak, she had always been more interested in carving out a place in the realm of women's rights alongside such illustrious names as Lucy Stone and Susan B. Anthony.

With a pointed finger, she mindlessly traced her initials on the smooth surface below Meg's name. Catching herself, she quickly pulled her hand away. The realization that she would gladly marry Rick if circumstances permitted not only startled her, but almost broke her heart.

With a shake of her head, she lifted the

hope chest lid. No matter how much she reminded herself that marriage would hold her back and keep her from accomplishing all that she intended to do, she couldn't help wondering what might have happened had Rick been found innocent.

Woodman's wife had filled the chest with clothes for the poor farm. Now, she pulled out a woman's blue calico dress and bonnet and shook out the wrinkles. Fortunately, the fire hadn't penetrated the wood, and the clothes inside were good as new. The frock looked a bit small, but it would have to do.

Slinging the dress over her arm, she reached for the key on the wall. Bracing herself with a deep breath that brought her lungs no relief, she walked to the door separating her office from the cellblock.

Her hand froze on the brass doorknob. Panic began to well up inside her. But then a distant memory echoed from the deepest regions of her heart. *You can do it, Amanda.*

THIRTY-THREE

Where was she?

Rick hadn't seen Amanda all day. Not since last night. Had she been purposely avoiding him? That's how it seemed.

Had he really held her in his arms? Had he only imagined seeing what looked like love shining in the depth of her eyes?

Each time the office door opened, his spirits soared, but it had only been Hobson checking on him or members of the Red Feather posse bringing him baked goods. It took a tremendous amount of energy to greet his visitors without showing disappointment that it wasn't Amanda standing before him.

One by one, the ladies filled his cell with his favorite food and offered tearful prayers for his soul. Mrs. Mooney hinted that since she was the bank president's wife, her prayers were given special consideration. Mrs. Granby offered to sing at his funeral and, God love her, demonstrated with a loud, shrill voice that would do a screech owl proud. Halfway through the song, the former schoolmarm, Miss Read, fell to her knees. It was hard to know if she was praying for him or Mrs. Granby.

By the time they had all left, he was exhausted from having to assure them that not only was he ready for the pearly gates but worthy of entrance.

He had no intention of hanging. He'd rather be shot in the back while running than make Amanda do something she was loath to do. It wasn't the most courageous way to die, but it would save Amanda from the grisly task, and that was all that mattered.

At long last, he heard the door open again. This time, it was Amanda, and his breath caught between his ribs. He searched her face. The dim light from the flickering gas lantern revealed little beyond her solemn expression. If only he knew how to lessen her pain. Nothing that happened was her fault.

He once thought he'd die a happy man if he knew she believed in him, believed in his innocence. Now he knew what a selfish thing that was. It would be easier for her if she thought him guilty. A better man would see that she did.

"You're working late," he said.

She made no comment. Instead, she surprised him by inserting a key into the keyhole of his cell.

The iron door swung open with a clank, and he froze.

She stepped aside, indicating what she wanted him to do. He now had full rein to walk out of there. To escape.

He shook his head. "I'm not leaving."

"It's the only chance you have."

"I'm not leaving," he repeated.

"Why are you punishing yourself?"

He frowned. "Punish? Why would you think such a thing?"

"You blame yourself for your wife's death. You said as much."

He drew in his breath. "I am to blame. I should have protected her. I should never have let Cooper —" His voice broke. "But that's not why I'm staying. If I leave tonight, the blame will fall on your shoulders."

She tossed a previously unnoticed bundle at him. "Put this on."

He stared at the ball of fabric in his hands. The *enormity* of what she was doing hit him with such force, he took a step backward. "Did you not hear what I said?"

"Do it!"

"I can't." He grimaced from the pain and longing caused by her nearness. "Everything you worked for . . . If I leave, they'll have your neck. Helping a prisoner escape carries a serious price. You could go to prison. Your life would be ruined."

Her expression softened. "Without you . . ." She shook her head and was once again all business. "Hurry. There's no time to lose."

He grabbed her arm. "Amanda, listen to me. You're puttin' yourself in serious jeopardy."

She pulled away. "I don't care."

"I do." The stubborn look on her face was all too familiar, and his heart sank. The escape she offered was tempting. Nothing he would like better than to walk out of there tonight and vanish. But how could he in good conscious leave her holding the bag?

"Okay, I'll do what you want me to do, but not this way. We have to make it look like I escaped of my own accord. That you tried to stop me. Tomorrow. When you lead me to the gallows . . . That's when I'll make my escape."

She shook her head. "It's too dangerous. You'll be shot."

He drew in his breath. "Maybe. Maybe not. Either way, you won't be blamed."

They stared at each other, their rigid stances showing no signs of giving in. "Put the clothes on." Never had he heard her sound so adamant, not even when she was fighting her critics. "Now!"

In a softer voice, she added, "If you can't do it for yourself, then do it for me." Her luminous eyes beseeched him. "I'd rather spend the rest of my life in prison than have to walk you to the gallows or see you shot trying to escape."

A short time later, the outside door flew open, and the Red Feather ladies strolled into the office right on time, dressed for business.

Instead of chatting as usual, the women seemed especially quiet and kept glancing at the closed door between the office and cells. A few were teary eyed, and Miss Read buried her face in her hands, sobbing quietly.

No one paid any attention to Rick, seated upon the hope chest, back propped against the scorched wall. In addition to a long-sleeved dress, he wore a Mother Hubbard hat tied beneath his chin.

Amanda had borrowed one of her mother's embroidery hoops and instructed him on how to use it. She couldn't think of any other way for him to keep his head down and face hidden. She only wished he didn't look like he was pounding nails instead of making dainty stitches.

Mrs. Mooney cast a disapproving look at Goldie, whose painted face and low-cut shirtwaist offered a disruptive contrast to her plain divided skirt and sensible boots.

"You do know that it's against town ordinance for women of *doubtful* virtue to be out after dark."

The comment caused even Mrs. Perl's knitting needles to pause, and a brittle silence followed.

Fortunately, Goldie took no offense. Instead, she ran her fingers along her bare neckline and smiled sweetly. "The ordinance doesn't apply to me. There's no doubt about my virtue. We all know I don't have any."

This brought relieved laughter from the others, and Mrs. Perl resumed her knitting.

Mrs. Wellmaker was next to speak. "Deputy Hobson said we have an important job to do tonight."

Amanda stood in such a way as to draw as much attention away from Rick as possible. "Yes, thank you for coming." She cleared her voice. "I got a report of possible horse thieves camped about five miles out of town." Fortunately, no one questioned the validity of her statement. "I thought we could sneak up and surprise them."

As if their horse-drawn vehicles could surprise anyone. A person would have to be deaf not to hear them coming from miles away. On the plus side, no one would suspect a noisy cluster of wagons and buggies of hiding an escaped prisoner. Talk about hiding in plain sight.

"Ohhh," squealed Becky-Sue. "This is sooo exciting."

Amanda hated lying, but it was better if the women were kept in the dark. That way, no one could blame them should something go wrong.

"We have a new posse member. Her name is Janet." Curious glances shot to where Rick sat. He raised a hand in greeting but kept his head lowered.

Some of the women exchanged glances, but no one said a word.

Amanda forced herself to breathe. "Claudia, would you mind if Janet rode with you?"

T-Bone's wife cast a dubious look in Rick's direction but nonetheless nodded, her sausage curls bouncing up and down. "Yes, of course."

After giving them further instruction, Amanda stuck her head outside and called to Scooter, who was standing guard. The mayor had been seen earlier escorting his guests around town. So far, he'd seen fit to avoid her office, probably because of the scorched walls. Or maybe he just didn't want to call attention to the sheriff being a woman. Should he change his mind, Scooter would sound a warning.

A bigger concern was the small group of church people gathered outside singing hymns and praying for the soul of the prisoner. Sneaking Rick past them could pose a problem.

"Is everything ready, Deputy?" she asked.

He stepped into the office and saluted her. "Yes, sir, Sheriff!"

She let out her breath. So far, the hardest part had been getting Rick to cooperate. "All right, ladies. Lead the way."

The women solemnly followed Scooter outside and into the dark of night.

Rick waited till the others had left before grabbing her by the waist, surprising her. With one easy move, he swirled her into his arms.

She gasped, but before she could say a word, he had effectively snapped a handcuff around her wrist. "What are you doing?"

For answer, he pushed her down on the hope chest and attached the other cuff to the trunk's handle. Only then did he explain.

"When they find me gone in the morning, I don't want them blamin' you." With that, he leaned over. Looking deep into her eyes, he lifted her chin and kissed her tenderly on the lips. For an amazing but fleeting moment in time, she was transported to a tropical isle, and then, just like that, he was gone.

Knowing that she would never see him again, she wanted to call him back but didn't dare. Instead, she stared at the closed door, her mouth and body on fire. Never had she known that a man's lips could be so tender and sweet. Oh, why did he go and kiss her? Why? If he had a sensible bone in his body, he would leave Two-Time and not look back. That meant she would never see him again. Now, thanks to his kiss, neither would she forget the feel of his lips on hers.

She squeezed her eyes shut and focused on the sound of wagon wheels until the last rumbles faded away. The voices of the church group singing "Rock of Ages" never wavered. The group's voices faded as the vigil ended and they drifted away.

Her breath whooshed out of her. Scooter and their posse had succeeded in safely smuggling Rick out of town. So far, so good.

She yanked on the handcuff attached to the handle of her hope chest, but it held tight. Recalling that the keys were in a desk drawer, she struggled to her feet but was unable to stand upright. The steel bracelet prevented her from getting behind the hope chest. The best she could do was pull the heavy chest inch by inch across the floor. Dragging a dead mule couldn't have been any harder, and the going was frustratingly slow.

Gunfire rent the air, and the window exploded into shattered glass. She practically jumped out of her skin. What the . . . She froze a second before reaching for her Colt with her one free hand. She then aimed it at the side of her hope chest and fired. The charred wooden handle shot across the room, freeing the iron cuff from its hold.

More gunfire ripped through the air. Ducking, she ran across the room and hunkered beneath the window, the iron bracelet dangling from her wrist.

"I know you're in there, Lockwood," a man's voice shouted. She recognized the owner at once as Gopher, and her blood ran cold. Apparently, he'd come to make good on his threat. "You think you run this town. Come out and prove it."

Crouched beneath the windowsill, she

fought to steady her nerves. The crazy fool was challenging her to a duel. "Go home, Gopher. You're drunk!" she shouted.

He fired again, and the bullet whizzed over her head.

"Don't make me shoot," she cried. *Please, please, don't make me do that.* The thing she most dreaded was having to kill or injure someone.

Another bullet splintered the wooden window frame. Okay, she would have to fire her weapon. There was no getting out if it.

Holding both hands over her head, she balanced the barrel of her gun on the windowsill and thumbed back the hammer. "This is your last chance," she yelled. If he fired again, she'd pull the trigger.

He fired again.

Okay, she'd give him one more chance to see the error of his ways. "Go home," she shouted. *Please go home.*

The next bullet hit the top of the window. Chips of wood and pieces of old paint rained down on her.

This time, she did what Rick told her not to do — she jerked back on the trigger, and the gun fired. The recoil sent her flying backward. Her ears were still ringing when she heard a man cry out.

"Help, I've been shot!"

Amanda jumped up and looked out the window. Gasping in horror, she dropped her gun. Mayor Troutman was on his knees, holding a bloody arm, and he looked fit to be tied.

THIRTY-FOUR

The following morning, Amanda arrived at the office on her pony and was shocked to find Rick's saddled horse tied up in front.

Oh no! Something went terribly wrong!

Scooter had left Spirit at a predestined location, waiting for Rick's arrival. Bedroll, food, and other supplies had been left there too, enough to last for several days.

Stomach churning, she tied her pony to the railing and ran inside. Scooter was sitting at his desk. "What happened?" she cried. "Is Rick —" She glanced at the cells in back.

"He's not here," Scooter said. "Found his horse waiting outside this morning."

Her heart sank. She tried thinking of every plausible explanation for Spirit returning to town without a rider, but only two came to mind: Rick was either injured or dead.

Her knees buckled, and she grabbed hold of the desk.

The door flew open, and Mayor Trout-man stormed inside, his arm in a sling. He glared at her from beneath a furrowed brow like a vulture on a telegraph wire.

She felt terrible. Of all the people in town she could have shot, why, oh why, did it have to be the mayor? Her bullet hit Trout-man in the fleshy part of his upper arm. It could have been worse. A lot worse, but knowing that didn't make her feel any better.

Still, how could she have known he'd taken it upon himself to sneak up on Gopher in an effort to impress his out-of-town guests, just as her weapon fired?

"We're waiting for you," he said without preamble.

She'd almost forgotten she was supposed to appear before the town council. "I'll be right there." She waited for the mayor to walk outside before tuning to Scooter.

"Summon the posse. We need all hands on deck to find Rick."

Scooter jumped up from his desk. "Will do, Sheriff."

On the way to the old schoolhouse where the town council meeting was to be held, Amanda ran into Mary-Louise. The two hadn't talked since Mary-Louise walked out of the hotel dining room.

Amanda peered at the sleeping infant in the baby carriage, nudging the blanket away from his face to get a better look. "He's getting so big," she said. His cheeks were as chubby as a chipmunk's.

Mary-Louise smiled. "Yes, isn't he? And he's such a good baby. He hardly ever cries."

Amanda drew her hand away from the child, and a horrid realization washed over her. She now knew what had bothered her at the bank. She must have given her thoughts away, because a look of dismay crossed Mary-Louise's face.

"I-I gotta go," Mary-Louise said and wheeled the carriage past her.

"I know how the fire started," Amanda called after her.

Mary-Louise stopped, her back straight as a ramrod. "I told you it was an accident."

"Yes, I believe that part is true."

Mary-Louise turned to face her. "Then what are you saying?"

Amanda walked up to her. "When I found your baby, he was covered with a white cloth. I didn't think anything about it until I happened to spot a payroll being brought to the bank. I just now realized that to protect your baby from the fire, you covered him with the first thing you could find. It just so happened to be an empty money bag. Just like the ones I saw at the bank."

Mary-Louise said nothing, so Amanda continued. "Now I have to wonder what you were doing with bank property."

"John uses the bags for his business. When I saw the flames, I panicked and grabbed one."

Amanda shook her head. A small business would have no need for such a large money sack. "You can't protect him. Not anymore. I found a charred banknote in the ashes, but I didn't know what it meant at the time. Now I do. You were trying to burn the loot John stole from the bank. That's how the fire started."

Mary-Louise looked like she was about to deny it, but then her shoulders sagged, and her breath whooshed out of her. "I was in labor and went to pull a clean sheet out of an old chest when I found the loot. I knew John was worried about finances, especially with the baby coming and business down, but I had no idea . . ." Tears welled in her eyes. "I didn't know what to do."

"So you decided to burn the money."

Mary-Louise's eyes filled with tears. "The canvas bag was too large to fit into the stove, so I tossed the money in separately. The pains started coming fast and . . ." She looked like she was having trouble breathing, but she continued. "I forgot to close the grate. A spark flew out, and the curtains caught on fire. But I couldn't do anything. Baby coming . . . I . . . I don't remember much after that."

"Oh, Mary-Louise, I had no idea things had gotten so bad. Why didn't you or John ask for help? You have friends and family. Even the church . . ."

"John wouldn't let me ask for help. You know how proud he is." She beseeched Amanda with a hand to her arm. "Please . . . he swore it was only the one time and he would never do anything like it again." Her lips quivered. "He's a good man, Amanda."

Amanda drew in her breath. A good man doesn't rob a bank, no matter how desperate, but she didn't want to say as much. How she hated the thought of having to arrest an old friend. Whatever made her think she was cut out to be sheriff?

"I'm so sorry . . ." Amanda wanted to say more, but no words seemed adequate. By the time this was over, Mary-Louise would hate her, and there wasn't a darn thing she could do about it.

Mary-Louise drew her hand away. Tears rolling down her cheeks, she reached for the baby carriage and hurried away.

Moments later, Amanda dragged herself into the old schoolhouse. She was worried about Rick. That and the encounter with Mary-Louise had depleted her energy. She wasn't sure how much more she could take.

The members of the town council, including Mayor Troutman, were seated behind a long table.

Nerves wound tighter than a watch spring, she stood in front of them and felt as if she were facing a firing squad. She hid her shaking hands by her side. What did the council have in mind? Whatever it was, she hoped they'd get it over with quickly so she could look for Rick.

No one had seen fit to provide her with a chair. There were five of them, including the mayor, and every last one of them harbored ill feelings toward her for one thing or another.

T-Bone, Mr. Perl, and Mr. Granby were married to posse members and continued to blame her for their wives' neglect of household duties. Mr. Levy owned the Red Rooster Saloon and Dance Hall and still hadn't forgotten how she tried closing him down on Sundays.

The fifth and newest council member was the dogcatcher, Mr. Mutton. He and Amanda, along with her sister Meg, had more than their share of disputes. To him, a dog was a dog, licensed or not, and none were safe from his snare.

Mayor Troutman glowered at her, his face as white as the sling holding his injured arm in place. The county director had arrived on the morning train, and Troutman had the unenviable task of informing him that the hanging had been canceled.

"*Miss* Lockwood. Suppose you tell us how your office allowed the prisoner to escape?"

Anxious to get the inquiry over with as quickly as possible, she curbed her impatience. Feigning a look of horror, she allowed her gaze to travel from man to man. "Surely, you're not suggesting that one of your wives . . ."

Looking appalled, Granby turned to the mayor. "That's not what you meant, is it? You're not saying that my Myrtle would help a killer escape . . ."

"Harrumph." Mr. Perl fingered the woolen scarf at his neck. "My wife would never do such a thing."

"Mine neither!" T-Bone said, though he sounded more certain than he looked.

The mayor chomped down on his cigar. "Relax. No one is blaming your wives. They're all fine women, I'm sure."

"Or were till they decided to wear long

handles," Mutton muttered.

Mr. Perl cleared his throat. Judging by his expression, Mrs. Perl's divided skirt, which looked like stovepipe trousers, were a sensitive topic. Or maybe the dour expression was due to the heat. The poor man was swathed in more wool than a flock of sheep, thanks to his wife's ever-present knitting needles. Like a Norwegian fisherman, he wore a knitted cardigan and woolen hat. That, along with his long narrow scarf, made Amanda feel hot just looking at him.

The mayor glanced at his notes. "As I understand it, you and the . . . others . . . were called away to check out a complaint."

"Yes, that's right," Amanda said, trying to keep the impatience out of her voice. "I received a report of suspicious activity out by the Freeman homestead." Recalling what John had done, she clenched her hands tight.

"I see," the mayor said. "According to Hobson, you were to follow him and the . . . others. Is that right?"

"Yes. My posse" — she paused for effect and cast her gaze toward Granby, T. Bone, and Perl — "including your very fine and noble wives, left with Deputy Hobson." The three men might be less willing to blame her or her posse if reminded of their wives' involvement.

Troutman took a puff on his cigar before asking, "Why didn't you leave with them?"

"I fully intended to. But I was attacked by Rick . . . Mr. Barrett. As I told you before, he handcuffed me to my hope . . . uh . . . wooden chest." At first, she'd resented Rick making her stay behind. In retrospect, she knew he had done her a favor.

Recalling the feel of his mouth on hers, she forced herself to breathe. *Oh, Rick, please be safe.*

Mr. Perl's impatience was as evident as the wool around his neck. "None of this explains how the prisoner escaped."

"I'm afraid that must have happened when I was occupied with Mr. Coldwell."

Troutman's eyes widened. "Are you saying that Gopher had something to do with it?"

She shrugged. She hated to falsely accuse someone, but it served the man right. Also, it *was* Gopher's fault that she shot the mayor. "I figure there was a reason he created a distraction." Fortunately, the council members didn't know that Rick had escaped before Gopher showed up.

T-Bone looked dubious. "Letting a prisoner escape is no more than what we expected from a woman sheriff. First, she corrupts our wives and nearly burns down the town. Then, she shoots the mayor. Now this!"

"What do you have to say for yourself, *Miss* Lockwood?" the mayor asked.

Corrupted their wives? She was tempted to give them a piece of her mind. Knowing it would only make things worse, she bit back her angry retort. *Grace and charm, grace and charm, grace and charm . . .*

"We have a dangerous killer on the loose. If you gentlemen would kindly let me do my job, I intend to track him down."

"Track him down?" T-bone snapped. "He could be in Mexico by now. He could even be in a foreign country."

The mayor elbowed him. "Mexico *is* a foreign country, you idiot."

Amanda stretched to her full five-foot-five height. "If he crossed the border, he won't be our problem anymore, will he?" Mexico was exactly where Rick was supposed to be by now. The thought of him lying somewhere in the hot sun injured and possibly dead filled her with horror.

The men huddled their heads together, their hushed voices failing to conceal a heated discussion.

Finally, the mayor pulled away from the others and sat upright. "That will be all.

For now. But be warned — we are holding another election for sheriff and expect to swear in a new one by next Friday."

Amanda said nothing. It was no more than what she expected and maybe even deserved. As far as she was concerned, Friday couldn't come soon enough.

T-Bone's eyes glittered. "Just so you know, me and the others are formin' our own posse. If Rennick or Barrett or whatever he calls himself is anywhere within a hundred miles, we'll find him."

Amanda left the town council meeting in a hurry. Already, a group of horsemen gathered in front of the butcher shop, including Pepper and other members of his lynch mob.

Her heart sank. Even if, by chance, Rick wasn't injured, he wouldn't get very far without a horse. The sooner she found him, the better.

Quick strides took her to Spirit's side. She unwrapped his reins from the hitching post and glanced around before slapping the horse on his rump. "Go. Find Rick." As soon as he took off, she would follow on her pony.

The horse moved a few steps forward, then stopped and turned his head to look back at her. "Go on," she said. "Find Rick."

The horse stood staring at her as if to say, *Get on, you dummy.*

After several more tries, she gave up. That's all she needed. A stubborn horse.

"Psst."

Amanda swung around, seeking the owner of the whispered voice. Finally, she spotted Mrs. Mooney motioning to her from the side of a building. Thank goodness.

Making sure that no one was watching, Amanda quickly slipped into the alley and was greeted by Scooter and the entire Red Feather posse.

She couldn't believe that Scooter had rounded up the ladies so quickly.

Mrs. Mooney stepped forward, looking unbearably important. As if to acknowledge her self-appointed position, the red quill on her hat stood rigid as a tin soldier.

"As the bank president's wife, I speak for all of us when I say your secret is safe."

"My secret?"

Mrs. Perl looked up from her knitting, but her needles kept moving. "You know . . . Janet."

Amanda glanced at her deputy, who simply shrugged. "You mean . . . you knew all along."

Mrs. Granby held her lorgnette glasses up to her eyes and made a face. "There had to be a reason for his hairy arms."

Becky-Sue giggled.

"Yes, and no woman would stab at her needlework like he did," Miss Read said in a voice once used on disruptive students. "He sewed like he was digging a well."

Amanda couldn't believe it. "You knew it was Rick, and you still went through with it?"

Mrs. Granby sniffed. "We all know that the dear man didn't do the things he's accused of. Since you arranged for his release, we assumed you believe him innocent too."

"That's true," Amanda said. Her heart swelled with gratitude. "Thank you. I didn't mean to involve you all but . . ."

"Don't apologize," Mrs. Perl said, waving a knitting needle. "Helping Mr. Rennick escape was the most exciting thing I've ever done. Wait till my son hears about that!"

"Even so, it was wrong of me to involve you without your permission. I'll take full responsibility and —"

"Nonsense," Mrs. Mooney exclaimed. "We couldn't let a poor innocent man hang."

"We would never have forgiven ourselves," added Mrs. Perl.

Ellie-May Walker nodded in agreement. "Deputy Hobson said you needed our help.

Tell us what you want us to do."

Amanda peered around the corner of the building. The number of men had doubled in the last few minutes and now rose to more than twenty.

Mrs. Mooney peered over her shoulder and gasped. "Is that my Gilbert?"

Next to her, Ellie-May made a rude sound. "How dare my husband take the law into his own hands!" she said, as if she hadn't done the same thing by helping Rick escape.

Mrs. Perl was equally appalled that her husband had joined the bloodthirsty mob. "And he's wearing his good knitted scarf."

"Shh," Amanda said, turning to face her posse. Maybe Rick was miles away; maybe he wasn't. In either case, she had to know for certain.

"Rick's horse returned without a rider, and I'm afraid Rick might be injured."

This brought cries of alarm from the others.

With a finger to her mouth, she reminded them to keep their voices down. "I need to find him. Do you think you can keep Pepper and his gang from following me?"

"We can do that," Scooter exclaimed, and all the women agreed with bobbing heads. "What's the plan?"

Her mind scrambled. She didn't have a plan. "Do you think you can find a way to delay them?"

"How're we gonna do that?" Mrs. Wellmaker asked.

"I've got an idea," Mrs. Mooney said, taking charge. She lowered her voice to a whisper. "We've got a dozen wheeled vehicles, and they've only got a bunch of horses." She smiled. "Come on, gang. Follow me. It's time to circle the wagons."

The women all ran for their wagons and in no time flat had formed a circle around Pepper and his men.

Wasting no time, Amanda took off, urging Spirit along the curving dirt road, past limestone knolls, groves of cypress trees, and stunted oaks. How long her posse could hold Pepper and his lynch mob trapped inside the circle of wagons was anyone's guess, but at least it allowed her a head start. Upon realizing they weren't going anywhere, Pepper and his men rent the air with enough curses to make even a sailor blush. Oh my . . .

Spirit's pounding iron-clad hooves triggered a cloud of blackbirds to rise from the treetops and take flight. On the ground, small rabbits, prairie dogs, and wild turkeys raced for cover. An armadillo scrambled into the bushes.

Halfway to her destination, she spotted vultures circling overhead. Fear unlike any she'd ever known gripped her until she saw the object of their attention was a dead steer.

Riding off, she guided Spirit into a grove of maple trees. She slipped from the saddle, holding the reins, and stood perfectly still, ears alert. A slight breeze rustled the leaves and rippled the tall grass. Overhead, a jaybird hopped from branch to branch, protesting her presence with a raucous cry.

She peered around the tree trunks to the road. In the distance, a train wound its way to town like a slick metallic snake. The lack of dust calmed her worries. So far, no one had followed her.

Satisfied, she left the safety of the grove. A few miles down the road, she reached her destination.

The white stucco building had once been part of a thriving Mexican village. Pulse quickening, she tugged on the reins. Called a cabana, the main building had long been deserted, as had others dotting the area. Now, only ghostly walls and overgrown weeds remained.

Sitting on the open plains, the small village offered both a risk and security. Easily spotted from the road, it also allowed a clear view for miles around. This is where Scooter left Rick's horse and supplies.

She reined Spirit in in front of the archway leading to a courtyard and called Rick's name.

The only answer she received was the sound of the breeze whistling through the deserted corridors. It didn't take long to find the supplies where Scooter had stashed them. It was hard to know if anything had been touched. The bedroll was rolled up, but Rick tended to be neat even while in jail and had straightened his cot every morning.

Frantically, she ran through the buildings, calling to him while something died inside. She'd hoped that Rick was safe somewhere far away by now, though it meant she would never see him again. She wanted to believe he'd already crossed the border into Mexico. Or had even traveled up north.

Now, she didn't know what to think. He couldn't have gotten far without his horse. She stood in the center of the courtyard and tried to decide what to do next. Spirit nickered and pawed the ground.

"What's the matter, boy?"

Then a distant memory came to the fore. Something Rick said. *I'm not worried about him. He'll always find his way back to me.*

Eventually.

Her breath caught in her chest. Shading her eyes, she surveyed the surrounding area. A cloud of dust caught her attention in the far distance. Something . . .

Mounting, she gave Spirit full rein and clicked her tongue. "Find Rick!"

Spirit galloped at full speed for nearly a mile before stopping in front of a thick grove of trees, ears alert.

"What is it, boy?" The horse acted skittish and refused to go any farther. Instead, he shook his head and tugged at the bit.

She slid off the saddle just as gunfire rent the air. A flock of noisy blackbirds rose from the treetops and took to the sky. Spirit bolted, pulling the reins from her hands, and vanished amid the trees.

She called to him beneath her breath. Blast it all. Just her luck to have a horse with a yellow streak.

Gun drawn, she ducked among the trees, senses alert. A slight breeze whispered through the silvery leaves overhead. A twig snapped beneath the sole of her boot, and she froze for a moment before moving again.

Another gunshot ripped through the air, this time closer. Heart pounding, she gripped her weapon with both hands and mentally ran through her checklist. *Arms straight, wrist solid. Don't jerk the trigger . . .*

Suddenly, a hand shot out and grabbed her by the arm.

THIRTY-FIVE

"Rick!" Gasping, Amanda's knees nearly caved beneath her. Never had she been so happy to see anyone in her life. "Where have you been? Spirit —"

He shushed her with a finger to his mouth and pulled her behind a tree with a nod toward her weapon. "I hope that thing is loaded this time," he whispered.

"It is," she whispered back.

"Good. Let me have it."

"Why should I?"

"My aim is better than yours."

"I wouldn't be so sure of that," she said. "I shot Mayor Troutman last night."

He reared back. "You shot the mayor?"

"It was an accident."

"A likely story." He put out his hand. "Let me have the gun before you shoot me."

With a sense of relief, she handed him the Colt, remembering to do it grip first. She searched his face. "When Spirit showed up,

I thought something bad had happened to you."

He checked the gun's chambers. One chamber had been left empty for safety's sake. "Spirit was gone by the time I reached the cabana. I figured someone stole him."

"He wasn't stolen. He came back to town looking for you."

He shook his head. "I should have known." He held out his hand. "Let me have another bullet."

"That's it. I don't have any more."

His eyebrows shot up. "You're jokin', right?" He glanced at her gun belt and groaned. "How do you plan on winnin' a gunfight with only five bullets?"

"My plan was to avoid gunfights," she said. Her shoot-out with Gopher was enough to last a lifetime.

The blast of gunshot made her jump and fall into Rick's arms with a gasp. They both dropped to the ground. Clinging to him, she shook so hard, she could hardly breathe.

"You hurt?" he murmured in her ear, his voice thick with concern.

Head pressed against his chest, she panted for air and struggled to find her voice. "No."

"Okay. Much as I hate to say this, you're gonna have to get off of me."

She lifted her head. "What?" With a start,

she realized she was flat on top of him. "Oh!" She rolled off and hunkered down behind the dense shrubbery.

A second bullet whizzed over their heads, this time, by mere inches.

He yanked the feather from her hat and tossed it into the ground. "May as well wave a flag."

"What's going on?" she whispered. "Who's shooting?"

"Listen."

At first, she heard nothing, but then a lowing sound broke the silence. "All I hear is cattle."

"Not just cattle." He flashed her a meaningful look. "Calves."

She stared at him. "Are you saying . . ."

"Take a look." He scooted over so she could see through the bushes.

In the distance, calves moved inside a barbed wire pen. Her jaw dropped. "Are all those stolen?"

"Bet my boots on it. Heard them bawlin' last night and decided to take a look, and that's when I saw him."

"Who? Who did you see?"

"The man who shot Cooper."

Her eyes widened. "You saw —"

A horrifying thought came to mind. Some serious outlaws were shooting at them, and it was her job as sheriff to do something about it. At the moment, she wasn't even holding the gun.

She forced herself to think like a sheriff. "Whose . . . property is that?" she asked, willing her heart to stop pounding. They were off the beaten track with nothing for miles but the remains of the long-deserted Mexican village. Suddenly, the gun in Rick's hand looked mighty inadequate.

"Soon's we find that out, we'll know who's runnin' the show."

Moving a branch away from his face, his arm brushed hers, and her already fast-beating heart pounded. It was hard to know which was the most disconcerting — Rick's nearness or the men shooting at them.

For the longest while, no more shots were fired. "Do you see anything?" she whispered.

He craned his neck. "Just cattle."

For several long moments, they crouched side by side, still as statues, gazes riveted on the opening in the trees ahead. Seconds passed. Minutes. Her breath whooshed out, and Rick stirred by her side.

She glanced at his profile. "Do . . . do you think they gave up?"

"Probably not."

It wasn't what she wanted to hear. Dying was a real possibility, and all the things still left undone flitted through her mind like leaves in the wind. Far from accomplishing the work she'd set out to do, she regretted the time she'd wasted. She was sorry for giving Papa so much trouble and for not appreciating Mama more. But there was something else she regretted as well. Something that shocked her.

She regretted not having known love, the kind between a man and a woman.

She glanced at Rick's profile and swallowed hard.

"Last night . . ."

"What about last night?"

She drew in a breath and reminded herself that she could die there in the dirt. This was no time for false modesty.

"Why'd you . . . you know?"

The question brought a rush of heat to her face, but the urge to know was greater than any embarrassment. Such things were not discussed in polite company. But huddling on the ground trying not to get shot hardly seemed the time to worry about protocol.

He turned his head to look at her. "Don't tell me you're turning all ladylike on me all of a sudden. Say it. I kissed you, plain and simple."

Nothing plain and simple about it. "Why?"

she asked, trying to sound as matter-of-fact as possible under the circumstances.

"Why'd you think?"

She looked away. "To show gratitude."

"Gratitude?"

She glanced at him askew. "For letting you go."

He gave his head a careless nod. "I guess that was part of it."

She moistened her lips. "What's the other part?"

His gaze dropped to her mouth. "I just wanted to know if your lips tasted as good as they look."

A thrill rushed through her like a speeding train, and she felt all flustered. *Grace and charm, grace and charm, grace and charm.* "And did they?" she asked, unable to curtail her curiosity. "Taste as good?"

"Better." His gaze found hers. "Didn't you ever wonder 'bout my lips?"

"Absolutely not," she said, just as her traitorous gaze lowered to his mouth. Okay, so they both knew she was lying.

She was about to admit as much when something made him stiffen and peer through the bushes. After a while, he said, "Never met anyone who didn't think about kissin'. You sufferin' women really are a different breed."

"It's not that I don't think about . . . things like that. It's just that . . . things like that lead to . . . other things."

"Other things, eh?" He glanced at her. "Would that be so bad?"

"For me, yes." If they were lucky enough to get out of this mess alive, he would leave, and she would go back to doing what she did best: trying to change society. It was foolish to think there was room in her life for anything more. For love.

"You know my work is important to me." When he made no response, she added, "I've been asked to speak at the next suffragist meeting in Austin." She groaned. Being asked to speak there was an honor she might not live long enough to enjoy.

"Congratulations," he said, keeping his gaze focused on the cattle pen.

"If I'm good enough, I may be asked to speak at other places." For reasons she didn't quite understand, it seemed essential to remind herself of the goals she had set for herself. "I might be asked to speak all over the country. Maybe even New York and Boston."

"Is that what you want?" he asked, keeping his attention on the distant calves.

Of course it was what she wanted. It's what she'd always wanted. "Women need a voice, and my lectures will give it to them."

"Don't imagine many outsiders will hear you speak. So you'll be preachin' to the choir."

"Perhaps. At first. But if I could inspire and motivate other suffragists, that would be something." Sensing his disapproval, she added, "Oh, Rick, don't you see the importance? I've worked hard for this." Almost all her life.

He craned his neck above the bushes. "If it'll make you feel any better, we'll just call it a good-bye kiss then and be done with it."

She tried to ignore her sinking heart. "Yes, that's probably for the best." It didn't make her feel better. Truth was, it made her feel worse. A whole lot worse.

"I don't expect we'll see each other again," he said. "After today. 'Less it's at the pearly gates."

She sucked in her breath. "I expect you're right," she whispered.

They stared at each for a full minute. "Stay here," he finally said.

"Wait." She grabbed him by the arm. "Where're you going?"

His gaze dropped to her hand before lifting to meet her eyes. "To circle behind them. Gotta make these five beans count for all they're worth."

She released him. "It's too dangerous."

He arched a dark eyebrow. "Got any other ideas?"

Her mind whirled, and she thought of something. "Spirit."

He frowned. "What are you doin'?"

"I'm calling your horse. We can use him as a distraction." She cupped her hands around her mouth and whispered as loud as she dared. Dogs had good hearing; did horses? "Spirit."

"His name is Killer."

She whipped her head around to gape at him. "What?"

He shrugged. "What can I say? He thinks he's a warhorse."

"Some warhorse. He ran at the first sign of trouble." For all she knew, he was miles away by now.

Just as she was about to call again, a male voice cut through the woods, "Come on out. I know you're in there!"

Rick pulled her down to the ground, and they crawled on their bellies to a fallen log.

"How many are there?" she whispered.

"Three that I know of."

"Not very good odds."

"I've faced worse."

A bullet ripped through the air, barely

missing Rick's hat and hitting a nearby tree.

A gunshot sounded from behind.

Rick grimaced. "We're trapped."

A barrage of gunfire followed. Rick fired back until the deathly sound of a shallow *click* announced his gun was out of bullets.

"Oh no," she whispered.

"This is where it gets interestin'," he said, shoving the empty gun into the waist of his trousers. "Stay here. I think I might have shot one of them. We need his weapon."

"I should go. I'm the sheriff."

"You also got that speech to make in Austin, and I aim to see you live to give it."

Her fingers dug into his arm. "Be careful," she pleaded. The sudden silence made her nervous. If anything happened to him . . . "It could be a trap."

He signaled for her not to move or make a sound.

She held her breath. If only she could mute the thumping of her racing heart.

He removed her hand from his arm, holding it a tad longer than necessary before gently releasing it and moving away. Crouching low, he vanished among the trees.

Gaze riveted to the spot, she pressed a knuckle against her mouth. *Please don't let him do anything foolish . . .*

She heard something and froze. A snap of a twig. A flash of blue. A glint of sun off metal. One of the bad guys was following Rick . . . and it sure did look like Gopher's brother, Buster.

Oh, dear heaven!

She had to do something, but what? A weapon. She needed a weapon. A rock. A stick. Something to create a distraction.

Finding nothing, she quietly left her hiding place, shoulders bent, head low. Somehow, she had to warn Rick. She crept through the woods. She was close enough to see that it was Buster Coldwell, all right. No question.

Buster stopped, and she stopped too, taking cover behind a tree.

If only she could sneak up behind him and clobber him with something — but what?

A nearby rustling startled her, and she jumped. A ropelike tail moved next to a boulder. Fearing it was a rattler, she froze, but a closer look revealed the owner was a "possum on the half shell," otherwise known as an armadillo.

A slow smile curved her mouth. Now *that* would make a great distraction, providing she could get it to run in the right direction. All she had to do was grab the animal by the tail and . . . She blew out her breath

413

and rubbed her hands together. Racing an armadillo to win a contest was one thing, using it to distract a gunman quite another.

You can do it.

Her gaze rolled up to the sky. *Easy for you to say, Grandmama. You're up there, and I'm down here.*

Mouth dry, she crept closer, careful to tread lightly. The creature stopped foraging in the dry leaves, and she stopped, one boot midstep. It turned its head from side to side and, after apparently deciding it was safe, poked its long pointed nose into the leaves again, grunting.

It's now or never. With a swoop of her arm, she grabbed the animal by the armored tail. Trouble was, this armadillo had no intention of playing her game. Instead, it twisted and turned and spun so hard, Amanda had to use both hands to hold it. Even then, her body quivered like a fiddle string.

Before she could set it down on the ground in the right direction, the animal's high-pitched squeals brought Buster running. Bursting through an opening in the trees, gun in hand, he aimed and fired.

The bullet glanced off the armadillo's hard shell. The startled animal popped up with an ear-piercing squeal, almost pulling her arm out of its socket. Screaming,

Amanda let go. The armadillo dropped to the ground with a thud and quickly vanished into the bushes, unharmed.

Then something strange happened. Buster did some sort of a slow-motion dance, and the whites of his eyes showed. His weapon fell from his hand just before his knees buckled and he crashed to the ground.

Rick came running out of the brush. Startled eyes met hers as he dropped to his knees by the man's side. He indicated Buster with a shake of his head. "Who shot him?"

"He shot himself."

"What?"

She explained. "The bullet ricocheted off the armadillo I was holding and hit him in the head." Hands on her waist, she grimaced. "Serves him right for shooting a defenseless animal."

Rick stared at her in astonishment. "Why were you holdin' an armadillo?"

"I planned on using it as a distraction."

"It looks like your plan worked." He chuckled and picked up the man's gun.

"Is . . . is he dead?" she asked.

Rick shook his head. "Looks like the bullet just grazed him, but he hit his head when he fell. Let me have your gun belt."

"What?"

"Your gun belt."

Amanda unbuckled her belt, and Rick used it to secure the unconscious man to a tree.

"Did you find anything?" she asked.

He shook his head. "So what happened to our armored friend?"

She glanced at the bushes to the side. "It took off running. I sure hope it wasn't hurt."

The smile died on Rick's face. "What *I'm* hopin' is that it has a nearby relative."

"What do you mean?"

For answer, she heard a click behind her followed by a male voice. "Drop the gun, or say good-bye to the lady sheriff."

Amanda whirled about. Her startled gaze fell on the barrel of a rifle pointing straight at her. She lifted her eyes. Something about the gunman looked vaguely familiar . . .

And then she knew.

THIRTY-SIX

"Mr. El?" It couldn't be. Her eyes must be deceiving her. Or the light was playing tricks.

Mr. El was . . . well . . . old. But this man stood straight and tall. Without his spectacles, he looked younger, and his hair was brown, not white, and shorter. Only his voice remained the same. That and the gold tooth showing beneath his evil grin told her that either this was Mr. El or a close relative.

"So we meet again," Mr. El said.

"Do you know this man?" Rick asked.

"He lives at the Wendell poor farm. Only he disguises himself as an old man."

Mr. El shrugged. "Brilliant. Wouldn't you say?"

Rick scoffed. "Yeah, especially for a murderer."

Amanda stared at Rick. "Murderer?"

Rick stood rigid. "This is the man I saw

leave Cooper's room the night he was found dead."

"Are you sure?"

"Oh, I'm sure. The hall was dimly lit. I mistook his gold tooth for the glow of a cigarette and his white hair for blond, but it's him all right. That's not all. He shot out of the room like a young man, but when he saw me, he hobbled away."

She nodded. "Like an old man."

Mr. El shrugged. "I didn't expect to see anyone in the hall. I hoped that you'd remember the limp and not the face."

Rick glared at him. "I didn't think much about the limp until last night. You didn't see me, but I saw you herd those cattle. I couldn't believe that someone so old could move so fast. Then you removed that white wig. That's when I knew."

Amanda couldn't believe it. Talk about hiding in plain sight. The things that had previously puzzled her about Mr. El now made perfect sense. His expensive watch. The odd way he moved and never looked anyone in the eye. The cough, which now appeared to be fake, had succeeded in getting him his own room. That way, he could come and go as he pleased.

"So why'd you kill him? Why'd you kill Cooper?" she asked.

Mr. El's lips thinned. "Never said I did."

"You were seen leaving Cooper's room."

"You can't prove a thing, and you aren't gonna be 'round long enough to try."

Amanda's mind scrambled as she recalled her last visit to the poorhouse. "Did you have anything to do with stocking the Wendell pantry?"

Mr. El shrugged. "It was the least I could do to show my appreciation for letting me use it as a hideout."

She doubted appreciation had anything to do with it. More likely he was tired of living off county food rations. "And the story you told about seeing six men steal the horses?"

"There were only three of us."

"Do the Wendells know who you are?" Amanda asked.

"Nobody knows, and I aim on keepin' it that way. That spells trouble for the two of you." His kept his rifle pointed straight at her. "Sorry, Sheriff. But a man's got to do what a man's got to do."

A loud boom shook the ground, and something streaked by them, barely missing Mr. El. The black object — a cannonball — hit a tree and fell to the ground, creating a crater.

Taking full advantage of the distraction, Rick made a diving leap toward Mr. El, and the two wrestled for the weapon. It was only after another cannonball whizzed by that Mr. El took off running like a scared rabbit.

Rick grabbed Amanda by the arm, and they both fell to the ground.

Huddled next to his side, Amanda thought of something and burst out laughing.

He looked at her as if she'd lost her mind. "What's so funny?"

She pointed through a small opening in the trees. "I know who's firing those cannons. It's the Rain King, and we're in for another rainstorm."

He rolled his eyes. "That's all we need." Rising, he helped her to her feet. He picked Mr. El's rifle off the ground and started through the woods. "Come on before the king fires again."

Rick held her hand as they cautiously emerged from the thick growth of trees. She blinked against the sun that suddenly peered through the clouds. That's when she got the biggest shock of her life. The two remaining cattle rustlers were on their knees, surrounded by Deputy Hobson and her Red Feather posse.

Holding Mr. El at bay with his Colt, Scooter greeted her with a grin. "Sure is good to see you, Sheriff."

"Good to see you too," she said. "But

what are you all doing here?"

"We had just arrived at the deserted Mexican village when we saw Spirit run by with an empty saddle," Scooter explained.

"Then we heard gunfire," Becky-Sue added and giggled. "So we came running."

"But you could have all been shot," Amanda said. "I mean . . . we're talking serious criminals here."

"Yes," Mrs. Mooney said with a nod. "But Deputy Hobson told us it was better to be taken by a big crocodile than eaten by little fish."

Shaking her head in wonder, Amanda's gaze swung to the captives who glared back at her. That a Coldwell was involved hadn't surprised her; seeing John Freeman did, though it probably shouldn't have. Evidently, he'd lied to his wife about the bank holdup being his one and only crime.

Mrs. Perl had wrapped John in red yarn until he couldn't move his arms. The red wool against his white shirt turned him into what looked like a living barber pole.

Mrs. Mooney looked unbearably smug. "As the bank president's wife, I'm putting the two of you under arrest."

"You can't arrest anyone, Maude," Mrs. Granby said. "You're not the sheriff."

"That's your job," Rick said, turning to

Amanda.

Never did she relish a job more, but first things first. "Not so fast," she said. She walked up to Mr. El. He didn't look so cocky now. "I asked you before and I'll ask you again. Why'd you kill Cooper?"

"I told you I didn't kill him. He did." He tossed his head in the direction of Freeman.

Amanda stepped in front of John. "Why'd you kill him?" For Mary-Louise and her son's sake, she hoped he didn't.

John glared at her. "I didn't kill him. Buster did."

Had Buster been conscious, he probably would point his finger back at Mr. El.

She turned to Scooter. "Empty their pockets."

"Yes, sir, Sheriff." Her deputy holstered his gun and started on John Freeman's pockets. He tossed coins, a money clip, wire cutters, and spare bullets onto the ground.

He then started on Mr. El's pockets, pulling out a handkerchief, keys, a rabbit foot, and hard candy. "Check his shirt pocket," she said.

Scooter stuck his fingers into the pocket and pulled out a small peacock feather.

It was all Amanda needed to see. She stood directly in front of the Welshman, hands at her waist. "I repeat. Why'd you kill

Cooper?" He started to deny it, but she stopped him. "Save your breath. Not only do I have a witness, but now I have actual proof."

"What kind of proof?"

"You'll find out in court."

His lip curled, and the pupils of his eyes dilated with hate. "We did all the work, and Cooper reaped the benefits."

"Oh, wow!" Scooter said. "That sounds like a real confession."

Rick frowned. "So Cooper was the brains behind the crime spree?"

Freeman made a face. "Until he got greedy and started demanding more than his share. That's why we held back . . ."

Amanda completed his sentence. "The loot stolen from the bank." That explained why Mary-Louise found a bag of money hidden in the house.

Mr. El sneered. "We were supposed to be living it up in Europe by now, but Cooper kept holdin' out on us. Said it wasn't time to leave till he said so. Then we found out he blew all our hard-earned money on the faro tables."

"By hard-earned, I take it you mean robbing stages and banks," Amanda said.

"Don't forget cattle rustlin'," Rick added. "It sounds to me like Cooper got the best of the deal."

"What do you mean?" Freeman asked.

"He's dead, and you're not."

Amanda stepped forward. "I'm placing you both under arrest for murder, horse and cattle theft, stage robbery, and animal cruelty." Someone had to pay for practically scaring an armadillo out of its armored wits.

She wanted to add "and taking advantage of Wendell hospitality," but far as she knew, there was no law against that.

"How'd you know about the stage?" John Freeman asked.

She took the peacock feather from Scooter. She was willing to bet that the feather came from the hat that blew off her head during the attempted holdup. Just like the feathers found in Cooper's room and Pepper's saloon.

She slipped the feather in her vest pocket. "A little birdie told me," she said with a wry smile. "Make that a big birdie."

After Amanda, Rick, Hobson, and the posse had collected Buster and hauled the prisoners a mile up the road where the wagons and horses had been left, Pepper and his lynch mob caught up to them.

Her posse had tricked them into going on a wild-goose chase, and Pepper looked like he was about to spit nails. His face practically turned purple when he spotted Rick leaning against a tree with a casual lack of concern.

"What in the name of Sam Hill is going on? Why are these men handcuffed?" He pointed at Rick. "And why isn't he?"

Amanda quickly explained everything that had happened. Well, almost everything. She left out the part about the armadillo.

Pepper listened with a look of disbelief. "That sounds like a lot of bull," he said, aiming his gun at Rick. "A jury found you guilty, and that's good enough for me." He signaled to his men. "Get the rope. Since the sheriff can't do her job, it looks like it's up to us."

Amanda's heart practically stood still. But then the most unexpected thing happened. John stepped forward and gave a full confession. "Everything Amanda said is true," he said, sounding more like her old friend than an outlaw.

Pepper frowned. "What about him?" he asked, tossing a nod at Rick.

John's gaze traveled to Rick and back again. "Mr. El killed Cooper. Nobody else." He sounded relieved to get it off his chest.

Oddly enough, Amanda felt sorry for him. He'd obviously never thought things would turn out so badly. Certainly, he had no idea that his decision to turn to theft would involve murder.

Mayor Troutman adjusted his sling. "That's good enough for me," he said. "Sorry, gentleman, but there'll be no hangings today."

Pepper lowered his gun, but he didn't look happy about it.

Mr. Mooney spoke up. "As the president of the bank, I say we give these little ladies a round of applause."

"I ain't givin' 'em nothin'." Pepper groused.

Ignoring him, T-Bone pulled off his hat. "I have to say, Amanda, you ain't such a bad sheriff after all."

Amanda smiled. That was high praise coming from the butcher. "Why, thank you, T-Bone." Aware that Rick was watching her, she felt warm currents inch up her neck. "I just want to say that I'm the one who let Rick go. I believed him innocent of the charges lodged against him, and it turns out I was right."

Mr. Steele stepped forward. "We're grateful that you did. You saved us from sendin' an innocent man to the great beyond before his time."

"You can say that agin." Mr. Perl gave his knitted scarf a tug. "Finally, Two-Time's got itself a decent sheriff."

"Had," Amanda said. "Soon as I lock these hombres up, I'm handing in my resignation." Even Rick looked surprised by her announcement.

"You can't do that," Mrs. Mooney said. She nudged her husband's arm with her elbow. "You're the bank president. Tell her she can't do that."

"You're darn tootin' she can't!" T-Bone agreed.

Amanda laughed. Things sure had taken an unexpected turn. Now people were actually begging her to stay. Incredible.

"I have to admit being the sheriff had its moments, but . . ." Facing death had made her realize how fragile life really was. She'd been shot at on two separate occasions as sheriff, and frankly, that was more than she'd bargained for. As for carrying out a hanging . . . she'd sooner walk on fire. And she still had the dreaded task of telling Mary-Louise the full extent of John's involvement.

"I think the town would do better with another sheriff." One with a stronger stomach.

She looked straight at Deputy Hobson when she said it. If he could just curb his enthusiasm a bit, he would make a fine sheriff. But he probably had little chance of landing the job. No doubt T-Bone and the rest were thinking of running for sheriff themselves.

"Does this mean we get our wives back in the kitchen where they belong?" T-Bone's horseshoe mustache twitched as he cast a beseeching look at his wife.

Mr. Perl blew out his breath. "That's what I want to know."

Mr. Walker inched up to his gun-toting wife. "So what's it gonna be, Ellie-May? Me or them?"

Ellie-May opened her mouth to say something, but Mrs. Mooney stopped her. "As the bank president's wife, I say we return to our kitchens on one condition."

T-Bone scratched his head, and Mr. Mooney drew his eyebrows together.

"Well, speak up," Mr. Steele said with an impatient wave of his anvil-sized hand. "What is it?"

"The condition," Mrs. Mooney said, staring down her nose, "is that we women are allowed to vote for the next sheriff."

Smiling to herself, Amanda met Rick's gaze. Amusement danced in his eyes, and he winked at her. "Sounds like a great compromise to me," he said.

"Now wait just a darn minute," Mr.

Mooney said, but his objections were over-ruled by the other men.

"If letting the women vote for the next sheriff puts supper back on the table, I say go for it!" Mr. Granby shouted, rubbing his stomach and no doubt anticipating his next meal.

After much discussion, the majority agreed with Mrs. Mooney's proposal, which pretty much assured Scooter's win.

Becky-Sue threw convention to the winds by throwing her arms around Scooter. He got all red in the face and seemed momen-tarily speechless but soon recovered.

"Oh, wow!" he said.

THIRTY-SEVEN

That night, the citizens of Two-Time celebrated by turning the town into one gigantic party. Music and laughter filled the air as couples danced the length of Main Street. Scooter's father provided trays of baked goods, and the ladies of the Tuesday Afternoon Quilting Bee supplied pitchers of lemonade.

Amanda couldn't stop smiling, even during the mayor's long, drawn-out speech. Who would have thought that things would turn out so well? Some of the stolen cattle and horses would soon be returned to their rightful owners. The crime spree that had plagued Two-Time these last few months had now come to an end.

That wasn't all. Husbands had their wives back, but nothing would ever be the same. Having had a taste of excitement, none of the women wanted to go back to the way things were. Almost all of them had signed up to join the suffragist group, and Amanda couldn't be happier.

Best of all, Rick was a free man. If only it wasn't for Mary-Louise, Amanda's happiness would be complete. The bank was the big loser, as none of the stolen money had been recovered. No doubt it had all gone up in smoke at the Freeman farm. Having to tell Mary-Louise the extent of her husband's criminal activities had been one of the hardest things Amanda ever had to do, and it near broke her heart. Fortunately, she was able to tell Mary-Louise that John had acted honorably at the end. His full confession had helped to exonerate Rick, and for that, Amanda would always be grateful.

The mayor continued to speak, ignoring all efforts to stop him. His arm still in a sling, he took full credit for the way things turned out.

Amanda didn't care. It was enough knowing that the crime spree was over and people felt safe again.

Mrs. Mooney gave a disgusted sigh. "The way he's praising himself, you'd think he was speaking at his own funeral."

The mayor might have gone on all night had Mr. Pendergrass not stolen his thunder by appearing in the buff. No one objected when the minister's wife chased the naked man down the street yelling, "Stop, or I'll have your hide!"

By the time the ruckus was over, the mayor had lost his audience.

Amanda was still thinking about the unexpected turn of events when Rick snuck up behind her and slid his hands around her waist. "May I have this dance?"

Swinging around in the circle of his arms, she gazed up at him, and her heart felt like it had wings. "I thought you'd never ask," she said.

He arched a brow. "Why so sad?"

"I was just thinking about Mary-Louise. I can't imagine what she must be going through right now."

"Yeah, it's gotta be tough."

Nodding, she melted against him. She couldn't take her eyes off him. His strong physique had attracted her from the very start. She especially liked the way his muscles shaped his arms and legs. But now that she knew the pleasure those same arms could bring when wrapped firmly around her, there was so much more to admire.

And his lips . . . She'd sampled those velvet-soft lips of his and wanted more. So much more.

A warm glow threatened to set her body

on fire, and laughter bubbled out of her.

He arched his eyebrows. "What's so funny?"

"You're supposed to move your feet. You dance like you're still behind bars."

He laughed too. "Sorry, but these feet are better suited for stirrups."

She exhaled with pure happiness. "Oh, Rick. I can't believe how things worked out."

His lopsided grin stole her breath away. "I'm just glad that they did, and I owe it all to you."

"Not all of it," she said. "I'm not sure what would have happened had Scooter and my posse not shown up when they did."

"And don't forget that Rain King fellow and your armadillo friend," he added.

"Oh, no, we can't forget them." So far, the Rain King's cannon had failed to bring a single drop of rain. She suddenly thought of something. "Now that you're a free man, I guess you'll want me to return Spirit."

"You mean Killer the warhorse?"

She laughed. "I mean the horse that took off so fast at the start of trouble, he left his shadow behind."

"He didn't take off. He went to get help."

"Help, eh?"

"It worked, didn't it? If it weren't for

Killer, you might never have found me."

"Can't argue with you there," she said.

He gazed down at her. "Now that you're no longer the sheriff, I guess you won't need him anymore."

"Guess not," she said. Though riding her pony would take some getting used to. "Now I can concentrate on writing my speech for the suffragist convention. Wait till they hear what happened here in Two-Time. Oh, Rick! Things are bound to be different now. I mean, women get to vote for the next sheriff. Who would have thought such a thing possible?"

"Who indeed."

"Maybe next time, they'll get to vote for the mayor and . . ." On and on she went, joy bubbling out like water from a spring. "And the best thing of all," she added without stopping to take a breath. "All my posse members joined my suffragist group. They'll no longer be fighting crime, but they'll be fighting for a different type of justice."

"Imagine that."

It was late by the time the music stopped. Couples, including Scooter and Becky-Sue, drifted away, walking hand in hand.

Rick escorted Amanda to her parents'

house on Peaceful Lane. He'd seemed especially quiet during the celebrations. But considering all that had happened, that wasn't too surprising. He had gone from a man condemned to hang to being somewhat of a hero.

"So what do you plan on doing now?" she asked when they'd stopped just short of her front porch.

"I'm heading to the Panhandle. Hope to hire on as a wrangler there. Once I get my bearings, I plan on startin' a horse ranch of my own."

Her earlier joy left like a speeding train. She swallowed hard and tried to be happy for him. If only it didn't feel like her heart had suddenly cracked down the middle. Even the bright, starry sky had suddenly lost its luster.

"A horse ranch?" She could hardly form the words around the lump in her throat. "Better watch it. Warhorse might get jealous."

"Think so, eh?"

They stared at each other. *Don't go,* her heart cried out. *Please don't go.* "W-when are you leaving?" she asked. *Why are you leaving?*

"Tomorrow."

She sucked in her breath. "So . . . so soon?"

He looked away. "Nothin' keeping me here."

She struggled not to show how much his words hurt. *Grace and charm, grace and charm, grace and . . .*

"Are you saying that Mrs. Granby's fudge isn't enough?" How normal she sounded. How in control. No one would ever guess that inside, she was dying.

He met her gaze and chuckled. "Yeah, I'll miss that for sure."

She searched his face. *What else will you miss?* Catching herself staring, she did a mental shake. "You've made a lot of friends here."

"I know, but . . . it's better this way. You and me . . ." She heard his intake of breath, and it matched her own. "We have different goals," he said at last. "I see nothin' but trouble ahead for us."

She moistened her lips. "Because of my suffragist work?"

"That and . . . you want to change the world. I only want to change a few hundred acres."

"So you're saying we can't be . . . friends?" she asked, battling to control the quiver in her voice.

He rubbed his chin. "Sometimes, a dream becomes so big, there's no room for anythin' else, friendship included. My mother —"

She cut him off with a shake of the head. "I'm not like your mother. I would never turn my back on my responsibilities. Certainly, I would never leave a child!"

The passion in her voice seemed to surprise him, and he stared at her with raised eyebrows.

"I can change, Rick," she said in a softer, quieter voice. "I know I can." But even as she said it, she wondered if that was true.

His eyes grew dark with sadness. "That's the crazy part. I don't want you to change. I love you just the way you are."

Her breath caught in her throat. Never had three little words affected her so deeply. "I love you the way you are too," she whispered.

His eyes flared with smoldering flames, startling her with their intensity. He shrugged in mock resignation. "Don't we make a fine couple?"

Only we don't, she thought and swallowed the sob in her throat. Rick was leaving, and life would go on without him. Life always went on. Oh, but how she wished things could be different. If only she could be more like her sisters. If only he wasn't so against women like her . . .

Gazing deep into her eyes, he cupped her chin and tilted her head upward. Their mouths met, and the sweet tenderness of his lips sent waves of desire spiraling through her.

Giving in to the divine ecstasy he offered, she rose on tiptoes to deepen the kiss. If this was to be their last kiss, by George, she meant to make the most of it.

The sudden urgency of his kiss suggested a similar thought had crossed his mind. Crushing her to him, his lips grew ever more persuasive, and her senses reeled. Nothing experienced in the past — none of the stolen kisses of her youth — compared in scope to this one. How was it possible that a kiss could both quench an inner need and leave her hankering for more? Much more.

The door flew open to her father's voice. "Amanda? Is that you?"

They drew apart like two guilty children, the space between them now torture.

Her lips still warm and moist and tingling with pleasure, she managed a breathless reply. "Yes, Papa. I'll be there in a minute." She turned back to Rick. "I better go," she whispered. "I can vote in the next election, but Papa still rules the roost."

"I guess this is good-bye then," he said, his voice thick with emotion.

Her heart squeezed tight. Never had a single word sounded so final. "Maybe . . . maybe you'll come back for a visit."

"Maybe." They stood mere inches apart, but it felt like they were on different continents.

"Good luck with your speech," he said.

She blinked back the threatening tears. "Good luck with your horse ranch."

"Just so you know, I admire what you're doin'. All that sufferin' stuff . . ."

"Amanda!"

"Coming, Papa."

Rick squeezed her elbow, the warmth of his touch sending flames of longing rushing through her. "Take care of yourself, Amanda. And just remember: I'll always be rootin' for you."

Backing away, she held him in her vision until the tears hid him from view. Only then did she turn and run to the house.

As Amanda hastened away, Rick felt like his whole world had collapsed. With a quick wave, she vanished inside, and he nearly doubled over with pain. The soft thud of the closing door wouldn't have sounded more final had it been a coffin lid.

He was tempted to chase after her, but that would have been a mistake. For both of them. It would only end in disaster. It hurt like the dickens, but better now than later. Had his father walked away in the beginning, he would have saved himself years of heartache. Instead, he married a woman totally unsuited to marriage and family. A woman who would eventually walk away from him and his two small children and never look back. How Rick hated what his mother had done to him. To the whole family. Hated how her actions dictated his life, even now.

Hands in his pockets, he started down the street. No sense dwelling on the past. At last, he was exonerated. The man who had killed his wife was dead. The nightmare was over. He was a free man. He could hardly wait to break the news to his sister.

Rick inhaled the night air, but the gnawing pain in his chest was hard to ignore. He should be happy. Ecstatic. Jumping with joy. Instead, he felt . . . what? Lost. Miserable. Lonely. Dejected.

I love you the way you are too.

The memory of those soft-spoken words pierced his heart. Of all the dumb, stupid, idiotic things he could have done, falling in love with Amanda Lockwood had to be the worst.

Even the night sky reminded him of her. Whenever she spoke of her suffering work, her eyes shone as bright as any star.

He once asked why his father didn't stop his mother from leaving. His father replied that it would be easier to hold back the wind. As a child, the answer made little sense, but now, he understood.

The single-minded purpose driving Amanda was as strong as any hurricane. A woman with such ambitious goals would never settle for the quiet life he longed for. She dreamed of changing the world; his dreams were far more modest. Home, family, horses . . . the good life.

Growing up, he thought he was like his mother, with the same restless spirit. But it turned out he was more like his father than he knew. Prison could change a man in unexpected ways. Or maybe it just stripped away all pretenses, revealing the true self.

If only he could stop thinking of Amanda's sweet smile or the alluring way she tilted her head. Or forget the soft feel of her lips and velvet smoothness of her touch. Even the craziness and havoc she created intrigued him and, at times, made him laugh and love her more.

He groaned. Here he went again. Dwelling on things best left behind. In an effort to erase the painful memories, he picked up his pace, pounding the ground with his peg-heeled boots.

Horses, that's what he had to think about. Once he went back to raising horses, he would no longer think of Amanda Lockwood. She had her priorities, and he had his.

And that's the way it was meant to be.

THIRTY-EIGHT

Amanda was the lone passenger on the stagecoach that hot summer day in June. That was a very good thing; she had much on her mind and was in no mood for company.

The trip to Austin and the suffragist meeting had been a tremendous success. At last, she had accomplished something worth sharing. The applause and cheers of congratulations still rang in her ears. But the real satisfaction came from knowing what her short stint as sheriff did for the town.

Three of the worst outlaws Two-Time had ever known were now behind bars, and the gang leader, Cooper, was dead. That wasn't all. Women had turned out in droves to cast votes for her replacement. After having a say in civic affairs, they were no longer willing to go back to being second-rate citizens. The men of Two-Time had been warned — things would be different from now on.

Best of all, Sheriff Scooter Hobson was doing a terrific job of keeping law and order, though he still tended to hoot and holler in delight whenever he made an arrest.

Even Lucy Stone was impressed by the way things had turned out. Amanda sighed. If only . . .

She shook her head. No, everything *was* perfect. She couldn't be happier. *Happy, happy, happy.*

Pulling a handkerchief out of the sleeve of her blue traveling suit, she dabbed at her eyes. *Happy, happy, happy!*

But she couldn't smother the thought. *If only* Rick was waiting to share her success. Without someone to share it with, the applause, the congratulations — all of it — rang hollow.

Closing her eyes, she sighed. No sense wishing things could be different. They wanted different things from life. As much as she understood his feelings, it still hurt. It hurt a lot.

Oh God, when would the pain go away so she could once again feel like herself? How long before the tears stopped? Before the broken pieces of her heart stopped cutting into her very soul?

When she left Two-Time a week ago, she

honestly thought that the excitement of being with like minds would put her feelings in perspective. She fully expected to return home with a new sense of purpose and commitment. But rather than pick up her spirits, the trip to Austin only made her feel worse.

That was the least of it. She couldn't concentrate. Even Lucy Stone's rousing speech had barely made an impact. Later, Amanda was hard-pressed to recall a single word that anyone had said. She barely remembered giving her own speech.

The worst part was bursting into tears at the most inopportune moments. Fortunately, the others believed her when she said she was just touched by all that been accomplished these last three months. Not just by her but others. Marilyn Hock even got her company to raise women's pay, though it was still way below what men were paid.

Now, sniffling into her handkerchief, she promised herself no more tears. The next suffragist meeting was in September, and there was still work to be done.

Tucking her handkerchief away, Amanda stared out the stage window. *Happy, happy, happy.* The scenery blurred past. *Happy, happy, happy.*

The stagecoach driver's voice brought her

out of her reverie. For some reason, he was urging the horses to go faster, and the stage picked up speed. Oh no! Not again. Not more bandits!

Alarmed, she flew to the window. The coach hit a bump, and she almost lost her balance. Grabbing hold of the windowsill, she pushed her head between the leather curtains. The wind tossed sand and grit in her face and tugged at her good peacock hat.

Far as she could tell, no one was chasing them. Then why . . .

The stage lurched around a boulder, forcing her to hold on tight.

"Stop!" she yelled, throwing herself onto the seat. Was the man off his rails? "Stop this minute!"

Banging on the ceiling with her parasol, she pleaded with the driver to stop or at least slow down. But the stage kept going, tossing her from one side to the other like a cork in a stormy sea.

"Ooh. There better be bandits chasing us, or I'll have your head! You . . . you . . ." She called him every name she could think of.

Finally, mercifully, the stage rolled to a stop.

Gasping for air, she righted her hat and straightened her skirt. "It's about time."

The door flew open, and Bullwhip's head appeared. He glowered at her over his full red beard. "Call me names, will ya?"

"No more than what you deserve!" she shot back. "Why were you driving like a . . . Wait. What are you doing?"

She practically fell out of the coach in her hurry to stop him, but it was too late. He'd already tossed her traveling trunk from the roof of the stage and into the dirt.

"You can't leave me out here!"

"Wanna bet?"

He slammed the door shut and climbed onto the driver's seat.

"Wait!" she cried. Oh fudge. She would have to apologize to the man. But before she could bring herself to do the dreaded thing, he drove off, leaving her stranded in the middle of nowhere.

She watched the fast-departing stage, seething with fury. "Just wait!" she yelled after him, tossing her parasol to the ground.

The man had some nerve, that's for sure. If they didn't finish the railroad line between Austin and Two-Time soon, she'd be tempted to lay the track herself. Just so she'd never have to deal with the temperamental stagecoach driver again.

Now what would she do?

Hands at her waist, she turned slowly and

447

stopped. She blinked, and her heart practically stood still. Was that . . . No, no, it couldn't be. She was seeing things.

"Rick?" she whispered in disbelief, then yelled at the top of her lungs. "Rick!"

Ignoring the six-inch rule, she hiked up her skirts, revealing a shocking display of red satin bloomers beneath the hem. But she didn't care. She ran so fast, her high-button shoes barely touched the ground.

Face shaded by his wide-brimmed hat, Rick greeted her with a grin as wide as the Texas sky.

Shamelessly, she ran into his open arms and sent his hat flying.

His lips brushed her forehead, her nose, and finally settled on her mouth. With a happy sigh, she flung her arms around his neck to shower him with kisses of her own.

By the time he finally pulled back, they were both out of breath.

"What are you doing here?" she asked when at last her brain kicked in. A short distance away, Spirit (she couldn't bring herself to call him Killer) was hitched to a wagon. "I thought you'd left and —" Confused, she dropped her arms and stepped back to gaze at the thing by his side. "And why is my hope chest here?"

"Woodman did a fine job of fixin' the

damage, don't you think?" He indicated the new handle on the side and ran his hand across the newly varnished top. "You'd never know it was shot at twice and barely survived a fire."

"No, you wouldn't," she said, puzzled. "But that still doesn't explain . . ." She shook her head in confusion. She must be dreaming. Nothing else made sense.

He laughed. "I wish you could have seen the look on your face when Bullwhip tossed you out bag and baggage."

Something dawned on her, and she slanted a look of suspicion at him. "You didn't —"

He scooped up his hat and placed it on his head. "Cost me a pretty penny to get him to leave you out here in the wilderness."

"But . . . but why?"

He grew serious. "You and me have some discussin' to do, and I don't aim on havin' any interruptions."

His heated gaze made her quiver with anticipation. "What . . . what kind of dis-cussing?"

Seating himself on the hope chest, he reached for her hand and pulled her down by his side. He stared at her palm. "I told you I'd never get entangled with an inde-pendent woman."

"Yes. Yes, you did say that. Several times

in fact."

"Well . . ." He cleared his throat and released her hand. "While you were gone, I did some thinkin'."

"Oh, Rick, I did some thinking too."

He touched a finger to her lips. "This is my party, so I get to talk first."

"But why here?" Cactus and yuccas were all the eye could see for miles around. "In the middle of nowhere?"

"This isn't nowhere. This is where I first fell in love with you. Only I was too pigheaded to know it at the time."

Her heart skipped a beat. He'd mentioned *love* before, but not with such urgency or passion. Not with such depth of emotion.

"Oh, Rick . . ." Feelings she'd tried to ignore rose to the surface. She had so much she wanted to say, but words failed her. When had she first fallen in love with him? Hard to know. Love had somehow snuck up on her when she least expected it. In some ways, it felt like she'd loved him all her life.

"When I first saw you standin' there beside your hope-a-thingie" — he pointed to the place beside the road — "I thought you were a mirage." He chuckled. "You looked horn-tossin' mad."

She laughed at the memory. "That . . . that was also the day I ran for sheriff."

"Little did I know at the time how that would change my life."

"Both our lives," she whispered.

Being sheriff gave her a unique perspective that enabled her to take a long hard look at herself. She thought she knew what she wanted out of life. How foolish of her to think that her charitable causes and suffragist work would be enough. She now knew she wanted more — so much more than she'd ever imagined. She wanted a husband and children too; she wanted to love and be loved. She wanted a personal life as well as a public one. But was such a thing possible?

"These last couple of weeks . . ." He shook his head. "Each day we were apart felt like a year."

"The days were long for me too. I thought they'd never end."

"I couldn't sleep," he said.

She nodded. "I couldn't eat."

"I couldn't think of anythin' but you."

She blinked in an effort to keep the tears from falling. "I almost flubbed my speech. I kept wishing you were in the audience."

His eyes smoldered. "I like myself a whole lot better when I'm with you."

She drew in her breath. "I like us too." Before meeting him, she saw everything that was wrong with the world, everything that needed fixing. Now, she saw everything that was right too.

He heaved a sigh. "Sounds like you and me have it bad."

"Real bad," she agreed.

He arched a dark eyebrow. "The question now is what are we gonna do 'bout it?"

She moistened her lips. "I . . . I could give up my work." Certainly, she could give up traveling. It would cause her great pain, but no more so than losing him.

"I got a better idea. If you could give this cowpoke a chance . . . I'll try my darndest not to complain when you're off givin' speeches. The only thing I ask in return is your promise to always come back to me. Because if I lost you . . ." He grimaced as if the thought was unbearable.

She held her breath. Was he saying what she hoped he was saying? *If this is a dream, please, no one wake me.* She didn't even know she was crying until he handed her a clean handkerchief.

Air rushed out of her lungs as she dabbed away her tears. "Does this mean you plan on staying in Two-Time?"

"A lot depends on whether the bank approves a loan so I can start my horse ranch here."

"Mr. Mooney will. I know he will. That is, if he wants his meals on the table."

Rick laughed and brushed a peacock feather away from his face. "Let's hope it doesn't come to that."

"Oh, Rick . . . I've been such an awful fool. I thought being a modern, independent woman meant I had to turn my back on convention. But what it really means is I get to choose what's right for me. And Rick Barrett, I choose you."

The warmth and desire in his eyes almost took her breath away. "You don't know how much it means to hear you say that. I choose you too."

"And that business about coming back to you . . . I don't need to make that promise, because I don't intend to ever leave you. Not for a day. Not for an hour. Not even for a minute."

He drew back. "Don't make promises you can't keep. I could never ask you to sacrifice your sufferin' work for me."

"Sacrifice? Oh, no, Rick. Anything I do for you would be done out of love, not sacrifice."

At last, she understood why Mama always put Papa and her girls first; why Josie had so willingly left everything behind to travel to Arizona for Ralph's health; why Meg would follow Grant to the moon if necessary. Amanda now knew what it meant to be madly, deliciously, head over heels in love. She *would* find a way to have it all.

"What about your speeches?" Rick asked.

"I'll write them and have someone else cross the States to deliver them. I love traveling through Texas, and I'll want to continue working with the groups here, but watching Josie go, I realized I didn't *want* to leave home." She thought of something. "I'll ask Miss Read. As a schoolteacher, she must have given lots of speeches. She once mentioned she would so enjoy traveling and meeting new people and . . ." On and on she went as new ideas occurred to her.

A look of approval crossed his face. "You've got it all planned, don't you?"

"Not all, but I will." Now that she thought of it, she could get several people to deliver her speeches. Her messages could spread across the country without her ever leaving the home and family she loved.

"Oh, Rick, this will work, I know it will." A similar plan worked for Elizabeth Cady Stanton, who stayed home with her family and put pen to paper. So why wouldn't it work for her?

Instead of taking her in his arms as she hoped, he surprised her by jumping to his feet. "I'm mighty glad to hear that, or I might have been in trouble."

Confused, she stared up him. "Why would you be in trouble?"

"For puttin' the cart before the horse."

She laughed. "I haven't the slightest idea what you're talking about."

He pulled her to her feet and pointed to the hope chest.

She bent over for a better look, but there was no mistake. Beneath the four initials of her grandmother, mother, and sisters, were two freshly carved letters that read *A. L.* Gasping, she looked up.

He shrugged. "Woodman was havin' trouble with that particular spot, and I suggested he hide the damage by carvin' your initials. It would save us the trouble of havin' to do it later."

She stared at him. "Later?"

He grinned and rubbed the back of his neck. "You know. When we tie the knot." He gave a sheepish grin. "I know . . . I know . . . You've got speeches to write and sufferin' women to organize and . . ."

"You've got a horse ranch to run," she said.

"Yeah, well . . ." He gazed deep into her eyes. "Speakin' of horses, the best kind are not the ones that walk behind or ahead. The best ones walk by your side. I reckon the same is true for people, and that's what I aim to do. Even if it means joinin' your sufferin' group. You won't find anyone who will love you more than me. So what do you say? Are we in for the long haul?"

Joy unlike any she'd ever known filled her heart until she thought her chest would burst. Still, she held back. She was surprised to learn that in matters of the heart, she was every bit as old-fashioned and traditional as her sisters.

"Was there a proper proposal in there somewhere?" she asked with a coquettish turn of the head.

He arched a dark eyebrow. "You're not turnin' all ladylike on me now, are you?"

"Certainly not." She pointed to the ground. She was willing to compromise on many things, but this moment would remain with her forever and couldn't be rushed. "But I have my standards."

"Do you now?" Grinning, he pulled off his hat and dropped to one knee. "Amanda Lockwood, would you do me the honor of marryin' this ol' horse wrangler?"

"Oh, yes, yes, yes!" She threw her arm around his neck and practically knocked him backward in her effort to kiss him ever so thoroughly on the lips.

Like she said, she had her standards.

Epilogue

A couple of days later, Amanda and Rick stood in the newly painted sheriff's office sharing the happy news of their betrothal with the now-disbanded Red Feather posse.

Scooter yelled, "Hold it!"

She turned and laughed. Two-Time's newest sheriff stood behind his camera. With a boisterous whoop, he pulled a black cloth over his head and ducked. "Say cabbage."

She gazed up at Rick. Mr. Mooney, with some pressure from his wife, had approved Rick's loan, and he'd already made an offer on some lovely property outside of town.

"I have a better idea for softening the mouth," she whispered. And with that, she rose on tiptoes to kiss him. Such a bold move would make even a suffragist blush, but then, it had already been determined that she was no lady.

Mrs. Perl giggled and dropped a stitch.

Becky-Sue got all red in the face. Miss Read, who had been practicing her suffragist speech, stopped to stare. Mrs. Mooney beamed with approval, and the other women averted their eyes. But no one objected, not even when Amanda kissed Rick a second and third time.

"Oh, wow!" Scooter called from beneath the black cloth. "Shall I shoot? Shall I shoot?"

Amanda pulled her mouth away from Rick's warm lips and gazed deep into his eyes. "Yes, Scooter, you can most definitely shoot."

AUTHOR'S NOTE

Dear Reader,

I do so hope you enjoyed Amanda and Rick's story.

Amanda had good reason to worry about the feathered hat craze that hit the country in the late 1800s. Believe it or not, there was a plume rush in effect, and it rivaled even those nineteenth-century gold rushes. Hats sporting feathers and, in some cases, entire birds became so widespread that by the middle of the 1880s, five million birds a year were killed by the millinery industry to keep up with the demand.

Egrets and herons provided the most popular feathers, especially the "bridal feathers" grown during mating season. But even tree sparrows and woodpeckers weren't safe from plume hunters.

Things became so bad that when ornithologist Frank Chapman walked down the streets of Manhattan in 1886, he documented forty species of birds — not in the trees or sky, but perched upon women's heads.

In that same year, bird feathers were selling for more than twenty dollars an ounce (more than five hundred dollars in today's currency). This increased to thirty-two dollars an ounce during the start of the twentieth century, which made them worth twice their weight in gold. "That there should be an owl or ostrich left with a single feather apiece hardly seems possible," *Harper's Bazaar* reported during the winter hat season in 1897.

The feather trade wasn't confined to the east. Much of it occurred in the American West, and Oregon, California, and Texas were prime hunting grounds.

Women were called a "bird's worst enemy," but in time, they also became a bird's greatest advocate. Alarmed by the decimation of birds, Harriet Lawrence Hemenway organized a boycott of feathers and helped form the Massachusetts Audubon Society, the oldest in the nation.

Eventually, the society was able to get the feather trade outlawed in Massachusetts, and the first wildlife protection movement spread across the country. Hats still remained high and wide, but they were trimmed with ribbons, lace, and flowers instead of feathers.

Why did women go overboard with hats? Hats made women feel more powerful and gave them a presence that was otherwise denied them. Historians credit World War I for making large, outrageous hats go out of favor. But one can't help but wonder if the amendment giving women the vote might have lessened the need to show power through headgear.

As for Two-Time, Texas, there are still more changes ahead, not just for the town, but for the Lockwood family as well. Hold on to your hats, folks. It's going to be a wild ride. Meanwhile, you can reach me through my website: margaret-brownley.com.

Until next time,
Margaret

ACKNOWLEDGMENTS

Writing a book is never easy, but because of my husband's illness and passing, writing *A Match Made in Texas* was especially difficult. If it wasn't for you, my readers, I might never have gotten the book written. Thank you for your notes of encouragement and for making me smile when I thought I had nothing to smile about.

I also want to thank my fabulous agent and friend Natasha Kern, whose loving concern and prayers helped me through some very dark days.

Words can't convey how much I appreciate my terrific editor, Mary Altman, whose skillful eye and keen insight helped make my book better than I thought it could be. I've always valued her advice, but never more so than I did for this book. Also, I simply must thank art director Dawn Adams, artist Judy York, and photographer Shirley Green for the great cover of the original publisher's version. That's exactly how I envisioned my heroine.

Finally, I want to thank God for my dear husband, George, who always believed in me and encouraged me to keep going during the many years of rejection. Among his last words to me was his wish that I keep writing. He truly was and will always be the wind beneath my wings.

ABOUT THE AUTHOR

Bestselling author **Margaret Brownley** has penned more than forty novels and novellas. Her books have won numerous awards, including Readers' Choice and Award of Excellence. She's a former Romance Writers of American RITA finalist and has written for a TV soap. She is currently working on her next series. Not bad for someone who flunked eighth grade English. Just don't ask her to diagram a sentence.